VENGEFUL COMMANDER

LAYLAH ROBERTS

Laylah Roberts.

Vengeful Commander.

Cover Design by: Allycat's Creations.

Editing: Eve Arroyo

Photographer: Golden Czermak; Furious Fotog

Cover Model: Nick Pulos

❀ Created with Vellum

LET'S KEEP IN TOUCH!

Don't miss a new release, sign up to my newsletter for sneak peeks, deleted scenes and giveaways: https://landing.mailerlite.com/web-forms/landing/p7l6go

You can also join my Facebook readers group here: https://www.facebook.com/groups/386830425069911/

BOOKS BY LAYLAH ROBERTS

Wilde

Sinclair

Luke

Standalones

Their Christmas Baby

A Cozy Little Christmas

Haley Chronicles

Ally and Jake

1

rund!

Victor smashed his fist into his opponent's face. The roar of the crowd barely registered. He wasn't here for them. The other guy stumbled back, his hand on his face as blood poured from his broken nose.

Come back at me.

Give me a decent fight.

It would be easy to end the fight now. A few punches to his ribs. A kick to the back of the knee. A choke hold when he fell.

But Victor wasn't ready for the fight to be over. He could still feel that burning, sizzling need inside him. And he had to do something to release it.

So, he waited for the asshole to shake off the pain of his broken nose, wipe the blood away, and move back to him.

Smack! Smack!

He pummeled the guy, punching his torso then darting back.

Come on, asshole.

The guy groaned, swaying while the crowd's roar increased. They could scent his desire for blood. To make this asshole suffer.

In these underground fights, there was only one rule. Do not kill your opponent. Because no one wanted the hassle of taking care of the body.

Come at me!

But the dickhead just crumpled to the floor in a heap.

The crowd was on their feet as Victor gave the bastard a final kick in the stomach. Yeah, it could be seen as unsportsmanlike. But then, this wasn't a sport down here.

It was dirty, nasty, bloody survival.

Just the way he liked it.

Besides, he had his reasons for hating this asshole. His friends rushed forward to drag him away as Victor glanced around.

Did he have time for another fight?

He hit the cold gaze of his oldest brother. Regent shook his head, knowing what he was thinking.

Fuck. He clenched his hands into fists but didn't let anything show on his face.

It wasn't enough—not nearly.

He nodded as George, the guy Regent hired to manage the fights, approached, talking about how he wanted Victor to fight this new up-and-coming fighter next week.

He'd heard it all before. This was getting . . . mundane. Boring.

It wasn't enough anymore. The fights were barely touching his need to do something . . . anything to help relieve the demons inside him.

Walking to where Regent stood in their private, secure area, he picked up the T-shirt he'd dropped and slipped it over his huge frame. He'd always been big, even as a kid he'd towered over all the other kids. He'd seen the way other parents had eyed him warily, as though worried he'd attack their children.

If they could only see him now.

But his size was his one advantage over other people. He

wasn't a leader like Regent with a cunning mind, wasn't driven and smart like Jardin, or charismatic like Maxim.

Victor was strong, muscular, and he could fight. That's all he had to contribute.

Regent met him part way. His bodyguard, Jose, stood behind him. Victor wanted him to start traveling with more bodyguards, but Regent didn't trust many people. He had a couple of guards at the house and his lieutenants. That was it.

And he got it. After Alice, they were all on edge and less trusting.

"Let's go," Regent said, eyeing him as they walked out the back door. Their car was waiting for them at the curb.

Jose held the door for both of them. Regent slid into the car with a nod, making it all seem so easy.

Victor always felt awkward when Jose or one of the other guards did this. He'd have been happier being the bodyguard.

That's what he'd been born to do. To guard his brother. To take a bullet for him if necessary. That's what his father had always impressed on him.

How disposable he was. How it was his responsibility to keep Regent alive.

Victor knew Regent didn't see it that way. But it was what it was.

He should have fucking realized what Alice was up to. They'd let her into their house, close to their precious sister, and none of them had realized she was the rat.

He should have guarded Regent better.

Instead, Regent had been poisoned. He'd nearly died.

After he'd climbed in, Regent handed him an ice pack and some antiseptic for the scrapes on his knuckles. The privacy screen was already up, separating the back and front seats.

"I'm fine," he grumbled as Jose shut the door.

"You don't know where that asshole has been. Clean the cuts or I will."

Victor shot his brother a look. He sounded stressed. That wasn't normal for Regent, but there had been a lot of shit going down lately.

Since they'd discovered Alice had been working for Patrick McMahon, Regent had grown even colder. Removed. Detached.

It probably didn't help that Lottie had moved away with her two men. Lottie had always given Regent someone to fuss over. To take care of.

His oldest brother needed someone to protect and look after to keep himself from becoming an emotionless robot. To keep him human.

Maybe he was the same.

"You hear anything?" he asked as he applied the cream with a wince.

Punch a guy in the face until he broke his nose? No issue. Put antiseptic cream on open cuts? Yeah, he wasn't so fond of that.

But he did it. Then he applied the ice pack to his right hand which was worse off than the left one.

"Nothing."

After discovering that Alice had been feeding information to Patrick, Regent had gone on the warpath. He'd destroyed anything that was even related to Patrick McMahon. The destruction hadn't ended until they'd discovered the slippery asshole had left town.

At the time, Regent had been furious. He'd wanted to chase him to the ends of the earth. Unfortunately, they'd had little to go on.

That was until a few weeks ago, when the rumors had started up. Whispers that Patrick was back in town.

"All smoke and mirrors," Regent said. "All rumors. But no one is willing to say for sure that it's him. Someone has to be helping him. I made sure there was nothing for him to return to," Regent said grimly.

"Why come back? He has to know that we'll be coming for him. I don't like it."

Regent grunted. "I want him found. I've got all our lieutenants and their soldiers on the lookout, ferreting out any sightings of the bastard. He's going to pay for what he did."

Not only had he placed Alice in their house and had her poison Regent in an effort to take over their territory, but he also had to be behind the FBI issuing a search warrant for their house.

In the months since the FBI raid, things had been mostly quiet. Regent had tightened his control over the city.

"We'll find him. And if he's working with someone, we'll find them too."

"They're playing the long game. They've been too quiet. They should have made a move by now."

And he knew that was pissing Regent off.

"MAYBE YOU CLEANED out the city too well," Victor said. "Perhaps we should have tried to get someone to turn on him."

Regent grunted. "Maybe. I wasn't thinking that clearly."

Yeah, Victor had noticed.

"You pulverized that guy tonight." There was a note of question in Regent's voice.

"I did."

"There something I need to know?"

"Fucker's a rapist."

He saw Regent stiffen out of the corner of his eye. "What? He works for Santiago, doesn't he?"

Santiago owned most of the strip clubs in New Orleans. Many of them had brothels out back with added extras. Not something that Regent was interested in getting into. He might be the leader of the largest criminal syndicate in New Orleans, something that would've made the old man proud, but he drew the line at getting into selling skin.

Sometimes Victor wondered if he even wanted to run any of it. If he wanted to be the criminal King of New Orleans.

But Regent had never confided in him whether this was something he wanted. Regent played his cards close to his chest. Almost as close as Victor did.

"Yep. Raped three hookers last week. He claimed it wasn't rape."

Fucker.

"Why didn't you tell me?" Regent asked. "You know I would've taken care of him."

"You can't go around murdering Santiago's men."

"I can when they're fucking rapists," Regent snapped.

"Well, now you don't have to. Because I took care of it."

"He's still alive."

Victor allowed himself a slight grin. "Not for long."

There was a long moment of silence. "You've taken care of it?"

He tried not to let the words get their claws into him. He told him that Regent didn't mean it to sound as though he doubted him.

As though he couldn't complete a job. As though he couldn't organize a fucking hit. That was child's play for him. Their father might have spent the majority of his time teaching Regent how to run the organization, but he'd taught Victor his role.

"Yeah. I did."

"Vic, I'm not doubting you, brother."

Victor shrugged. "I'd get it if you were."

"Victor, I have never fucking doubted you. Ever. You've always been there for me. You know how much I value you."

"Let's not get all mushy and shit, yeah? I'm not fucking hugging you."

There was a beat of silence then Regent let out a small sigh. "Yeah. Right."

Guilt swirled in his gut. He knew all his siblings wished they could get closer to him. That he'd open up to them. Let them in.

But that was another of his father's lessons. To protect all of his siblings, and keep them from getting too dirty.

And if he let them in, let them get close, they might just find out how fucking filthy he'd had to get in the name of protecting them.

He'd done shit that he knew he could never do enough penance for. But if he could take care of a motherfucking rapist now and then, well, he thought that might somehow balance out the scales.

"We need to find someone close to Patrick who'll talk or turn on him," Regent said.

"We'll find someone. And when we do, I'll get him to cooperate."

That's what he did best, right?

"I know you will. But you know you don't have to, right? You mean more to us than your ability to make someone talk. To make a rapist pay by pulverizing him. You don't have to get your hands dirty."

"Sure."

Regent sighed. "Glad we cleared that up."

The rest of the drive home was in awkward silence. Victor stared at the huge house that held more bad memories than good. At least for him. Regent seemed to like this place. Lottie had shut herself up in here for years, hiding from her demons, from the world. Not that he blamed her.

He clenched his hands into fists as he remembered everything she'd been through. They should have protected her better.

He'd failed her.

He glanced at the time. He still had a few hours to get some sleep before he was needed elsewhere.

"You're going to bed?" Regent asked as they walked into the dark house.

"Yep."

"And you'll be leaving again at four-thirty?"

He stiffened. He hadn't been aware that his oldest brother had noticed him leaving every morning.

"Yep."

"And you'll return by eight?"

"Is there a problem?" He turned on the stairs to look at Regent. "Did you need me for something?"

"At that hour of the morning? God no." Regent had always been a night owl. "But you can't keep surviving on a few hours' sleep."

"I'm not going to slip up and make a mistake," he growled. "I'm fine."

Regent ran his hand over his face, looking tired. "I'm not saying that you're going to make a mistake, brother. I'm worried about you. Someone could get to you."

Victor scowled. "I'd like to see them try. I'm a grown man. I can look after myself. You're just looking for someone to cluck over like an old hen now that Lottie is gone. I don't need the overprotective shit, Regent."

Regent threw his hands up in the air. "Sorry for caring. I'll stop clucking."

"Good. Why don't you go visit Lottie? You can fuss all over her until Liam kicks your ass."

"Liam will never be able to kick my ass," Regent growled. "Where's the brotherly loyalty?"

"Go see Jardin if you want that."

"And what would I come to you for?" Regent asked, sounding disgruntled.

"You come to me if you want brute force or someone to help bury the body. You know that."

A FEW HOURS LATER, he stood in the shadows and waited.

Like clockwork, the tiny red car rattled its way into the parking lot.

He frowned at the funny noise it was making. That wasn't usual. Had she gotten that looked at? If there was something wrong, then it could break down on her when she was driving around at five in the morning.

That wasn't safe.

But then nothing she did was with her own safety in mind. She parked in a parking lot that was an entire block away from her bakery, *Make It Sweet*, when there were perfectly good spots behind the building she could use. But no, she left those for her customers.

Instead, she parked here, paid a monthly parking fee that he wasn't certain she couldn't afford, and walked in the dark to the bakery.

At least he'd gotten the city to do their fucking job and fix all the streetlamps. It was easy to get shit done when you had the right sorts of tools to work with.

In this case, a video of a councilman having an illicit affair with his son's teacher.

Yep, these lights had gotten fixed surprisingly fast, along with the cracks in the road.

Sometimes it seemed like no one in this town was innocent.

Except for her.

Gracen.

She was gorgeous. Petite, but with curves that made his mouth water. She'd look ridiculous next to him. He towered over her, and he was too brutish, too violent to ever touch anyone so precious.

But that didn't keep him from keeping an eye on her. Someone had to. A few weeks after he started watching her, he'd stopped some asshole from trying to mug her—or worse. He'd grabbed the guy, dragged him into an alley, and taken care of him.

Bastard didn't deserve to breathe the same air as his angel.

Neither do you.

No, but at least he knew it. And he was doing what he could to keep her safe. He was burning himself out, but there was no way he'd stop. Because if something happened to her, no one in New Orleans would be safe from his wrath.

He suddenly realized that she'd stopped. Fuck. He was too close to her. He froze. Logically, he knew he was hidden in the shadows. But if she looked closely enough she might make out a hint of him standing there, watching her.

And then it would be all over.

Because there was no way she'd ever understand what he was doing. That she'd see it as his way of keeping her safe.

No, he'd terrify her.

And if his actions didn't scare her, his size would.

Or his reputation.

Yep. He wasn't the guy that good girls like Gracen took home to their parents.

He was the guy your parents warned you about. The one good girls needed to steer clear of.

She was searching through her bag, cursing quietly. He wanted to grab hold of her and shake her.

Or better yet, put her over his knee and spank her ass until she promised him that she'd never do anything foolish like this again. That she wouldn't put herself in danger. That she'd take every care because she knew that he couldn't live without her.

Stop being an idiot.

She'll never be yours. Your filthy hands don't deserve to touch her delicate, soft skin.

Putting her over his knee was a regular fantasy, but that's all it was. He'd always been careful of his strength around women.

But it still fucking killed him that she was standing here in a quiet, run-down area of the city in the dark, searching for something in her handbag.

Did she have no situational awareness? Couldn't she sense eyes on her? Watching her?

Of course, it suited him that she couldn't. It made his job watching over her easier.

Finally, she gave a huge sigh and drew out her keys. "Thank God I didn't leave these behind. That would have been a disaster."

He shook his head as she moved away. Why the hell hadn't she checked that she had her keys before leaving her apartment? And she should have had them in her hand before she even left her car.

He swore to God if she were his . . .

Easy.

He watched her unlock the door and head inside. This was the part he fucking hated. But he'd checked the cameras when he'd first arrived, the cameras he'd secretly put in. No one was inside the building. No one had set off the silent alarm he'd also installed without her knowledge.

He had to do whatever was necessary to keep her safe. It wasn't like he could sneak into the bakery before she got there to ensure it was safe. He couldn't be in two places at once and breaking in carried the risk of her finding him.

So, he'd installed the cameras and an alarm.

Getting cameras into her apartment was a bit trickier. She lived in a multi-level complex so there was often someone coming or going.

It might still be doable, but he'd likely have to hire someone for that job. And he didn't want anyone to know about her.

About what she meant to him.

That was another reason she couldn't ever be his. There were too many people who'd want to get revenge on him by hurting someone he cared about.

So instead, he'd gotten the landlord to install good locks on her door.

He checked the app on his phone, watching as she bustled around in the kitchen, getting ready for the day. He sighed in relief, then headed across the road to his usual perch until she opened up for the day.

Another day where she was safe was another day where he could breathe a little easier.

2

Gracen Stall froze as she heard raised voices coming from the front of the shop. Shit. Wiping her hands on her apron, she rushed out the front.

"You can't just jump the line, man," Russ, one of her regulars, was getting in the face of a younger man she'd never seen before.

She swallowed heavily, fear thumping in her chest. The younger guy had a shaved head with tattoos over his skull. His jeans were halfway down his ass, and he had the swagger of someone who thought he was invincible.

She didn't want to jump to any conclusions, but he looked like trouble.

"I can do whatever the fuck I want, old man. Get to the fucking back and out of my face before I rearrange yours."

"What's going on?" she asked Anita, stepping forward.

"Uh, Russ was next in line when this guy came in and barged his way to the front. I think we should just serve him, though. He looks dangerous."

Gracen didn't like the note of admiration in her niece's voice.

But that was something to worry about later. The younger guy was starting to ramp up. Then he pushed Russ.

With a gasp, Gracen moved around the counter and got in between the two, facing the younger guy. She wasn't going to let anyone harass one of her customers. There were several other customers in the bakery, but they were all standing back. No one liked to get involved in a conflict in this neighborhood when there were gang members involved in almost everything.

"You need to leave. Now," she said firmly.

His eyes were moving around wildly and he was twitchy, like he was on something.

"Get out of my way, you fat bitch. I'm going to teach this asshole a lesson."

She was dimly aware of the front door to the bakery opening, but she didn't want to move her gaze from the jerk in front of her.

"Leave before I call the cops."

"Fine, you want to be taught a lesson as well?" He smiled, showing off yellowed, crooked teeth. He drew his hand back, forming a fist, and she closed her eyes, bracing herself for impact. But nothing happened. She heard a crash and opened her eyes to see the younger guy pressed against the wall. A large man held him there, his hands on each of his arms.

Her breathing quickened.

It was him.

She didn't know his name, but he came in for a sticky bun nearly every morning. He was huge, barely ever said a word, and he tipped really well.

And he'd just saved her.

Turning his head, he moved his gaze over her. "Are you hurt?"

"N-no," she managed to replied.

"Stay here."

She hadn't been planning on going anywhere.

"Fuck, let me down, you asshole!"

"Shut. Up." His voice was cold, commanding and even the jerk he was holding against the wall grew quiet.

"You, get the door," he said to Russ, who hurried over to open it.

He dragged the guy outside. They could all hear him protesting as they disappeared down the street.

Her heart was thumping wildly. What had just happened?

"Fuck, do you think he's going to kill him?" Anita asked.

"Anita!" she snapped, looking around at the other customers. Shit. This wasn't a good look for the bakery. "I'm really sorry. Anita, give everyone a free cinnamon roll." She rushed to Russ. "Are you all right?"

"Yeah, young punks, trying to ruin everything for the rest of us, thinking they can do what they want," he muttered angrily as she got him his order.

Feeling exhausted and wrung out, she waited out the front while Anita served the rest of the customers.

Where was he? What had he done with that guy?

When everyone was cleared out, she moved into the back of bakery. Was he coming back?

Unable to concentrate, she found herself moving around aimlessly.

"Aunty G, he's here," Anita called out through the door.

Heart in her throat, she rushed out and saw him standing there. He looked unruffled in his navy blue shirt and dark pants. His dark hair was short, his eyes intense as he ran them over her.

"Are you all right?" she asked frantically. "Are you hurt?"

He raised his eyebrow. "I'm fine. Are you certain he didn't touch you?"

"No, you stopped him." She could feel herself blushing. "Thank you." She gave him a smile.

Instead of smiling back, he scowled. "You shouldn't have stepped in between them. Don't do that again."

Her mouth dropped open at his words. That was it? He'd come back to growl at her? He took the bag that Anita handed him.

After slipping some bills into the tip jar, he left.

Wait. He was leaving? She rushed out after him without thinking. "Wait!"

He stilled, then looked back.

"What did you do with him?"

"Made sure he wouldn't be bothering you again."

Maybe that should have scared her.

Instead, she felt a warm rush at his protectiveness.

What was going on with her?

"Aunty G, he's here again."

Gracen looked up from where she was tidying up one of the workstations. Next on the list was to get some white chocolate and raspberry muffins in the oven. They were a favorite with her customers.

She placed her hand over her stomach, which was complaining that she hadn't eaten anything this morning.

There was always so much to do and so little time to do it in. It didn't help that Anita had slept in and hadn't arrived until just before seven. The bakery opened at six so she'd had to serve out the front while getting more goodies into the cabinet.

"Who?" she asked Anita.

"The big guy. He's back."

Gracen frowned at her niece. At nineteen, she was unreliable and flighty. She wasn't sure if it was Anita's age or if that was just who she was.

Gracen couldn't remember ever being so carefree and irresponsible.

Then again, her grandpa had installed a good work ethic in

her. He had always emphasized that the only way to get anywhere was through hard work.

She should have been further ahead by now with how hard she worked. Six days a week, she worked from five in the morning until four in the afternoon in the bakery, and then she often went home to more paperwork than she knew what to do with.

When would she start to feel like she was getting somewhere? Sometimes it felt like it was never going to happen.

Stop feeling sorry for yourself.

Wiping her hands on her apron, she glanced up at the clock. Seven twenty, like clockwork. Right as the first morning wave was waning off. It wouldn't be dead out there, but people wouldn't be crammed in like sardines either.

Not that anyone would dare try to get close to him. He was big enough to intimidate even the scariest gangster wannabe. Like he had the other day. She didn't even know why he'd interfered. Heck, she didn't even know his name. And she was just the lady with the sticky buns.

Okay, even she heard how bad that sounded.

Whenever he was around, she instantly felt safer, though. Once, when a customer had gotten irate because Anita had given them the wrong change and he'd calmed him down with just a look. And another time when she'd been carrying a heavy box out to a customer's car, he'd taken it from her and carried it out.

Sometimes she wondered if he'd had something to do with the fixed streetlights as well as the cracks in the sidewalks and roads.

But that was just silly.

"Don't call him that, Anita," she scolded.

"Why not? He is big. Anyway, you better get out there and serve him."

"What? You mean you just left him out there? Damn it, Anita. You're here to serve customers."

Anita scowled. "I'm trying to do you a favor. He's only got eyes for you."

"That's not true." She tucked her white-blonde hair behind her ears as she hastily made her way out to the front.

Please don't let me have flour all over my hair or face.

That happened way too often when Anita had something else to do and she had to duck out the front to serve.

If she wasn't family, she'd have fired her a long time ago. Never hire family. Another of Grandpa's lessons. One she hadn't taken heed of.

Pasting a smile on her face, she headed out to serve the big beast . . . no, she couldn't think of him like that. She might not know his name, but she did know he wasn't a beast.

She didn't know why he came here for his sticky bun fix. He didn't look like he lived in this area.

Anita had speculated a lot about him, her favorite theory was that he was some wealthy underground fighter or criminal kingpin.

That girl sure did have a healthy imagination. If only she'd apply herself so diligently to her work, then Gracen's life would be much easier.

She took a brief moment to study him, from his broad shoulders to his beefy biceps. All of him was thick and muscular. But it was his face that called to her. He had dark hair and deeply-tanned skin with a short beard. Maybe he couldn't be called classically beautiful, but there was something so mesmerizing about him.

When he walked into a room, everyone's gaze went to him immediately. She'd seen it before when he'd come into the bakery. Everyone would pause and stare. No one dared come close to touching him. He gave the impression he could break a body in half with one hand.

And yet . . . when she looked into his hazel eyes, she got the impression he was kind of sad.

But that was just stupid.

She smiled at him brightly in an attempt to hide her thoughts and how flustered she was by his good looks. "Good morning. Are you here for my sticky buns?"

Oh, Lord.

Did she just say that? She didn't, did she?

Please don't let me have said that.

To her shock, she thought the corners of his lips twitched. But she was certain she'd been mistaken when she looked again, and he appeared as serious as ever.

He simply nodded.

"How many today?" she asked, trying to sound professional. She heard Anita snort with laughter from the back room.

Great. She'd hear about that for the rest of the day. Probably the week. With a sigh, she gave the big guy a tired smile. She didn't even know his name. She knew the names of all her other regulars. And all their family members too.

Not him. He came in for a sticky bun, left a big tip in the jar they kept on the counter, and left.

Anita usually snuck off with most of the tip money, but Gracen had learned early on that it was just easier to let some things slide with her niece.

"Two, please."

She nodded. "To go?"

"For here. And coffee, black."

That was surprising. He didn't usually stay. She nodded with a smile, grateful he wasn't going to bring up her embarrassing gaff.

"I'll bring it over."

He paid then moved to a seat at the back of the small bakery. She'd taken over the shop next door when they'd gone out of business and put a wide doorway in so people could sit and eat and have a cup of coffee.

All of her savings had been sunk into the renovation that the landlord had thankfully agreed to.

Picking up a plate with the sticky buns and his coffee, she moved toward him after making sure Anita was back out serving.

He'd chosen a seat with his back to the wall, so he could look out at everyone coming and going. She got the feeling that it wasn't an accidental choice, that he did everything with purpose. Did he feel like he had to guard his back constantly?

She set down the plate and his coffee, staring at his hands for a moment. He often had scraped and swollen knuckles. She knew what that likely meant, and it should have worried her. He was a huge guy, and if he regularly got into physical fights . . . but perhaps he was a boxer or something?

Whatever he did, for some reason she wasn't as intimidated by him as she should have been.

As she turned to walk away, though, he reached out and grabbed hold of her wrist.

She paused with a small gasp.

"Sit. Eat with me."

It wasn't exactly a request, but she was working. She didn't really have time to sit and eat because he'd ordered her to. But then he lifted his gaze to hers.

And there was something in his dark gaze, something that called to her. She recognized it all too well because she felt it herself.

Loneliness.

"All right," she said. "Just give me a minute to check in with Anita."

He nodded.

She turned and walked toward the counter. Anita finished serving someone and spun to her as she poured a coffee.

"Well?"

"I'm just going to have something to eat."

"With him?" Anita's eyes widened.

"Yes. You all right here?"

She wasn't sure if she wanted Anita to say yes or not. Anita nodded, a bit too excitedly.

"Go, go. I'm good."

Gracen eyed her for a moment. Anita was acting a little odd. Usually, she'd moan and groan if she thought she was having to do all the work. But she was overly enthusiastic.

Shaking it off, hoping that maybe her niece was starting to think about other people more, she dumped a heap of creamer into her coffee, then moved back to where he sat.

The buns were still sitting on the plate. His gaze was intent on her. Watching her every movement. Although she had the feeling that he was aware of everything else going on in the bakery at that moment too.

He looked like he could look after himself. And anyone that was under his care.

Would you like that?

She hadn't had anyone take care of her in a long time. Her last boyfriend hadn't been that protective or all that interested in anything she was doing—other than when it affected him.

They'd drifted apart. He'd told her that she had unrealistic expectations of him. She'd just wanted him to give a shit. To check in if she was late getting home and ask if she was all right. Or for him to be concerned if she was sick, rather than keeping away so he didn't catch anything.

She paused, worry filling her. "Aren't the sticky buns good? Would you like me to replace them? Do you want something else instead?"

He frowned, staring down at the buns, then up at her. She set down her coffee and reached for the plate. But that large, scarred hand landed on hers, stilling her.

"They're perfect. Why?"

"Oh, sorry. You just weren't eating, and I was worried . . . sorry."

"Nothing to be sorry about," he told her in that low, rumbly voice. She swore she could feel her nerve endings dance into life.

Suddenly the thought of him ordering her around in the bedroom with that voice flitted through her mind.

Jesus, Gracen. Stop it, he's a customer. The last thing he wants is to come in here and have you lusting all over him.

How embarrassing. She hoped that he hadn't caught her watching him closely. Or heard the small sound of pleasure escape her lips when he touched her.

That would be mortifying

"Sit. Please." The please was definitely an afterthought. It sounded rusty coming from his lips. Drawn to the command in his voice, she moved toward the chair opposite him. He stood and drew out the chair to the right of him. "Here."

"Here?" she asked as she slid into the chair. She looked to him for reassurance.

His nod filled her with warmth. Shoot. She liked pleasing him. She wasn't sure why it made a difference where she sat. Did he want her close to him? Or maybe he didn't want her blocking his view of the room. That seemed more likely.

"Here." He took one sticky bun and pushed the plate over to her. "Eat."

"Oh, no, I couldn't. Those are for you." And from the look of him, the two buns would be a mere snack, not an actual meal. It must take a lot of calories to fuel him.

"Bought one for you."

"You . . . you didn't have to do that." She owned the place, after all.

"You don't like them?" he asked.

"Oh no, I do. I don't bake anything that I don't like." She laughed self-consciously. She was well aware that she was at least ten pounds overweight. Hmm, probably more. Between sampling the product and working long hours, she didn't have the time or energy to worry about her health.

Besides, she kind of liked her curves. Sure, they weren't what was trendy. But she didn't think she had the type of body that wanted to be super thin.

"You're not hungry?" he asked.

"Oh, uh, I . . ." Her stomach chose that moment to grumble. Stupid stomach. She glared down at it. "Way to betray me there, buddy."

Heat filled her face, and she knew she'd gone bright red. She heaved in a breath.

Wow, Gracen. First, you mention your sticky buns, then you talk to your stomach. Way to act crazy.

"Eat. You're hungry. You haven't had breakfast?"

So, he was going to ignore the fact that she'd just spoken to her stomach like it was sentient?

Suited her.

"I don't usually eat breakfast."

"You should."

"I usually sleep in till the last minute. And I'm always snacking as I bake, so I figure I don't need the extra calories of breakfast on top of that. I'm hardly at risk of fading away here." She gave a self-conscious laugh, gesturing at herself.

You're an idiot, Grace. Way to point out your flaws to the gorgeous guy that just bought you breakfast.

"No," he said firmly.

"What?" she asked, confused.

"No, you're not doing that."

"Doing what?" Was her body doing something she wasn't

aware of? Her foot wasn't touching his, was it? She wasn't subconsciously rubbing herself up against him like a cat.

Because sometimes it felt like her body acted without consulting her brain first. But all of her limbs seemed to be behaving themselves, so she shot her gaze back to his.

Were his lips quirking? Or was she imagining that? If they had been, they'd stopped already.

"Why did you say no? What was I doing?"

"Saying ridiculous things about yourself. Things that aren't true and that you won't say again."

"I won't?"

"Nope."

"Why won't I?" she asked, tilting her face to the side.

"Because I said so."

Her eyebrows rose. "Do people often do as you say, Mr. . . . ?"

"Call me Victor."

"Okay, Victor. Do people often do what you say?"

"Yes. Always."

She swallowed, a sense of daring washing over her. "Oh, yeah? And you think I'll be the same?"

His gaze moved over her face slowly. "Of course."

"You might be disappointed then. If all you want is someone who says yes."

"Oh, I won't be disappointed."

She wasn't entirely certain if he meant he wouldn't be disappointed because she'd be doing what he said or if he'd been implying that he could never be disappointed in her.

The former, for sure.

Thinking otherwise was just foolish.

"You all right?" he asked.

She realized then that he'd been saying something, and she'd totally tuned him out. Rude.

She blushed. "Sorry, sometimes my mind wanders."

He just studied her for a long moment.

"You can't stop me from calling myself fat, you know."

His gaze grew dark.

"I can't believe I just blurted that out. I think it's because I live alone. You know . . . you start talking to yourself, then you start thinking you need a cat so that you have someone to talk to without looking like a complete moron, then you think you don't have time for a cat, so you get a goldfish only they don't live long and when they die you fall into a funk and declare that you'll never get a pet again. So, then you go back to talking to yourself. And are you really not going to stop me from rambling?"

He should have stopped her by now, right? Put her out of her misery or something.

Lord, this was embarrassing.

"Do you tell a lot of people that you live alone?"

That was what he wanted to focus on? She ran her hand over her face. "No. I don't."

She saw his skeptical look.

"I really don't. I do have some self-preservation skills. There's just something about you . . ."

He raised his eyebrows.

"You feel safe," she blurted out. "I know that's stupid."

She waited for him to say something. To make some excuse to leave. Although, she'd have thought he'd have taken off after she started talking to her stomach.

"You're always safe with me, Gracen," he said instead. He spoke in such a solemn voice, it settled like a blanket around her shoulders.

She was safe with him.

"You know my name?" Perhaps she should be concerned. What if he was some sort of weirdo stalker?

This time his lips definitely twitched, and warmth filled his eyes, lightening them. "You have a name badge."

She closed her eyes.

Idiot.

"I really shouldn't be allowed to talk to people. Sorry if I implied that you're, well, a . . ."

"Stalker?" he prompted.

And she knew she was bright red again. "Uh, yeah. Sorry." Was there an appropriate way to apologize for basically accusing someone of stalking you?

Not exactly.

"Eat," he urged. She opened her eyes and noticed that he hadn't touched his sticky bun. Was he waiting on her? She picked off a piece of the bun, settling it in her mouth with a hum of pleasure. These really were good, even if she said so herself.

His gaze was watching her, satisfaction filling his face. She wasn't sure why. When she started eating, he did the same.

"Thank you for the other day," she told him. "You didn't have to help, but I appreciate it."

"You shouldn't have stood between them. That was unsafe. Don't do it again."

"Don't do it again?" she repeated.

"Yes, don't do it again."

Wow. He really did like to give orders.

"You could have been hurt." He frowned.

"So could you."

He scoffed. "Hardly."

She wanted to ask again what he'd done with that guy. But she also felt like maybe she didn't want to know.

He finished off the last bite of sticky bun.

"Would you like another one? On the house," she said, feeling slightly awkward that he'd paid for this one.

She shifted in her seat, but he gently grabbed her wrist. "No, thank you. And if I wanted one, I'd pay for it."

"But you paid for mine when you didn't have to."

"Yes, I did."

"Why?" she asked.

"Because I wanted to." It was said so matter-of-factly.

"Do you always do what you want?" she asked.

"No. And I probably shouldn't have this time either. But I couldn't stop myself."

She was confused. Buying her a sticky bun was something he couldn't stop himself from doing? That didn't make a lot of sense.

But there was something so weary and worn down in his gaze that she didn't press him. Instead, she sat, and when he pointedly looked down at the sticky bun, she started to eat it again.

"Are you all right?" she blurted out.

His eyebrows rose. "Yes, of course. Why wouldn't I be?"

Don't ask about his knuckles. Don't ask about his knuckles.

"Eat," he pressed.

"You don't have some weird eating fetish, do you?"

Oh, holy crap. She smacked her forehead with the palm of her hand. What was wrong with her? Really? This is why she should just stay in the kitchen. Although she had no trouble talking to her other regulars.

It was him.

It was his fault.

That made her feel slightly better. Only, he was the last person she wanted to embarrass herself in front of.

Damn it. She needed to get her act together.

The worst thing was that she managed to ask him that at the exact same time as he took a sip of coffee. The liquid burst out of him, spraying over the table. She didn't know why, but that made her feel better. Seeing him have a human reaction. Doing something less than perfect. He choked, trying to catch his breath. She jumped up and whacked him on the back.

Dear Lord. He was solid. Like, how did a person get that hard?

"Do you have any fat on your body? Your shoulders are like rock."

When he stopped coughing, she sat back down. "Water. You need water." Jumping up, she raced over and got him a glass of water, ignoring Anita's shocked face.

Please don't let her ask about what was going on.

Rushing back, she handed him the glass of water. Taking it, he drank it down. Should that be sexy? Watching him drink?

She had it so bad. There was something wrong with her. Maybe she was ill. She put her hand on her forehead.

"Gracen?"

"Hmm? Oh, sorry, just checking for a fever."

"Do you feel unwell?" he asked, frowning.

"No."

He blinked.

"I just . . . I can't believe I said that. I'm so sorry. That's just embarrassing."

"What kind of eating fetish do you think I have?"

He didn't look offended, just a bit surprised.

"I don't know. I don't know why I said that." She twisted her fingers into each other. "I'm such a dork sometimes."

"Sit," he commanded.

She slipped back into the chair. Yikes, how did he do that? Reaching out, he placed his finger under her chin and tilted her face back. "You are not a dork. Don't say that. Understand?"

"Yes." She had to bite off the sir. Damn, that was hard. There was something about him that called to her. She'd often wanted to explore her submissive side. But the few times she'd tried to find someone . . . well, yeah, they hadn't been good.

"I can assure you that I don't have an eating fetish," he told her.

What about other kinds of fetishes?

Thank the Lord she didn't say that out loud.

His phone buzzed, and he frowned, looking down at it with a sigh.

"You have to go?" She should be relieved. It would end the disaster that had been the last twenty minutes.

But all she felt was a wave of sadness. Would he even be back?

"Yes," was all he said. Standing, he reached into his wallet to pull out some cash.

"You don't need to leave a tip," she protested. "I'll clean this up. And you bought me breakfast. My turn next time."

If that ever happened. Even if he came back, she should probably hide.

Without saying anything, he put a twenty down on the table. She shook her head. It was way too much, of course. Nearly four times what the coffee and buns cost.

She had to resist the urge to lean into him, even if his scent was so delicious it made her head spin. He smelled like leather and spice.

"Goodbye, Gracen."

"Okay, well, come back any time for more of my sticky buns!" she called out as he walked to the door.

Good Lord.

He didn't react. Maybe he hadn't heard her. A flood of mortification filled her. Had she seriously just said that? Looking around, she discovered that everyone in the bakery was gaping at her. Most of them were people she'd known for years.

Heat filled her cheeks. "Yes, I know how that sounded."

"Aunty G, that was . . . that was . . . terrible," Anita told her as she followed her out back. "Like truly awful. How are you not dying of embarrassment? I would be. I don't think I could ever leave my apartment again."

She rolled her eyes at her niece's dramatics. Although, to be honest, she kind of agreed. It was terrible.

"I don't have the luxury of dying every time I do something embarrassing."

"I always wondered why you were single. I mean, you do work all the time and you could lose a few pounds. But also, you're truly awful at speaking to men."

She snapped her hands on her hips and glared at her niece. "Got anything else you want to say?"

"I mean, no offense or anything."

Gracen just shook her head and turned away. She knew she shouldn't have gotten up this morning.

3

"Gracen? You okay?"

"What? Oh, yeah. Sorry. My mind was a million miles away." She smiled over at her best friend, Sammy.

"Yeah? Was it on anything interesting . . . or anyone?" Sammy asked slyly as they warmed up for their ballet class.

At thirty-four years old, they'd both decided to learn ballet.

The first lesson had been an absolute disaster. Actually, every lesson was a disaster. Gracen was so short that getting her leg up on the barre required a stepstool, a prayer, and some sort of sacrifice.

And while Sammy was a whole foot taller than her and looked every inch the ballerina, she had zero flexibility.

Plus, she was really clumsy.

But even though they were absolutely horrid at ballet, they kept coming back because it was fun watching the teacher's face every time they did something awful.

And across the street was this great bar which had half-price frozen daiquiris on Friday nights.

"Oh my God, who told you?" she asked as she bent over.

They'd been told to dress appropriately for the class. But there had been no way that Gracen was fitting her size twelve body into a tiny leotard. Instead, she wore some yoga pants, one of those boob tube things that attempted to tame her breasts, and a loose black T-shirt over the top. It was actually a guy's top, but it was comfy and soft and that was all she cared about.

"Um, only about five different people. There was a phone chain."

"Oh, shut up. There was not."

"Uh-huh. I got two phone calls and several text messages. I'm surprised there wasn't a social media post. I guess we should give Anita some credit for not going that far."

She groaned. "I can't believe everyone contacted you to tell you. What did they say?"

"Uh, nothing too bad," Sammy replied, trying to shove her leg up high onto the barre. Seriously, it wasn't even that high up for her.

"You need to stretch more."

"Tell me about it. I can barely even bend over to tie my shoes. And it's all Barry's fault."

Gracen raised her eyebrows. "How is it Barry's fault?"

Barry was Sammy's husband. He was a sweet, quiet guy who adored Sammy.

"Because he's not interested in sex anymore. And if he does want it, all he wants is missionary style. I mean, if he were slinging my legs around, I wouldn't be this inflexible, would I?"

The whole room went silent just as Sammy spoke. Gracen glanced around at everyone. Twelve women stared back at them.

"What?" Sammy asked, looking around at them all. "When you've been married twelve years to your childhood sweetheart, you'll find yourself in the same position as me. Literally. Over and over again."

Gracen couldn't stop herself from giggling.

"Right. Let usss get back to our ssstretching, ladiesss," their teacher commanded in her fake French accent. She seemed to think that all she had to do for a French accent was elongate her s sounds at the end or start of words. It really just made her sound like a talking snake.

"Please get into position."

Right, here she went. She could do it. She threw her leg up into the air and nearly toppled back onto her ass. Honestly, she had no idea how everyone else made it look so effortless.

Well, they were all far taller than her.

"Oh, they were all saying how you offered up your sticky buns to this big hunky beast of a guy." Sammy swung her leg back and up and right into Gracen's face.

The side of her face was engulfed in pain, and she cried out, falling back onto her ass.

"Oh my God! Gracen, are you all right? Holy shit! I just kicked my friend in the face. Someone call an ambulance!" Sammy yelled, kneeling beside her.

Shoot. Sammy panicked easily. She was terrible in an emergency. Gracen gasped for breath as she grabbed hold of Sammy's hand.

"I'm all right, babe."

"No, you're not. Oh my God. I'm so sorry! I can't believe I did that. Jesus, I'm a menace. What can I do? Wait, you want to take a shot at me? Go on! Punch me in the face."

"Sammy, I'm fine."

"No, do it. Punch me. It will make me feel better. Unless you don't want me to feel better. You shouldn't. You should tell me what a terrible, horrible person I am."

"Sammy, I'm fine.

"Get away from her! Quick! Quick! Here let me see." Madame Jeanne appeared in front of her, her face twisted in a frown.

"Someone get an ice pack from the freezer, or she won't be seeing out of her eye tomorrow." Madame Jeanne peeled back her hand, frowning down at her. "You're a mess."

"Thanks for the sympathy," she said dryly. "I appreciate it."

"I knew I should have kicked the two of you out of this class the second you walked in."

Wow. She was so empathic.

And what the heck had happened to her accent?

"I'm calling an ambulance," Sammy said.

"Sam, I'm fine. Honestly. I just need to go home and keep an ice pack on my eye."

"I kicked you in the face, there's no way you can be fine."

"You should take her home," Madame Jeanne said, sounding stressed. "And never come back again."

"Hey, we paid in full for these lessons," Sammy replied, putting her hands on her hips as she glared at the teacher.

"I'll refund you. Just go! Please go. I cannot put up with the burning hole in my gut every time you try to do something. You are both walking disasters."

"Yeah, well, your French accent just conveniently disappeared, didn't it, Madame Jeanne? Or should that be Jenny McDonald? Isn't that your real name? And aren't you from a little town in Ohio? Not Paris."

"Out! Out!" Madame Jeanne, or Jenny, screeched.

Sammy helped her up, putting her arm around her as they made their way out to the parking lot out the back.

As soon as they left the building, Gracen started to crack up. "Oh my God! I can't believe you outed Madame Jeanne in front of the whole class."

"This isn't funny!" Sammy told her. "How can you laugh? This is terrible! I just kicked you in the face. What if I've broken your cheekbone? What if I've permanently damaged your eyesight? Oh my God! What are we going to do?"

"Oh jeez, Sammy. I'm fine. Honestly. It's just a bruise." It was throbbing and her eye was swelling shut, but she was confident it would be fine by tomorrow.

"It's not just a bruise. I've got very powerful legs. I could have done some real damage. I think you should get checked by a doctor."

"Very powerful legs? What from? You sit at a desk all day and never exercise."

"Hey! I would be insulted by that if I didn't feel so terrible."

"Sammy, I'll be fine. I don't need the hospital."

They got to her car, and Sammy turned to eye her skeptically. "I don't think you should drive."

"I'm fine. But we need to talk about what's really important . . . did you see Madame Jeanne's face when you told everyone she was from a small town in Ohio?"

Sammy covered her face with her hands. "Oh, hell. I can't believe I did that." Then she started giggling too. "Oh, no. We can never go back there."

"No great loss. We were only going to it so we could go have a drink afterward. Now, we can skip the embarrassment of trying to move our bodies in ways they don't want to move and just go straight for a drink instead."

Sammy sighed as she gently pulled the ice pack away from Gracen's face, wincing. "Oh, Gracie."

"I'll be fine," Gracen told her. "I promise. If I ice it, I'm sure it won't be so bad in the morning. Think I better skip the drink tonight, though."

Sammy nodded. "I'll drive you home."

"No. I've got it. I need my car to get to work tomorrow."

"Don't you think you should take the day off?"

"No days off for me," Gracen said gently. "There's no one else who can do my job."

Sammy frowned with a sigh. "I don't like how much you work.

You're going to burn yourself out. Is the bakery still not making enough to hire some more help for you?"

"Unfortunately not. One day."

Luckily, Sammy was a good enough friend not to point out that she'd been saying since her grandpa died and she'd taken over everything herself.

One day still seemed a long way away.

"I'm going to drive behind you to make sure you get home safe, all right?"

"Thanks, Sammy. You're a good friend."

"Clearly not, or I wouldn't have kicked you in the face."

"It was an accident." Gracen patted her friend on the back with her free hand. "I'll be fine."

"I still feel terrible. It's my treat for daiquiris next week."

"Deal," Gracen told her.

Gracen had to drive home slowly since she could only see out of one eye. Luckily, it wasn't far. She winced at the noise her car was making. That wasn't normal. But she didn't have time to worry about it.

Driving with one eye swollen shut wasn't her brightest idea. She was trembling and sweaty when she slid into a spot in front of her apartment building. Getting out, she grabbed her handbag and the now-warm ice pack. Sammy tooted her horn and called out her driver's window.

"Text me after Mr. Sticky Buns comes in tomorrow morning. I want to hear all about it." She took off, driving too fast.

Gracen shook her head, then winced. The adrenaline rush had worn off and now she was really feeling the throbbing in her face.

She knew Sammy meant she wanted to hear what mortifying things Gracen said tomorrow. But it wasn't happening. She wasn't going to do or say anything to embarrass herself.

Hopefully.

That's if she hadn't scared him off for good.

V<small>ICTOR PARKED</small> his car outside the warehouse.

The only light came from his headlights. All of the streetlamps had stopped working a long time ago.

The warehouse appeared to be abandoned. Walking up to the big metal door, he spotted one of the younger guys who worked for them, standing guard.

The kid gave him a respectful nod as he walked in. It still looked like an old warehouse that had been forgotten once you got inside. Cracked windows, dust, cobwebs, that stale stench. But he moved confidently toward the back, to a door where another guard stood. Walking through the doorway, he strode to the trap-door set in the floor that led to a soundproof basement.

Regent had purchased this warehouse through a series of false companies so no one could trace it back to him.

Climbing down the ladder, he heard the sound of a fist hitting something solid. A grunt followed by a pain-filled groan.

He moved toward the sound. It was dark down here. Damp and cold.

Perfect.

A man he didn't recognize was hanging by his shacked wrists from a hook in the ceiling. Although not even his own grand-mother would recognize him now.

He didn't flinch at the sight. He'd long since desensitized himself to this sort of violence. He had no qualms dishing this sort of shit out to someone who deserved it. And he'd been briefed on this guy's background.

He had a rap sheet for possession and armed assault. But that wasn't what sealed his coffin. He'd been accused of raping and killing a woman about ten years ago in San Diego. The charges had been dropped when the one witness had disappeared.

So, yeah, Victor wasn't going to feel guilty for what this asshole was going through. They'd received a tip that Patrick had been seen in one of Santiago's clubs. Which didn't mean much, but then this guy, who worked for a bouncer in that same club, had started mouthing off about Regent. And all the things that Patrick intended to do to him.

He stood for a moment and watched Basilien, one of Regent's lieutenants, work the asshole over.

Lukas, another lieutenant, nodded respectfully, stepping up beside him. "Asshole shot one of our guys dead when they were bringing him in. Basilien is taking it personally."

Ahh, that explained it.

"He said anything else about where Patrick is hiding out?"

"Not yet."

All right then, time for some answers. He knew Regent wouldn't approve of him getting his hands dirty. But it wasn't like they weren't already black.

He tapped Basilien out and got to work.

SEVERAL HOURS LATER, he stepped out of the warehouse, needing a shower. Although no shower would ever make him feel completely clean.

But he had a name of a dancer that Patrick was fond of.

She worked in one of the club's that Santiago owned.

His name was coming up too much for Victor's liking. Getting out his phone, he checked the time and winced.

He wasn't going to make it over to the bakery in time to catch Gracen opening up.

Fuck. He hated being torn like this between his two worlds. He'd missed her dance class last night. Afterward, she and a friend would go across the road for a drink. He usually tried to get into the bar before they did, so he could take a seat in the dark at the back.

He wished he could have eyes on her all the time, but he couldn't be everywhere at once and he didn't trust anyone else to watch over.

And you want her to be just yours.

Yeah. That too.

Initially, he'd been worried about her driving after having a drink. Then he'd decided to order the same for himself and discovered it was more ice and flavoring than anything else.

Sitting in his car, he closed his eyes for a moment, thinking about her. The one good thing in his life. He loved his family, but this was different.

Gracen was like the angel sitting on the top of the Christmas tree. Untouchable, delicate, and out of his reach.

Yesterday had been a mistake. He should never have asked her to sit with him. But he hadn't been able to resist. He was just sick of everything in his life being dark.

For a moment, he'd wanted to bask in the sunshine that was Gracen Stall. Her smiles, her blushes, and the adorable way she blurted stuff out without thinking. She seemed extra flustered around him.

He'd briefly worried that she was scared of him. That his size might have intimidated her. But after thinking about it, he'd realized she was flustered around him for an entirely different reason.

And that was so damn tempting.

You can't have her.

Except touching her had been like eating a slice of her dark chocolate tart. Pure indulgence. Her skin was silky smooth, and he had no doubt that tasting her would be decadent.

And he wouldn't be able to stop at one taste.

Gracen was an innocent. She wasn't part of his world. And if she knew what he was . . . well, she'd probably run screaming.

With good reason.

He wasn't a good person. And she deserved far better. He could easily hurt her without meaning to.

Although he wouldn't mind putting her over his knee for being so reckless with her safety.

He shook his head.

However, that was an impossibility as well.

What he should do was stay far, far away from her. She'd accused him of being a stalker.

If only she knew.

4

Victor felt antsy as hell.

He'd stayed away from Gracen today and it was killing him. And not just because he didn't get his sticky bun fix.

It was her.

He wanted to talk to her again. To see her blue eyes spark with laughter. To feel the touch of her skin against his. But he should keep some distance between them. As difficult as that was to do.

"Vic? You with me?" Regent asked from the head of the table where he sat.

Gerald had just set out lunch, but Victor stared down at it without interest. He tapped his phone screen again.

Just take a look. See if she's all right.

"And then I murdered the lot of them. The cops are probably coming for me as we speak. I'll be out in fifty years."

"What?" He glanced up at Regent.

"Just making sure you were listening," Regent said dryly.

"Sorry," he muttered. He wasn't really.

"Gerald wants some time off. I'm not risking hiring someone else, so we'll have to fend for ourselves."

He frowned, glancing up from his phone. Great, neither of them could cook. But he also didn't want to order out. He didn't trust someone not to sneak something into their food. He foresaw a lot of peanut butter sandwiches in his future.

"Will he be safe leaving?"

"I'll make sure he is." Gerald had been with them forever, and he was like family. But that meant someone could use him against them.

Victor nodded and went back to staring down at his phone. He flicked the app on to display the cameras inside the bakery.

"Are you sleeping? You look terrible. Victor?" Regent pressed.

Ice cold rage filtered through his veins.

What. The. Fuck?

He gaped at the camera, certain he must be mistaken. The images were in black and white, but they were clear. He'd made sure to buy the best.

Jumping to his feet, he was dimly aware of his chair crashing back onto the floor and Regent's questions as he rushed out of the room.

Nothing mattered but getting to her.

Then killing the motherfucking bastard who ever had laid his hands on her.

SADNESS FILLED her like a dark wave, threatening to drag her under.

It was so silly. So, what if he didn't come in this morning? It didn't mean anything.

Sure, in the three months he'd been coming in for a sticky

bun, he'd missed less than a handful of days. But there could still be a perfectly good reason.

He could be ill.

There could be a family emergency.

He might have been in an accident.

Okay, whoa. Was she really hoping that he was ill or injured? Or that his family was? Had she sunk to a new low?

No, she was just praying that yesterday's stupid outburst hadn't sent him running and she'd never see him again.

"Guess you scared him off, Aunty G," Anita sang, walking out back. There were only twenty minutes left until close and most of their stock was gone. All that was left was some clean up and getting everything set up for Monday morning.

Tomorrow was her one day off and she desperately needed some sleep. Not that she ever managed to sleep in. Her body now seemed to be wired to wake up at four a.m. It sucked.

But not as much as not knowing whether or not she'd sent sexy, mysterious Victor running from her. And it really didn't help having Anita point out the obvious.

Anita leaned against the counter as Gracen swept. It wouldn't hurt her to pick up a rag and start cleaning. But Gracen bit her tongue. It would only take her a minute to do it and she'd do a much better job. Plus, she'd avoid an argument.

Avoiding confrontation was kind of her thing.

"I mean, I knew you were, like, awkward and stuff, but I didn't realize how bad you were at talking to guys." Anita shook her head and checked out her nails. "Guess when you've gone as long as you have without a guy you just get flustered and shit, huh?"

"It hasn't been that long," she muttered. Had it? How long since Jacob had broken things off with her? A year? No, wait, it must have been longer. Two? And she hadn't had sex since then.

Two years. Wow. She really was out of touch.

"If you want, I can hook you up with one of Ice's friends."

Ice was Anita's boyfriend. He was a little asshole who spent his days hanging with his friends and his nights doing things that Gracen really didn't want to know about. He was in his midtwenties, but as far as she could tell, he'd never had a job. Some of the guys she'd seen him hang out with belonged to the Ventura gang. They were becoming increasingly troublesome in this neighborhood.

She hated that Anita was dating Ice, but as usual, she wouldn't listen to a word Gracen said.

Their last big fight had been about Ice, and Gracen hadn't seen Anita for a week. Trying to keep the bakery open had been a nightmare. She'd had to call on Paloma, the older lady who usually only worked on Mondays, to come in to work full-time.

"Thank you, but no."

"Are you sure? Some of them are into fat older chicks."

"Anita!" she snapped. This was getting too much. There was only so much she could take from her niece.

Remember, she's the only family you have left.

Anita was the sole reminder of Christopher, her older brother. Her best friend. The only person who knew what it felt like to lose their parents. When he'd died four years ago, Anita had come to live with her. Her mother had died when Anita was young.

Anita had taken the death of her dad hard. He'd spoiled her, and when she came to live with Gracen, she'd started acting out. Getting into trouble. Gracen got it, she was angry at the world in her grief.

Then a year after Christopher's death, Gracen had lost her grandpa. That had almost killed her. If she hadn't had the bakery and Anita to take care of, she wouldn't have had much reason to get out of bed.

Then Jacob had left. Probably because she'd been so busy with everything else in her life. She couldn't blame him. But she . . . she was just so lonely and scared of losing someone else. And that included Anita, who'd moved in with her boyfriend, Ice as soon as she could. Ice wasn't a good influence on her, but Gracen hadn't been able to talk her out of living with him.

She knew she let Anita get away with too much, but speaking to her like this wasn't acceptable.

"You cannot call me old and fat, Anita," she said firmly.

"That's not a very nice way to speak to me," Anita said with a pout. "I'm just trying to help you. If you don't want my help, then just say so."

She stopped what she was doing to stare straight at her niece. "I don't want your help."

Anita's face screwed up in anger briefly before relaxing again. "Fine."

Great. Now she felt guilty. Sighing, Gracen closed her eyes for a moment. "Look, I know you were trying to be helpful. But Ice's friends aren't my type."

"You don't exactly have guys knocking your door down."

Gracen winced. She wasn't wrong. And the one guy that she'd hoped might be into her, had been scared off by her awkwardness.

Well, then she guessed he wasn't the man for her. Because she was pretty much always awkward.

"Look, we haven't had any customers for the last ten minutes. Why don't you leave early." There were fifteen minutes until close, and it wasn't like Anita was doing anything.

Turning, her face lit up with a smile. "Aw, thanks, Aunty G, you're the best." She raced off to grab her stuff.

Sure. Now she was the best. Before, she'd been a horrible person.

"Bye!" she called out as she sped off with a bag of goodies that were no doubt for Ice and his friends. Gracen sighed but didn't say anything. It wasn't a big deal if she took food to her boyfriend.

Gracen just wished that her boyfriend wasn't some gangster wannabe. She moved out to the front to tidy up. She'd stuck to the back for most of the day, not wanting the hundred and one ques-tions about her face. When she'd woken up this morning, her eye had been far worse than she'd anticipated.

She should have iced it more, but by the time she'd gotten home last night she'd been exhausted. She'd ended up crawling into bed without even taking time to eat dinner.

This morning, it had been hard to get up and moving. At least now she could open her eye slightly, but she knew it looked terri-ble. Even Anita had been concerned when she'd seen her, wanting to know who'd hit her. And offering to set Ice and his friends after them.

As if she needed Ice to fight her fights for her.

She hadn't realized how exhausting it would be to have to rely mostly on one eye all day. Or how painful it would become by the end of her shift.

She wanted to go home, take a nice, hot bath and then sleep.

She moved toward the door as a huge black truck pulled up in front of the shop. It made her freeze for a moment. An expensive vehicle in this neighborhood usually meant the person inside it was a pimp or a dealer.

Neither of which was someone she wanted to deal with at the moment.

Shock flooded her as she saw the person who stepped out.

He'd come.

But as she saw the fury edged into his face, she suddenly wondered if she'd spent all day hoping for something she shouldn't have.

She didn't lock the door. Instead, she stepped back and moved quickly behind the counter.

As if that's going to keep you safe.

Fear flooded her as Victor opened the door and stepped inside, slamming it behind him. He flicked the lock, then he started striding toward her. She ended up in the kitchen before he caught up with her, the bench pressing against her lower back as he moved in closer.

His gaze roamed over her face as he came to a stop mere inches from her. All she'd need to do was take a deep breath and her breasts would brush against his chest.

Suddenly, he reached up to touch her cheek, and she flinched back.

His eyes flared wide as he looked at his hand then down at her. Suddenly, he moved away, horror filling his face.

"You think I'd hit you?" There was raw agony in his voice.

And she realized then that she might have misread his intent. But honestly, he couldn't blame her. A man twice her size walking toward her with rage filling his face . . . well, wouldn't most people flinch away in fear?

"I . . . I . . ." she couldn't get anything more out. What could she say to make this right when she didn't even know what was going on?

"Who?" he demanded.

Huh?

"What?" she whispered.

"Who was it?" he asked. He'd backed off until he was across the room. And she stupidly found herself wishing he was closer again. That she could catch a hint of his scent, feel the warmth of his body pressed against hers. "Who hurt you?"

Was that why he was so upset? Because he thought someone had hurt her? Was his anger on her behalf? Her last bit of fear bled away as she realized this huge, scary-looking man was upset because he thought someone had harmed her.

"Nobody hurt me."

"Don't lie to me." His voice was whisper soft, but no less impactful because of it. If anything, it made her suck in a sharp breath.

She had a feeling she'd never be able to lie to him. All he'd need to do was give her the look he was giving her right now. The one that seemed to see through her, into her. The one that promised to fight all her battles.

She closed her good eye for a second. She had a raging headache. It had been there all day since she'd woken up, but now it was getting worse.

"Who hurt you, Gracen?" he asked again. "I want a name."

"Why? Why do you care?"

And how had he known that she was hurt?

"I want a name," he repeated without explaining himself.

"How did you know? Oh my God, are you on the phone tree?"

He didn't react to her wail of disbelief.

"I want a name."

Damn, he was like a broken record. "Nobody hurt me."

He turned around, giving her his back as he put his hands on the countertop. His shoulders were bunched, stiff. She heard him take several deep breaths. Without stopping to think about it too much, she stepped forward to place her hand on his back. He flinched, and she jumped back.

"S-sorry," she stuttered out.

Idiot, Gracen. He didn't want to be touched. He's obviously going through something, and you just go and put your hand on him.

Not cool.

"No, it's . . . it's okay. I just wasn't expecting . . . I'm not used to being touched."

He was killing her. No one touched him? Why didn't anyone touch him? Did he not have a family? Was he like her? Alone and lonely?

You're not alone. You have Anita.

Who cared more about her idiot boyfriend than her own aunt.

You have friends who love you.

You're loved. You're cared for.

But she didn't have someone special. Someone who put her

first. When she got home at night, there wasn't even a potted plant to greet her.

To think that this gorgeous, strong man might be in the same boat. That he could be lonely and in need of someone to see him . . . yeah, it floored her.

She reached up and ran her hand up and down over his back. "Damn, you're tight."

He let out a low noise that sounded like a chuckle.

"Have you ever considered getting a massage?" she asked.

"I don't really like people touching me."

Oh. So, when he said he wasn't used to touch, it wasn't because he didn't have anyone to touch him. He just didn't like it.

"Sorry." She snatched her hand back again.

A low growl filled the room, filling her with shocked surprise. But to her amazement, she wasn't scared of the noise.

"I didn't say stop."

"But you said you didn't like it."

"No, Gracen," he replied in that deep voice. She swore that he could say anything, and it would sound sexy in that voice. He could tell her he was going to poop, and it would send a shiver up her spine.

Okay, well, maybe not. That might be a step too far.

"I said I didn't like people touching me."

"Um, well, last time I checked, I'm people. Not an alien, I promise. Even though it might have seemed like aliens had taken over my brain last time we spoke. Actually, no, scratch that. You know what? Aliens had definitely taken over my brain. That's what happened. That wasn't me."

"Easy, baby. It's all right," he soothed.

He'd called her baby.

Cue swooning.

Her breath shuddered out of her in a long sigh.

"I don't think you're an alien."

"Is there a reason you can't look at me, though?" she asked.

She felt him take a deep breath, her hand rising as his shoulders moved. Then he slowly released it.

"Victor? Are you all right?"

"No," he replied.

Oh, no.

"Can I help?" she asked.

"Yes."

Oh, good.

"Do you need a hug? That always makes me feel better."

There was a beat of silence, and she thought he was going to reject her. Why wouldn't he? Why was she offering him a hug? He didn't like being touched. Plus, he wasn't a toddler who'd scraped his knee. Who still believed that there was magic in a kiss and a cuddle.

Although, at thirty-four, she still kind of believed in that magic.

But he likely thought she was ridiculous. She moved her hand slowly away. Perhaps if she backed up and pretended that she'd never said that, he'd think it was his imagination.

Yeah, that was a foolproof plan.

"Yes."

She stood there, frozen, her hand a few inches from his back.

"Yes?"

"Yes, I want a hug."

Right. What now? A hug? He wanted a hug. From her.

Her mind was spinning out of control. Until she saw the way he tightened up as though . . . as though he was expecting her to reject him.

Suddenly, her mind settled, and her body sprang into action as she threw herself at him. If she'd been thinking properly, she would have moved more slowly. Her face smashed into his hard back and she let out a groan of pain.

How had she forgotten about her face?

"Gracen?" He tried to turn to face her, but she was clinging to him like a baby monkey to its mama. And despite the fact that her arms didn't reach all the way around him, she wasn't letting go.

"Gracen, baby. Can I see you?"

"I'm giving you a hug."

He stilled then took another deep breath. No doubt he'd be doing that often if he spent a lot of time with her.

"I appreciate that. But can I please check on you?"

The please did it. She loosened her hold on him with a sigh of disappointment. "You're so warm, though."

Argh, had she said that?

He stiffened.

Great. She wasn't making any better of an impression than yesterday. If anything, this might be slightly worse.

Although at least she hadn't offered up her sticky buns to him.

"Oh, no! You didn't get your sticky bun today, and I don't think there're any left."

He gently grasped her hands, pulling them from him. "That's all right."

"I didn't think you were coming when you weren't here by seven-thirty."

Turning, he peered down at her. Then his hand slowly rose to cup her swollen cheek. "I'm sorry I wasn't here."

"No, that isn't . . . I wasn't saying . . . I mean, you don't have to apologize. I just didn't want you to miss out on my sticky bun—I mean your sticky bun!"

His lips twitched. "I do like your sticky buns."

She groaned. "It's become a really, really bad joke. I just have to stop speaking for the next ten years, and then maybe I'll forget about this whole thing."

"You want to forget about me?"

"What? No! Of course not." She felt herself growing red. "I

meant that I want to forget all the stupid things I've managed to say."

"Why? I think they're cute."

"Yes, well, maybe I wasn't going for cute. I mean, cute is what you say about puppies and kittens and baby elephants. It's not really sexy or anything."

"Hmm. Well, I like puppies and kittens and baby elephants. And I happen to think that cute can be sexy."

"You think baby elephants are sexy? That's kind of odd. You might want to get that looked at." She grinned to let him know she was joking.

His gaze moved to her mouth and his eyes darkened. Maybe with lust? Or perhaps he had a sore tummy.

Oh, she'd never been good at this sort of stuff.

He grasped her chin, holding her face still.

Yikes. Was this it? Was he going to kiss her?

"Gracen."

"Yes?" Her breathing quickened. She licked her lips. She was ready. So ready. It had been so long. Did her breath smell all right? Would he postpone the kiss for like thirty seconds while she tried to find a breath mint?

Stop thinking, Gracen.

"I want a name."

Huh?

"What's that got to do with kissing me?" she whispered.

Argh. Shit. Crap.

Dumb. So dumb.

She tried to step back, her face flaming with embarrassment. What an idiot. He hadn't grasped her chin to kiss her. He wanted her to answer his question about who'd hurt her. And like the fool she was, she'd just blurted her thoughts out loud.

This was the sort of humiliation that she couldn't come back from. When she tried to move away, though, he grabbed hold of her waist, lifting her onto the counter.

As she attempted to wriggle off, he moved between her legs, spreading them wide. She bit her lip to stave off the gasp of shock and need.

He hasn't lifted you up here because he wants to touch you, idiot. He just doesn't want you getting away before you answer his questions.

"Gracen," he said in that deep raspy voice.

Nope. She wasn't going to let it affect her.

"Gracen, look at me."

His hands went to her thighs. And it really wasn't fair because his touch scrambled her brain and made it hard for her to think. And she was already struggling to get her brain to work properly around him.

"Look at me, baby."

Damn it. Damn him. Calling her baby was like her kryptonite. Jacob had never given her an endearment other than the occasional babe when he wanted her to get something for him.

Babe, bring me a beer. Babe, get some dip, will you?

But this . . . this was different. He said baby with a note of cajoling. And that tone, the endearment, they spoke to that lonely person inside her. The one that wanted to give this man whatever he wanted.

And that was dangerous.

She raised her eyes to meet his dark ones. She studied him, taking in the long eyelashes. His thick beard. The small wrinkles around his eyes. A faded scar near the corner of one eye that she'd never noticed before.

"Who hurt you? Please tell me."

"Nobody."

His eyes narrowed. "Gracen."

Oh, wow. The command in his voice rocked her, dragging out the submissive in her.

When did she start to think of herself as having different personalities? That was disturbing.

"It was my friend."

"What friend? Give me his name. I'll take care of everything else. Just a name."

She opened her mouth, then shut it with a frown. Well, as much of a frown as she could manage with one side of her face swollen and bruised.

"Take care of what?"

"Of him. I'll make certain he never hurts you again."

Even though she knew there was no one to take care of and that his promise shouldn't turn her on . . . there was something about a man going all protective over her that made her go weak at the knees.

Maybe it was because it was something she'd rarely had. Her brother had been protective when they were younger. But then he'd moved away, and she'd lost that feeling of having someone who was always on her side.

And she wanted it back so desperately.

"That's a really nice sentiment—"

"It's no sentiment. It's a promise."

"Why would you care?" she asked hoarsely. She knew she should tell him the truth. Poor guy was going to give himself indigestion worrying over her. But at the same time, she was fishing for information. For something to tell her that this attraction wasn't one-sided. She thought she'd caught glimpses of his interest.

But maybe she'd been mistaken.

"Because no one hurts my . . ." he trailed off with a grimace, moving back away from her.

His face went stone cold, and she felt the loss immediately. Not just his body, but the warmth in his eyes when he looked at her. When it felt like all he saw was her.

"Your what?"

"It doesn't matter. I've asked for a name. I want a name." That tension was back in his shoulders.

"Nobody hurt me," she whispered. "I told you that. It was an accident."

"What sort of an accident?" he asked, giving her a skeptical look.

"My friend and I, we take a dance class for beginners, only we're really bad."

He appeared puzzled. "Someone at the dance class did this to you?"

"In a roundabout way," she told him. "My friend did it."

"What?"

"She was trying to get her foot up high, only she's kind of clumsy and she whacked me in the face with her foot."

"She kicked you?"

"Yes, but it was totally an accident. So, you know, there's no one to, uh, take care of."

He stared at her for a long moment.

Another deep breath in. Then out. Long and slow. "Why didn't you tell me that?"

"I was trying to, but you seemed rather upset. I should have tried harder to tell you right away." She stared down at her hands as she twisted her fingers together in her lap. "Sorry."

There was silence. Then to her shock, he moved closer and gently tilted her face back with his finger under her chin.

"You're telling the truth?"

"Yes. I'm actually terrible at lying. And do you really think I can make this stuff up?"

He studied her face. "Did you ice it?"

"Yeah, in the beginning, but I think I should have iced it more. It looks pretty bad, huh?"

"Yeah. It does."

Great. She knew she wasn't looking her best but having him confirm how bad it looked really made her feel down. She wanted Victor to see her as attractive and sexy.

"It looks sore. Did you take some painkillers?"

"Last night," she admitted. "I'm not fond of taking any sort of pills."

He gave her a curious look but nodded. "I get that. But it's fine to take pain relief if you're in pain. In fact, I'm going to insist on it."

"Why?"

"Because I don't like seeing you in pain." Reaching up, he ran a finger down her cheek, then he sighed. "Your skin is so smooth."

"Thank you." Emboldened, she ran a finger down his cheek and over his beard. "You're hairy."

Oh, God.

Did she really just say that?

"Thank you, I try."

"I didn't mean that negatively," she said hastily. "I like your beard. Not like hairy as in your legs need a shave, hairy. Like, sexy hairy."

"That's . . . good to know," he replied.

"I'm not usually this awkward . . . there's just something about you that makes me nervous."

He nodded solemnly. "I usually make people nervous."

She could be mistaken, but there seemed to be something lonely about the way he said that.

When he tried to step back, she reached out and grabbed his hand. "Not a bad sort of nervous. Not the kind of nervous where I think you'd hurt me or anything. For some reason, I feel safe around you. As if you'd protect me. I know that sounds silly—"

"It doesn't sound silly. I would protect you."

"And I'd protect you."

His gaze warmed. "That's good to know, little bit."

Oh, that was cute.

"So, you see, I'm not nervous for bad reasons. I guess I just get flustered when you look at me."

He placed his hands on her thighs, moving them around behind her to grasp her ass.

She let out a low moan of pleasure at his touch.

"I shouldn't be doing this."

"Why not?" she asked.

"Because I'm dangerous to be around," he replied. "I'd never harm you, but that doesn't make me a good person."

"You seem like a good person to me."

"You don't know me, little bit."

"Well, you tip well. And you hold doors open for little old ladies. And you like my sticky buns, so . . ."

"With each day that passes, my soul gets darker and darker."

"Victor, that's not true."

She hated that he thought that. She reached out to touch his face, but he drew back. And it was like a curtain came down over his face. She knew she wouldn't be reaching him now.

"Where are your painkillers? Do you have some here?"

"Uh, yeah, there's some in that drawer over there." She pointed over behind him, trying not to show how sad she was that he'd drawn back from her.

He found the painkillers and shook a couple of pills out of the bottle onto his palm. Then, grabbing a glass from where she had them set on a shelf, he poured her some water before returning to where she still sat on the counter.

She held out her hand and he put the pills in her palm and handed her the glass. She swallowed them down with a grimace.

"You eaten today?" he asked.

"Um, yep."

"What did you eat?"

"Uh, I don't know." What had she eaten? She couldn't remember. "I think I had a few bites of a cupcake and maybe some brownie."

"That isn't a proper meal," he said chidingly. "You need to take breaks and eat."

"Like I said, my thighs won't complain from a few missed meals."

"And like I said," he spoke in a voice that had delicious chills working their way up her spine, "you won't be saying things like that. Not without consequences."

"What sort of consequences?" she whispered.

Please let them be the most delicious kind.

But he drew back again. Damn, it was like one step forward, two steps back with him.

"You especially need to eat if you're taking painkillers, or you'll feel ill."

"Right. I guess. I think there's a protein bar around here somewhere."

He blew out a breath, then shook his head. "Are you finished here?"

"Hmm? Yeah, pretty much."

"What about your earnings for the day? It's been secured?"

"Mostly. I've just got a little bit of change left in the till to deal with."

"Go do that, then lock up and meet me outside." He lifted her down, then walked off. What were they doing?

5

This was such a stupid idea.

He studied his surroundings while he thought about how close he'd come to kissing Gracen's full, pink lips.

What he wouldn't give to see those lips wrapped around his cock as she knelt in front of him, trying to swallow him down. Her lips stretched, hums of pleasure coming from her as he fucked her mouth.

Shut it down.

She wasn't someone he could just fuck and get out of his system. Hell, he hadn't been with a woman in . . . in years. It was easier to use his hand than it was to worry about hurting a woman, about being too rough.

So, he'd closed off any thoughts or dreams of having someone.

Until he spotted her. And now all he could think about was all the ways he wanted to have her, take care of her, fuck her.

Own her.

It was torture. Watching her from afar was enough of a risk, being up close to her was just stupid.

So fucking stupid.

Yet, he wasn't walking away. He couldn't.

He'd make sure she ate some proper food and get her safely home.

Then he'd try to figure out how the hell to stay away from the one good thing in his fucked-up life.

"I'm ready."

He turned, studying her. He hated the bruises on her face. Her swollen eye. She winced as though the sunlight was hurting her.

"Your head still hurts," he stated.

"I'm all right. It will go away soon." She tried to give him a smile.

The desire to kidnap her and hide her away somewhere safe where no one would ever find her rode him hard. Fuck. He'd never wanted something more and he wasn't used to denying himself.

The restraint he was showing was award-winning.

"I was going to take you out for something to eat, but if you're too tired or sore, you could go home and I'll send for something."

"I'd really like to go out to eat something. If that's good with you."

Getting to spend more time with her was always all right with him. Even if it was a bad idea.

He nodded, then opened the passenger side of his truck. She got her foot up on the running board, then attempted to pull herself up, without much success.

"How high is this?" she grumbled.

Not that high. But then he was a big guy.

Wrapping his hands around her waist, he lifted her up and into the seat. She let out a small gasp as he settled her in, then pulled back quickly.

He walked around the front of the vehicle and climbed in. She was sitting stiffly, she hadn't even put on her belt. She looked like a small child who was too scared to touch anything for fear she'd get told off.

"You all right, little bit?" he asked.

"I feel underdressed for this car."

He frowned. He didn't want her to ever feel unsure. Or like she wasn't good enough. Because she was a queen and the whole world should bow down to her.

"Gracen? Look at me."

"Yes?" She turned to gaze up at him.

"It's just a fucking car."

She stared at him for a moment. Then she broke into a gorgeous smile. "It's just a fucking car?"

He winced. "Sorry."

"For what? For saying fucking? I don't care if you swear. I can swear like a sailor. Argghhh, me fucking hearties."

"Are you trying to be a sailor or a pirate?" he asked.

She giggled, and he felt like he was floating. Which was an odd feeling when all he'd ever done was sink.

"Obviously, I need to work on my pirate speak." She shook her head. "So, was that your way of saying I can touch what I like?"

"Yep."

"But what if I break it? I can't exactly afford to replace it. I can't even replace anything in my car and it's probably worth the same amount as one of your tires."

Likely less.

He didn't say that though. And he needed to figure out a way to get her car looked at. He still didn't like the noise it was making.

"You won't break anything."

"I wouldn't be so sure."

"I don't give a shit if you destroy the whole car, all right?"

"Well, I'll try not to do that. But okay."

Reaching across her, he grabbed the seatbelt and fastened it. Her cheeks filled with red, and he swore a shiver ran through her as his arm brushed against her breasts.

"I can do that."

"I know." That was all he said. She didn't make any more protests, which surprised him.

He liked doing things for her.

But he loved that she seemed to like him taking care of her.

It spoke to the protector inside him. The part of him that would wrap her up tightly to keep her safe from the dangers of this world.

If only he wasn't one of those dangers.

Turning back, he started his truck and drove toward Matteo's restaurant. He pulled into a parking spot, then he turned to her.

"This place good?"

"Yeah. I've never been in here." She bit her lip, and he could tell she was worrying again.

"What's wrong?"

She glanced down at herself, then over at the restaurant. "Maybe getting some takeout is a better idea."

Reaching out, he gently took hold of her chin, turning her face toward him. This was wrong. He shouldn't touch her, shouldn't look at her, and he definitely shouldn't be taking her out for dinner.

Yet here he was.

And there was no turning back now.

Not tonight anyway. Maybe tomorrow he'd be stronger. Once he was out of her presence.

Yeah. Right.

"You look beautiful no matter what you're wearing. You outshine everyone else."

She shook her head, and he moved his fingers away from her chin. "You flatterer, you. But seriously, I can't go in like this. Can I?"

"If it makes you uncomfortable, we won't go in."

"It doesn't embarrass you? Being seen with me?" she asked.

"Embarrass me? How the fuck could you ever do that? And who gives a fuck what anyone thinks."

Happiness filled her face, and she ducked her head shyly. "For a guy that doesn't talk a lot, you say the nicest things."

Christ. He'd never been accused of being nice. But around her, he could be different. He wasn't Victor, the fighter, the enforcer.

"All right then, I'd like to go in."

"Good."

She reached for her door handle, but he grabbed hold of her arm. "Wait for me to come around and open your door."

"I've never had someone open doors for me before you."

"Then you've been hanging out with the wrong people."

She gave him an intense look. "I think I have been."

She'd been right.

She really wasn't dressed for this place. She looked out of place beside Victor in his expensive-looking clothes. But to her surprise, no one seemed to bat an eye. In fact, as soon as the hostess saw him, she'd blanched white then started stammering.

Victor was an intimidating-looking guy, sure. But it seemed an over-reaction since he was being polite to the woman.

She guided them to a booth at the back. It was darker and again, Victor sat with his back to the wall, looking out at the room. After taking their drink orders, their server scampered off.

"Do you always like to sit where you can view the whole room?" she blurted out.

He glanced over at her with his eyebrow raised.

"Sorry," she said. "It's just I noticed you sat like that yesterday and today you're doing the same. But was that rude to ask?"

"Not rude, no. Observant."

She ran her finger over the veins in the wooden table. Reaching out, he placed his hand over hers. She sucked in a deep breath. The warmth of his skin infused her. His palm was rough, the top of his hand covered in scars. Not to mention the scrapes on his knuckles.

"You're nervous."

"Slightly," she agreed.

"Because of me?"

"Uh-huh."

"I'm sorry."

She gave him a surprised look. He didn't seem the type to apologize easily. And she wasn't quite sure why he was now.

"For what?"

"Making you nervous. Is it my size? The way I acted before? I was angry, but it wasn't at you. I thought someone hurt you and . . ."

"I get it." She placed her free hand on top of his, sandwiching his big hand between hers. "And I'm not scared of you."

He gave her a skeptical look. "I saw the way you backed away from me."

"All right, for a moment I might have been scared. You looked rather frightening when you entered the bakery. But then I understood that you were angry on my behalf and, well, it's been a long time since anyone felt protective of me."

He gave her a long, searching look. "You don't have anyone to take care of you?"

She smiled, aware it was slightly sad. "I can look after myself."

"Why don't I believe that?"

"Hey. I can." She straightened. "I'll admit that it gets tiring doing everything myself, though. I miss having someone to come home to."

And now you're starting to sound pathetic.

He didn't want to know about how lonely her life was, that was just depressing.

"What do you feel like for dinner? It's my treat," she told him.

If she lived on bakery leftovers for a few weeks, she could use her grocery money.

"Your treat?" he asked quietly.

"Yep. My turn to pay. The steak sounds good." It sounded amazing and her mouth watered at the thought of it. But she'd need to grab the cheapest item. A garden salad. Yuck. Cobb salad. Getting better.

But she'd make sure he had whatever he wanted. He was a big guy, he needed plenty of fuel.

"Your treat?"

She realized he wasn't repeating what she'd said because he hadn't heard her the first time. Instead, he sounded like he was in complete disbelief.

"Uh, yeah. I'm paying."

"In what world would you be paying?" he asked gruffly.

"It's my turn."

"Your. Turn," he said the words slowly, as though he didn't understand them.

"Because you paid for my sticky bun the other day. It's turnabout, see?" How was he not getting this?

He simply stared down at her. "No."

What? That was it? No?

"No, what? No, you don't want me to pay?"

"Correct."

"But it's only fair—"

"Fair? It's fair that you pay for a full meal when I bought you a sticky bun worth two dollars? That's fair?"

"Uh, well. Next time we go out you can pay for the meal. Not that there needs to be a next time. I mean, I'm not saying there can't be a next time. Or even that you have to pay. You're under no obligation to take me—" He reached out and placed a finger over her lips.

Oh, thank God. It was about time he shut her up. She swore her mouth was a runaway train around him.

He made her so darn nervous.

"I'll say this once. There will never be a time when you pay. We go out for a meal, I pay. We go do anything together, I pay. Got me?"

"That's not how turnabout works," she grumbled.

How was being dictated to like that so hot? It shouldn't be and yet . . . she liked that he wanted to look after her.

Even if she wasn't going to let him pay every time—that's not how friendship worked. And that's what this was, right?

"There is no turnabout. That's the way things are. Do you want a starter?"

"Huh? Oh, no, I don't need a starter," she replied. "And you can't pay for me all the time."

"Can't I? Who is going to stop me?"

She straightened her shoulders. "Me."

His lips twitched as he slid the iced tea she'd ordered closer. "No, you're not. Now, what are you eating?"

She sighed. "You're a frustrating man to argue with."

"That's what we were doing? Arguing?"

"Well, not exactly."

"You really object to me wanting to look after you?"

She stared at him as those words sunk in. "No, I'm not objecting to that. But looking out for me doesn't mean me taking advantage of you."

Shock filled his face. "You think that's what you're doing?"

"No, but I don't want you to think that." She ran a finger along the condensation on the glass of her iced tea that the server had delivered before running off again.

"Gracen, look at me."

Yeah, she didn't want to do that. He seemed to be able to

convince her of anything when she was looking into those hazel-colored eyes. "Baby, I wouldn't ever think that."

Damn it. He was bringing out the big guns by calling her baby. She shifted around on her seat, still unable to meet his gaze. "It's just obvious you have money, and I don't, and I don't want you to think that's why I . . . why I'm here."

She'd almost blurted out that she liked him. That was one way to have him running from her.

"You want me to give it all away?"

"W-what?" She gazed up at him.

He ran a finger down her cheek. "My money. Want me to get rid of it? Will that make you feel more comfortable?"

"What? No!" she protested even though she knew he had to be joking.

Although he wasn't exactly the joking type . . . but that was silly.

"Of course I don't."

"But you feel like things are uneven because I have money and you don't?" he asked matter-of-factly.

Their server approached, opening his mouth.

"We need a few more minutes," Victor told him before he could speak.

"O-of course," the guy stammered out. "T-take all the time you need."

"I think you made him nervous."

"I make everyone nervous. Except you."

"You make me nervous," she blurted out.

Idiot!

"But not in the same way," he murmured, watching her closely. "How do I make you nervous, Gracen?"

Oh, hell.

She wasn't going to tell him that.

Suddenly, she felt his hand brush against her thigh. Her breath caught, her eyes widening as a rush of arousal filled her.

"How do I make you nervous?"

"I just . . . I . . ."

"Do you think I'd hurt you?" His fingers brushed lightly up and down her leg.

Killing her. He was killing her.

This was insane. She could feel her nipples tightening, her clit throbbing. It was slightly embarrassing how easily she was getting turned on. He was touching her leg, for goodness sake. That shouldn't be sexy.

Only, he was moving his hand around to her inner thigh. Her legs were pressed firmly together. Should she part them? Did that seem like an invitation? Shoot. What did he want from her?

She really wished men came with instruction manuals. It would make her life a lot easier.

"Gracen?"

What? Oh, crap. He'd asked her a question. What was it, though? Damned if she knew.

"Are you listening?" He moved his fingers lower, toward her knee.

"I'm trying. But you can't expect me to think when you're touching me."

"I'm distracting you?" He moved his hand away. Reaching out, she grabbed hold of his wrist.

"Wait, no! Don't stop."

Oh, Lord, what was she doing?

"I mean, I . . . you don't have to stop unless you want to stop, that is. Whatever it is you want to do is fine with me."

"Hey, you're all right," he said soothingly, placing his arm over the back of her chair.

She heaved out a breath. "I am?"

"You are." He brushed a finger down her cheek then placed it under her chin, turning her face to his. "Do you think I'd hurt you, Gracen?"

"No, like I told you before, I feel safe around you."

"Good." His voice was filled with satisfaction. "You like my touch."

"Yes, I just . . ."

"You just what?"

"Don't exactly know what you want from me, and I don't want to make a wrong move. I just . . . sometimes I wish I knew what to do. And I don't want you to think that I'm interested in your money."

He hummed. "No one has ever offered to treat me. Trust me, I know you're not here for my money. I might not even have any. This could all be on credit. I could be horribly in debt."

Somehow she didn't think that was the case.

He ran a finger down her cheek, then closed his eyes as though in pain. "Christ, I shouldn't be doing this."

"Why not?"

"Because I can't have you, Gracen. You deserve far better than me."

She narrowed her gaze at him. "That sounds like a cop-out. Like, when you break up with someone and you tell them it's not you, it's me. Argh, I hate when people do that."

"Someone did that to you?" he asked in a gravelly voice.

She was too far in her own memories to hear the warning in his voice.

"Yeah, my last boyfriend said that. Of course, he also told me that I didn't give him enough affection, but I was also too needy. I mean . . . how can I do both of those things, right? Asshole."

"What's his name?"

Finally, she was aware of the danger permeating the air. She glanced over to find him staring down at her intently.

"Why?"

"I want to know."

She shook her head. "No. Nope."

He leaned in, and she realized he still had his hand around the back of her neck. Maybe it should have felt threatening, but it didn't.

It felt possessive.

And she wanted him to possess her. Own her.

Oh, hell. She was so out of her depth here.

"Don't say no to me."

"What do you want from me?"

"Everything. I want fucking everything."

Her heart raced.

"But you're such an innocent, Gracen. You live in the sunshine while I'm down in the filthy dark. I shouldn't drag you down with me."

"Yeah? Who says I won't pull you up with me?"

"I'm stuck where I am, baby."

"Nobody is ever stuck, Victor. They've just got to want to move."

"If I said I wanted to stay where I am?" he asked.

She got the feeling the question wasn't a casual one.

"What if this is me and I can't change?" he asked. "Won't change."

How could she answer that when she didn't know exactly who he was? It just highlighted how little she knew about him.

He dropped his hold on her, then turned to pick up the menu again.

"I don't know you well enough to answer that," she finally said. "But I want to get to know you better. You . . . I like you, Victor."

"Like you said, you don't know me."

"But I want to. And I have some idea about the important parts. You're protective. You're watchful, observant, sometimes kind."

"I'm never kind." There was almost a twinkle in his eyes as though she amused him.

"You're stubborn and have some very set ideas about things like whether I get to take a turn paying—"

"Never happening."

"And you seem to think I'm incapable of getting into a vehicle on my own—"

"You're too short."

"Plus, you can't tell the difference between a pirate impression and a sailor—"

"I can tell the difference, baby. You're just crappy at impressions."

She huffed out a breath, insulted by that. "But I guess I can work on helping you with those."

"You won't change my stubbornness or convince me to ever let you pay," he told her firmly.

"But I can still teach you about what a proper pirate voice sounds like. Noted." She rubbed her finger up and down her glass. "I know that I look forward to you coming into the bakery every morning, and I was upset when you didn't come in this morning."

He took hold of her small hand in his much larger one. "You missed me?"

"Yeah. And I was worried. I didn't know how to contact you to make sure you were all right."

"We'll remedy that," he promised.

Her breath hitched.

"I want you, Gracen. I like you. My life is dangerous and it's complicated and for your own safety I should walk away."

"I don't like the idea of you being in danger."

"No? I don't like the idea of you being in danger either."

"I'm tougher than I look." She straightened her shoulders. "You don't know, but I could be a closet badass."

"Are you?"

She sighed. "No. Damn it, sometimes it's a curse being so honest."

"Not for me, it's refreshing. I don't have many honest people in my life."

"Well, you can have me." She winced. "I just offered myself up on a platter, didn't I?"

"I like that you want me. Because you have no idea how much I want you. I just have to figure out a way to keep you safe."

"So, you're not walking away?" she asked hopefully.

"Right now, it would be impossible to leave you. But once you know the full truth about me, you might run."

"I'm not going to run. Don't really have the body for it. Obviously." She gestured at her body.

He moved in close once more, his mouth brushing her ear. "Told you what I think about you putting yourself down. And what I expect. Do it again, and you'll learn how you'll be punished."

Drawing back, he stared down at her, studying her. She got the feeling he expected her to fight back.

If only he knew what was going on in her body right now. He'd know that getting away from him was very, very far down the list.

She licked her lips. "Was that supposed to turn me off?"

"Fuck, baby. Keep saying stuff like that and I won't ever be able to let you go."

"I'm like red wine. I get better with age. Well, some red wines. There's some that I swear taste like cat piss. And wow, I wish I really hadn't said that."

Urgh. What was wrong with her?

"Look at your menu. You need to eat. What would you like?"

No one had ever told her that she needed to eat before. Jacob had been on the Anita-train of thought when it came to her weight. Meaning he thought she was overweight as well.

Honestly, it was refreshing. And the way he warned her off talking badly about her body?

Delicious.

She squirmed on her seat and his hand went back to her thigh. "Still."

She drew in a sharp breath but froze in place.

"Good girl."

Warmth flooded her at his words.

"What would you like to eat?" he asked.

"I was thinking of the Cobb salad."

He raised his eyebrows, staring down at her. "That's really what you want? Or are you choosing it because it's the second cheapest item on the menu? What's wrong? Couldn't stomach the garden salad?"

"Damn it, you're observant."

"There's very little about you I don't notice."

"That could be a good thing or bad thing, I guess," she muttered.

"Good for your pleasure," he told her. "Bad for your ass."

"W-what? Why?" And could they go back to that pleasure thing?

"Because you won't get away with much and that means that if you do something you're not supposed to, then your ass will pay the price."

She leaned into him. "Are you threatening to spank me?"

He stared down at her. "Scared?"

"Nope. I don't scare easily."

"Need you to remember that later."

Well, that wasn't ominous or anything.

6

Victor gestured for the server. The man rushed over, nearly tripping over his own feet. She winced in sympathy. She understood how Victor could look intimidating if you didn't know him. Hell, even once you did know him.

She was under no illusions that anything would last. She doubted that she was like any of the other women he'd been with. Frankly, she was shocked that she kept his attention at all.

But she had. So, who said she couldn't reap the rewards while she had it?

"C-can I help you, Mr. M—"

"Yes," Victor told him. "We'll both have the filet mignon, I'll take mine rare, no sauce and . . ." He looked at her.

"Oh, I'm allowed to choose?" she asked dryly.

"I can order it for you if you'd like."

"No, nope, that's okay. I'll have it well-done, thanks. With mushroom sauce." She'd never had mushroom sauce with her steak. It sounded rather delicious.

The waiter opened his mouth with a frown, then took one look at Victor and nodded.

"I'll put that right in." He disappeared and she turned her attention back to Victor.

"I don't know much about you. I mean, I only just found out your name." And she was already considering how she could get him into her bed.

"And yet, even though I hardly know you, it also feels like I've known you for years. Does that sound silly? Almost as though we've been in contact in a past life or something. Or maybe it's just because you're my stalker," she joked.

He stiffened. "What?"

"Remember, I accused you of stalking me because you knew my name?" she reminded him.

"Oh, yes. Of course. Your name badge."

"You're not really stalking me, right?" she said jokingly.

"If I did, it would only be for your protection."

"Right, ha ha. I'm certain you have more important and inter-esting things to do than follow my ass around. I'm so boring you'd fall asleep. So, what is it that you . . ." she trailed off as he narrowed his gaze at something over her shoulder.

"Excuse me," a pompous-sounding voice said from behind them.

"Yes?" she asked, turning.

The short man standing there was dressed in a chef's uniform that strained over his bulging stomach. He held a piece of paper in his hand.

"Did you order the filet mignon well-done, ma'am?"

"Uh, yes?" This was a bit weird.

"Well, you ordered it wrong. It's only cooked rare or medium-rare. Never well-done." His voice was snooty and condescending and she felt herself shrinking. How was she supposed to know? She'd rarely eaten steak and when she had, her grandpa would cook the crap out of it on the grill. She'd never eaten steak that wasn't well-done.

Victor leaned forward, resting his forearms on the table. The chef's smirking gaze went from her to him. And his expression changed in an instant. He visibly gulped.

"My girl wants her filet mignon well done. Is that going to be a problem?"

"Uh, well, yes, you see, that's not the way I cook this cut of steak."

"Then you best learn how to cook it that way. Because what she wants, she gets."

Someone needed to come cool her down because she swore her body was overheating.

Who didn't want to hear a sexy, commanding guy like Victor say that?

"It's all right, I can eat it, uh, medium-rare." Argh, did that mean there would be blood? She wasn't sure she could handle that. "Or maybe I should get the fish." There was no way she could muck up the order for that, right?

"No, you're having the steak," Victor told her firmly. "And it's going to be cooked how you want it to be cooked. Isn't it?"

"Yes, well, it will taste terrible though. Perhaps you'd prefer some porterhouse cooked well-done?"

"Yes, okay, thanks," she said hastily before Victor could say anything.

"I apologize for interrupting you." The chef waddled off.

"Just great," she groaned, sitting back in her chair.

"What is it?"

"He's going to spit in our food."

Victor narrowed his gaze. "He better not." He moved his hand back to her leg, running it up and down her thigh. She shivered.

"What do you do for a living?" she asked, trying to get her mind off how good that felt.

"What do you think I do?" he countered.

"Ooh, a guessing game. I like these. Do you own a gym?"

"No."

"Are you a businessman?"

"No."

"Lawyer?"

"Definitely not."

She clicked her fingers together. "Writer."

"Writer? Really?" he asked.

"Yeah, it was a long shot. But I thought maybe I should take a chance. I could have asked if you were a contortionist, but . . ."

"Definitely not that."

"Me either. You should see me trying to get my foot up onto the barre. It's pitiful. I'm way too short to begin with. But then, Sammy is a lot taller than me, and she can't manage it either."

"Sammy? She's the one who did this?" He ran his finger gently down her swollen cheek.

Argh, she'd nearly forgotten that she looked like one of Picasso's paintings. It was still hard to see out of her eye and even though the painkillers she'd swallowed earlier had taken the edge off her headache, she could still feel a dull ache in her temples.

"Yes, but she didn't mean to. It was a total accident," she told him hastily.

He just grunted. "You should have stayed home today. It's easy to see it pains you."

"No rest for the wicked." She grinned at him.

"Wicked, huh? Just how wicked are you, little bit?"

"Oh, very."

"Yes, I can tell. Very, very wicked." He moved his hand from her thigh up to her neck. She almost protested, until he started massaging. She moaned in pleasure, her eyelids closing.

"Jesus, baby. You can't make noises like that in public. It makes me want to do things you really aren't ready for."

She opened her eyes, staring over at him. "What makes you think I'm not ready?"

"You're not the type to just jump into something."

"No?"

"No, you're the type who is looking for her happy ever after."

And she was guessing he didn't think he could be that for her. But maybe she could show him differently.

He moved his hand back down to her thigh. "Part your legs."

She breathed out deeply as she moved her legs apart.

"More."

She missed the feel of his hand on her neck, massaging out the tension. But then his fingers grazed the inside of her thigh, making her gasp. And that was through the material of her pants. She could only imagine how good his touch would feel on her bare skin.

"Be quiet, little bit," he warned. "And widen your legs further."

He slid his hand further up her leg, toward her pussy. This was . . . he couldn't . . . it was insane. She'd never done anything like this before. Was she really doing this now?

But they were in a dark booth and the tablecloth went down to the floor, which meant no one could see what he was doing.

However, she felt certain that if they took one look at her, they'd know exactly what he was doing to her.

"Good girl," he told her, stilling his hand as the server returned with their food.

She stared down at the steak, potato gratin, and charred broccoli with little interest. She needed him to move his fingers up closer to where she wanted them the most.

Lord, she hoped that her vibrator had working batteries. Because there was no way she was getting to sleep tonight unless she took care of the need pulsing through her.

"Eat your dinner, little bit."

Turning, she stared up into his eyes and licked her lips. "I'm not that hungry anymore."

Well, not for food. But for something else . . .

He removed his hand with a shake of his head. She let out a noise of protest, wanting to snatch his hand back and put it where it would do the most good.

"Don't stop touching me," she whispered.

"Be a good girl and eat your dinner. Then you'll get a reward."

"Is this the equivalent of if you don't eat your vegetables, then you don't get dessert?"

His lips twitched. "Something like that."

"You do know I'm not a child."

"I know that you're still talking rather than eating. And that naughty girls don't get rewards."

Well, she didn't want to be naughty.

At least, she didn't think so.

When she started to eat, though, her appetite soon came roaring back.

"Oh man, this food is delicious." And she probably looked like a pig, stuffing food in her mouth. Especially when she took in his impeccable manners.

Honestly, he seemed to eat without even eating. There were no crumbs in his beard or down his shirt. He didn't chew too loudly. Or clang his knife against the plate.

How did he do it?

"Are you even human?" she asked, staring at him.

"Sorry?"

"You just eat so perfectly."

"Uh, well. I had lessons."

"You had lessons?" she asked. What did that even mean? "On how to eat?"

"Sort of. On table manners, etiquette, things like that."

"Wow. Don't take this the wrong way, but you don't look like the sort of guy to take etiquette lessons."

"Well, I didn't take them last week," he told her. "This was when I was younger. Keep eating."

"I don't know. I'm a mess. Look at me. Yikes. How did I spill something on my boob? Stupid boobs," she muttered, reaching for her napkin. "They're always catching food."

"Don't worry about it." He stilled her hand.

"But I look so messy, and you look so perfect."

"Appearances can be deceptive, little bit. I am far from perfect. And you . . . you are perfection personified."

Lord. He really did say all the right things. Could be he was just saying these things to get in her pants.

She finished eating and sat back with a groan. "That was delicious. And I'm full."

"You did an excellent job." He brushed his fingers along the inside of her thigh then cupped her pussy. "Well done."

"I've always been good at eating." She groaned. "And I can't believe I just said that."

"Did you always want to run a bakery?" he asked her.

"Not really. I really wanted to be a superhero, unfortunately that didn't pan out. My grandpa owned the bakery, and he taught me to bake. And I do love baking and creating things. Not so much the day-to-day business stuff."

"You work long days?"

"Yeah. I was nearly late this morning because of my stupid car. Which would have been a disaster since I don't have anyone else to do the baking. But you don't want to hear about my boring day."

"I want to hear everything about you. I doubt it was boring."

"Oh, it totally was. I got up, had to send several prayers to the car gods to get my car started, got to work, baked all day, hid out in the back, and had my niece tell me how terrible I am at talking to men. Oh, and she offered to set me up with some of her boyfriend's friends who like fat, older women. And then some sexy guy came racing into the bakery, swept me off my feet and brought me out for the best dinner I've ever had."

"Wait. Go back. She tried to set you up with her boyfriend's friends?"

"Yes, apparently, she thinks I need a lot of help in that department. Can't blame her for thinking that."

"I can blame her for calling you old and fat," he said in a cold voice.

She opened her mouth to say it wasn't exactly wrong, but the look on his face had her shutting her mouth once more. Yeah, that probably wouldn't go well for her.

"I've got to use the bathroom."

"Go straight there and back," he told her.

"Have you always been this bossy or is it special just for me?"

"Straight there and back."

As if she was going to go off somewhere else. Shaking her head at him, she headed into the women's bathroom. Whoa, even the bathrooms in this place were gorgeous.

When she came out of the stall, a gorgeous, well-dressed woman with dark hair was standing by the sinks.

"I can get you out," she whispered to her.

"I'm sorry, what? Get out of where? Oh, no, are we locked in? That's my worst nightmare, to get locked in a public bathroom. Or my own bathroom, I guess. Still, I guess at least I'm not locked in the stall. How did we get locked in here?"

"We, uh, we didn't."

"Oh. Sorry. I just assumed when you said you could get me out . . . I'm sorry, you probably weren't even talking to me."

Jeez. This had just become hugely embarrassing.

She turned to walk out of the bathroom, aware that her face was flaming.

"Wait, no! I was talking to you!" The other woman reached out and grabbed her wrist. "I was saying I can get you away from that guy."

"What guy?"

"The one you came in with."

"Victor? Why would I want to get away from him?" Frankly, all she wanted was to get closer to him.

"Because of what he did to you, of course."

This conversation was really confusing.

"What did he do to me?"

The woman was staring at her like she was a few cards short of a deck. "Your face."

"My face? Oh." It finally clicked. "I am such a doofus, you're talking about my black eye."

"Yes."

"Wait, and you're offering to get me away from Victor because you think he did it?"

"Yes. But we really have to go now before he comes for you. Come on."

"No, no, Victor didn't do this."

The other woman's face filled with a mix of pity and sympathy. Gracen studied her, there was something slightly off about her. "You don't have to lie about it. I can help you. I can get you to somewhere where he won't find you."

"No, no, I'm not lying. He really didn't do this. My friend kicked me in the face. It wasn't Victor."

"Right . . . that's a version of 'I walked into a door' I've never heard before. But you shouldn't put up with someone hurting you."

"I'm not. I promise. But thank you for caring. It's actually really brave of you to help a stranger you think is being abused." That wasn't an easy thing to do. A lot of people would prefer to ignore an injustice rather than put themselves out there to help someone.

"Thanks." The other woman had gorgeous dark hair and mesmerizing green eyes. Not many people had true green eyes and Gracen wondered if they were contacts. "When I needed help, someone came to my aid. Not that it worked," she muttered so quietly that Gracen knew she wasn't supposed to hear. "So, I'm trying to pay it forward by helping as many women like me as I can. I can help you. You don't need to be afraid."

"Thank you, but I'm not lying or making up excuses. Victor didn't hurt me. This really was dance-related."

"Right. Look, I'm sure your, uh, man will be looking for you soon and I don't want you to get hurt. I know the way this goes. My name is Lilia. Here's my phone number if you ever need help. Call me. I'll do whatever it takes to get you away."

Lilia slipped a piece of paper with her number on it into her hand, then stepped out of the bathroom.

Gracen slid the piece of paper into her front pocket. Not that she needed it. But somehow, it felt disrespectful to Lilia to just throw it away. When she walked out, Victor was waiting outside the door.

"Oh, hi."

He frowned, running his gaze over her. "I was about to come into the bathroom. Are you all right? You were taking a while."

"Yep, I'm fine. Sorry I took so long."

Great. He probably thought she'd been pooping or something.

"Ready to go?" he asked.

"Sure thing. Are you sure that I can't go dutch with you?"

His look would have sent a lesser person on fire. Luckily, she was made of tougher stuff. Well, not really. Which is why she caved immediately.

7

Victor escorted her through the quiet restaurant then out to his vehicle. He watched their surroundings, hovering close to her as he guided her back to his massive truck.

He lifted her in, doing up her belt before closing the door.

It probably shouldn't feel this good, being taken care of like this. But it did. It really did.

Starting up the truck, he didn't use the backing cameras. Instead, he placed his arm over the back of her seat and turned to back out.

His scent drifted over to her. It was subtle and delicious. She breathed him in as he turned around and put the truck into drive.

"Are you sniffing me, little bit?" he asked in that low voice.

"Uh, well, um, maybe?"

"Like what you can smell?" His free hand moved back to her thigh. He had a thing about putting his hand on her leg. And she was absolutely into it.

She relaxed into her seat. "Oh, yes, you smell edible."

"You want to eat me, huh?" His fingers slid between her legs.

She parted them slightly, and he ran his fingers up and down the seam of her pants, right over her pussy lips.

What she wouldn't do to feel him touching her bare pussy.

"Maybe."

"Just a maybe?"

"All right, more than maybe. Yes, I want to eat you." Her gaze drifted to his crotch. Was his dick as big as the rest of him?

Holy. Heck.

How do I prepare for that?

He rubbed his fingers back and forth over her pussy. And her heart started racing. She wanted more. Needed to feel him touching her clit.

"I need a bigger vibrator," she muttered.

"What?" he asked.

"What?" she repeated. Because she was absolutely going to pretend she hadn't just said that.

How embarrassing.

How could she have said that out loud?

She needed a muzzle or something. Dear Lord, she hoped he hadn't heard that. Or if he had heard it that he'd pretend otherwise.

"You just said that you were going to need a bigger vibrator."

"No, you must have heard me wrong. I said that I needed a bigger refrigerator." She winced. Right, because they sounded so alike.

She was an idiot. A complete and utter idiot.

"A woman approached me in the toilet. She thought you were abusing me and offered to help me leave you," she blurted out, hoping to distract him from her plans to buy a giant vibrator so she could get ready for his cock. Unless he didn't have a big cock. Just because he was oversized didn't mean all of him was.

"You're staring at my cock again, baby."

"What? No, I'm not. You have dick on the mind." She was so

hot she was certain she could fry eggs on her cheeks. How had this conversation gone so wrong?

"Do I?" he murmured. "What woman approached you?"

"Don't be mad," she said quickly as he started driving in the direction of the bakery.

"I'm not mad."

"She was only trying to help. It wasn't that she looked at you and thought you looked nasty or like someone who would hit a woman. It was because of my eye."

"Baby, I'm not mad at her or you. I'm just trying to understand what happened."

"Oh, good. I didn't want you to feel bad about yourself."

"I don't feel bad about myself. Is your car parked behind the bakery?"

"Ahh, no. It's at a parking lot about a block away." Sadness filled her. She wasn't ready for the night to end.

"You don't park behind the bakery?" he asked. "Don't you arrive early in the morning? When it's dark?"

"Uh, yes. But I keep those parking spaces free for customers. Some of them aren't very mobile."

He kept moving his fingers back and forth over her pussy. Why did she wear pants? If she'd been wearing a skirt, she'd be able to feel so much more.

"I'm going to drive you home."

"W-what?" she asked.

"I don't want you driving home in this condition."

"What condition? You mean because I'm really, really turned on right now?"

She groaned.

Did I just blurt that out? What's wrong with me?

"Yes, that's what I mean. Plus, I need to give you your reward, and I don't want to do it in my truck. Not this first time."

Oh, Lord. She was hoping that by reward he meant an orgasm.

Because she was going to be really disappointed if it was a cupcake.

Not that cupcakes weren't good. She liked cupcakes. But she could have them anytime.

An orgasm that she didn't give herself . . . an orgasm from a really sexy guy . . . those were much scarcer in supply.

"Gracen? Can I drive you home?"

"Y-yes. I can . . . I can get my car tomorrow." She'd bus in or something. She couldn't think right now.

"Good girl. Widen your legs as far as they'll go. That's it. Now, tell me about the woman."

"I don't . . . why does it matter?"

"I'm interested. She just approached you in the bathroom?"

"Yeah, she saw my face and was concerned that you'd hurt me. Actually, I don't think she believed me when I told her the truth of how this happened."

"Well, there aren't many dance-related injuries like yours, I'm sure."

She huffed out a laugh, then moaned as he pressed against her clit. "No, I'm sure there aren't. She said that someone once helped her, and she liked to pay it forward."

"What did she look like?"

"Ah, she was pretty. A bit younger than me, I think. With dark hair."

"I want you to tell me if you see her again."

"Why?"

"Just promise you'll tell me."

"You won't get angry at her, will you?" she asked with concern.

"Why would I get angry with her for trying to help you?"

"I don't know. I just guess some guys might feel insulted that she thought that."

"I'm not some guy," he reassured her before pulling his hand from her thigh.

She let out a distressed sound.

"Shh, baby. I need you to calm down a bit. And tell me where you live."

Oh, right. That would be helpful.

She rattled off her address while watching his hands on the steering wheel. He had gorgeous hands. Sure, they were scarred and rough, but she really wanted to feel them touching her bare body.

"Why do I have to calm down?" This was torture. All she wanted was his hands on her again, driving her insane, pushing her up and over that peak.

Was that really too much to ask for?

"Because if you wait, it will be that much sweeter when I give you what you're owed."

She eyed him suspiciously. "It better be an orgasm. Because if you're teasing me this much, then you just give me a gold star sticker or something I'm going to be pretty annoyed."

"A gold star sticker, huh? Like for a reward chart? Maybe we should get you one of those. Every time you're good, you get a sticker. Five stickers means a kiss. Ten stickers means an orgasm."

"Argh, Victor. Don't tease me. It's mean."

He let out a chuckle. An actual God-damned chuckle. She stared at him in amazement as he reversed into a spot.

"Why are you looking at me like that?"

"You laughed."

"I did?"

"Uh-huh. I heard it. Also, you just parallel-parked this big beast of a truck. I thought parallel parking was a myth."

"A myth? Really? You mean you can't parallel park?

"I can barely forward park. It's a skill that seems to be beyond me."

He nodded to the building ahead of him. "That where you live?"

"Yes." All of a sudden, she felt shy. "Do you want to come in?"

"Yes."

As she led him up the stairs to her place, she tried to think about how much of a mess she'd left it in this morning. He placed his hand around the back of her neck, keeping her close.

She reached into her handbag with a shaking hand. After three tries at getting the key in the lock, he reached over and placed his hand over hers.

"I don't have to come in if I'm making you nervous."

"Oh, no, I want you to come in. I just . . . it's been so long since I . . . since I was with . . ." She stared up at him nervously.

"We're not fucking tonight, little bit."

"Thank God. No, wait. We're not? You don't want me?"

He turned her, pressing her back against the door, his hands on either side of her head as he leaned into her.

Dear. Lord.

This was sexy as fuck. Nerves and excitement fluttered through her stomach. She adored how much bigger than her he was.

"I want you," he stated. "Going to take all of my control for me to walk away without taking you tonight."

"Then why don't you?"

"Because this isn't a casual fuck for me. And I won't treat you that way."

"I don't . . . I won't think that."

"I want to make sure you know it." He ran his thumb over her lower lip. "Open."

Immediately, she parted her mouth. He slid his thumb into her mouth.

"Suck."

She followed his order.

"Very good." He praised her.

Happiness flooded her. He slid his thumb free, and she made a protesting noise.

"Shh, little bit. All in good time. I just wanted to explore something."

"What?"

"How well you take direction."

"Take direction?" she asked. Did he really just say that?

"Have you ever been with someone who likes to take control, Gracen? Someone who will take charge, in the bedroom and out?"

"Like a . . . like a Dom?" she asked, feeling slightly breathless. This was taking a very different turn.

"I'm not talking about BDSM, but I do like to be in control. To make the rules. How do you feel about that?"

Her breathing sped up. "I kind of like the idea of you taking control."

"Such a good girl."

He moved his hand to the front of her neck, holding it there. His finger rested on the pulse in her throat, and she knew he could feel her heart race.

"You like when I hold you like this, don't you, little bit?"

"Yes," she groaned.

"Is there anything you don't like? Anything you don't want me to do?"

"I don't . . . I don't want anything too extreme. I'm not into blood play. I kind of get woozy at the sight of blood. Or humiliation. No, thank you. That is not a turn-on. And no food."

"No food?"

"Yeah, I don't like to be sticky. No whipped cream, no chocolate sauce, no food in the bed."

"But this is okay?"

"Yes, this is . . . this is more than okay."

He stepped back, and she leaned more against the door, her legs threatening to cave in on her. He held out his hand. "Key."

Gracen placed the key in his hand, and he wrapped his arm

around her waist before sliding the key into the lock on the first try.

"Show off," she muttered.

Opening the door, he pulled her into the small apartment. Then turning, he locked the door. There was a musty sort of smell inside that she couldn't get rid of. It was run-down. The laminate floors were worn and peeling up in places and the walls were a sickly-yellow color. And while she'd tried her best to brighten the place up, it was all too obvious that everything was tired and worn down.

Much like her.

"I'm sorry the place is a mess," she said nervously as she moved into the tiny living space. I didn't get a chance to clean up last night. I'll just go tidy—"

He grasped her arm and then gently turned her so she was pressed against the wall. Then his hand went back to her neck, and arousal flooded her. He tilted her head slightly back and pressed his lips to hers. She could feel his beard against her skin, rough and delicious. His smooth lips moved against hers. Pressure applied to her jaw had her parting her lips and his tongue swept inside to tease her.

When he drew back, she swore she was seeing stars. The room around them was a blur. There was just her and Victor.

"Put your hands above your head and keep them there," he commanded.

She slid her hands up the wall, pressing them against it. Satisfaction filled his face, making her feel like she'd conquered some mountain rather than just followed a simple order.

"It's so fucking sexy when you obey me." He raised his hands, pressing them against hers and entwining their fingers. Then he kissed her again.

And she swore if it wasn't for the fact that she was pressed between his large body and the wall that she'd have fallen flat on her ass.

"My beautiful girl. So gorgeous. So amazing."

Whoa. She couldn't believe what he was saying to her. No one had ever spoken to her this way. In fact, every guy she'd been with had seemed to get off on putting her down.

Not raising her up.

"Keep your hands where they are. Move them and you'll have to be punished, understand me?"

"Yes," she agreed.

"Yes, Victor," he corrected.

"Yes, Victor."

8

Victor reached for the bottom of her sweater, shoving it and her T-shirt over her breasts. She flushed with embarrassment as he took in her worn bra. She really hoped she had a decent pair of panties on—if that's where he was going next.

Please let him be going there next.

He cupped her breast, then tongued her nipple through the worn fabric before moving his hands around her back to undo the hooks of her bra.

Then he shoved that material up as well, exposing her full breasts.

"I know they're kind of saggy and big . . . " she trailed off when he stared down at her with a fiery expression.

Oh, whoops.

Why did I say that? Idiot.

"What did you just say?" he murmured, his hand going behind her neck as he glared down at her.

"I, uh, well . . . crap. Can we forget I just said that?"

He cupped her breast. "No." He ran his thumb over her tight nub, and she shivered. "I shouldn't let you come as punishment."

"What? No!"

"I've given you several warnings, little bit. It's time you learned I won't tolerate such comments. You have a choice. We stop now, you get dressed, and I'll put you to bed."

"Or?" she asked, hoping the alternative was better.

"Or you turn around, take down your pants, and stick your ass out for a spanking."

"I get to come with option two?"

"Yep."

He eyed her calmly. She wasn't sure what he was looking for. But she suspected he thought she'd freak out over the thought of being spanked.

She was gratified to see his eyes widen in shock as she stepped slightly forward then turned and reached for the top of her pants, drawing them down.

"Well, that is a surprise." He ran his hand over her ass, and she shivered. She tried to look down to see what panties she was wearing. The peach ones? Okay, not so bad. They were newer and had some lace at the back.

"I expected you to take option one. Seems someone needs to come. Badly."

God, yes.

He ran a finger lower, to her panty-covered pussy and along her lips.

"Your panties are wet, baby. Did you get turned on at the restaurant when I was touching you?"

She moaned as he flicked her clit.

Smack!

Pain flared over her right butt cheek, and she gasped.

"Answer me when I ask a question," he commanded.

"Yes, I got wet."

"I know you did. Damn, I bet you smell and taste delicious. But we have to take care of your spanking first, don't we, little bit?"

"Yes, Victor."

"Hope you don't think you're getting some light taps. Because I don't do anything by halves."

Yeah, she was getting that.

Suddenly, he stepped back and tugged her panties down her legs. She drew up her right foot, then her left. Now her ass was completely bare. She took in a shuddering breath, trying to push aside her insecurities.

"Spread those legs," he ordered. "Push your ass out, hands on the wall. That's it."

He ran his hand down over her ass, one cheek then the other. "This is a beautiful ass, baby. I love your curves."

"You do?" she asked, staring over her shoulder at him.

"I do." It was said in such a confident voice that she believed him. "I like every part of you, from this sexy ass to your beautiful hips and gorgeous stomach. Every. Fucking. Part. And every time you say something bad about this body, it insults me. Because I think you're fucking amazing."

She took in a shuddering breath. She could hear the sincerity in his voice, and it helped wash away some of those voices in her head that told her she wasn't good enough. That she'd never be thin enough, smart enough, successful enough.

She was enough for him.

"Stop thinking," he told her.

"I don't know how to do that." It seemed impossible.

"When you're with me, like this, all you have to worry about is pleasing me. Understand?"

"You think I should want to please you?" she asked dryly.

"When you please me, I please you."

Damn, all right when he put it like that, she could be totally down with pleasing him. He ran his hand up the inside of her thigh and she groaned. Then a single finger slid along her slick lips. He toyed with her clit, teasing it, flicking his finger back and forth over it before slowly circling the bundle of nerves.

"So wet. Listen to the sounds you're making. You want me, don't you, baby?"

"Yes. Yes."

He slid his finger away, and she let out a whimper.

"No! Please. Please, touch me. Make me come."

"Not yet. First you have to be punished, don't you?"

"Are you sure we can't just forget about that? I've learned my lesson."

"I don't think you have. And when you go to say or think something bad about this beautiful body, I want you to remember your hot ass. The count is ten."

Ten didn't seem so bad. She could handle ten. That would be over in less than twenty seconds, right? Twenty seconds of pain for what she hoped and prayed was going to be a spectacular orgasm.

Please let it be.

Smack!

There was a flare of heat. And she hoped like hell her butt hadn't wobbled like a bowl of jelly hit with a spoon.

Shoot. She tensed.

Smack!

His hand landed on her other cheek. Ouch! Crap.

"Remember what I said. All you have to worry about is what I want from you."

"But how do I know what that is?"

"I'll tell you."

Right. It sounded simple. But she wasn't sure how it could be.

Smack!

Instead of moving back to her right cheek, he'd surprised her by hitting her left side again. Ouch. Shit.

She swore the man had a hand like a wooden paddle.

He ran his hand down her stinging ass. "Are you regretting choosing the spanking as punishment?"

"No," she replied. There was no way a spanking could be worse than not getting to come.

"That's good. Because I don't think this will be the last spanking you'll get."

Well. She wouldn't go that far.

Smack!

Again, on the left side. Ouch. Shit. How long had this spanking been going for? She swore he was dragging it out.

"I'm a good girl, normally."

"Of course you are. But that doesn't mean you won't push your boundaries. Won't test me. And I'll be here to show you that I mean what I say."

Smack! Smack!

Two hard and heavy slaps landed on her right buttock. By this time, her ass was throbbing and so was her clit. She wasn't sure if she wanted him to stop or keep going.

"Why are you being spanked, little bit?"

Oh, hell. Oh, hell.

"Because I said bad things about my body."

"That's right."

Two slaps landed on her left cheek. Followed by another two. Then he drew her up, so she was resting back against him. His hand was around the front of her neck once more as he brushed his mouth over her ear.

"And I don't want to hear you speak that way, understand? Every time you do, it's just going to end up with you sitting uncomfortably. Because the next time, it's twenty spanks. Understand?"

She practically sagged in his arms. She loved the feel of him taking control. And she trusted him not to hurt her, not to take things too far. Maybe that was naive of her, but there was this feeling of safety that came with being in Victor's arms.

"Yes, I understand."

"Good girl." He removed his hand from her neck, and she stood there, trembling, her ass on fire.

"Raise your arms in the air." He grabbed the bottom of her top.

Oh, heck. She hadn't expected he'd want to completely strip her.

Well, that wasn't quite true. She'd been hoping they'd both get naked. But between the sheets in the dark, where he wouldn't see her imperfect, dimply body.

"Do I need to spank you again?"

"What? No! What kind of question is that?"

He placed his hand over her neck again, and that wavy, fuzzy feeling moved over her once more. What was it about that dominant move that just did it for her?

"Because you're not doing as you were told, little bit. And while I can usually be a patient man, I find that my patience is greatly challenged when it comes to you. And I need you to obey me, understand?"

"Yes, Victor."

"Good girl." He stepped back and with shaky hands, she drew off her sweater and T-shirt, then got rid of the bra.

"Turn around."

Yikes. Feeling tense, she turned, but couldn't meet his gaze. Because if she saw any sign that he didn't like what he saw . . .

He stepped into her space, putting his finger under her chin to tilt her head back. Then leaning in, he nipped at her mouth with his teeth. "You are fucking beautiful."

The tension started to ease. What was she so worried about?

Cupping her breast, he lightly pinched the nipple and she moaned.

"I love the noises you make. You are never to hold back, understand? Give me all the noises. All of your reactions."

"Yes, Victor."

"I want to fucking worship you like the queen you are and at the same time, I want to order you to your knees and take your mouth with my cock. I want to claim every part of you. Make every inch mine. But I'm trying to be good here."

"Maybe I don't want good. Maybe I've been the good girl all my life. And what I want is something real. Honest. Raw."

"Fuck. Fuck." He leaned in and kissed her again. This time, his teeth tugged at her lower lip, dragging it down so he could claim her with his kiss. When he drew back, they were both breathing heavily.

"I want you to go sit on the sofa and lean back against its arm with your legs spread."

She moved over in a daze. She couldn't believe she was naked while he was still dressed.

It was sexy as hell.

"Fuck yes, baby." He just stood there, staring at her. "Part the lips of your pussy. Show it to me. Show me the pussy that belongs to me."

Damn. She wished she could read more into those words. She wanted to be his. But she wasn't entirely sure if he meant it or not.

Reaching down, her fingers trembling with a mix of trepidation and excitement, she spread her pussy lips.

His face heated, his eyes staring down at her with utter precision and intent.

"Fuck, baby. You have no idea how much I need you right now."

He shocked her by getting on his knees. Right between her legs. She moved her fingers away from her lower lips.

"What are you doing?" He gave the side of her thigh a sharp smack. "Did I say move your fingers?"

"No, but are you . . . are you going to put your mouth on me there?"

"That a problem?" he asked. "Because if it is, you need to get over it."

"Victor!"

He stared up at her firmly. "I mean it, baby. There is no way that I'm not having a taste of you. Now, put your fingers back where they were like a good girl, or you'll be over my knee."

Her breath came in sharp pants as she moved her fingers back to her pussy. "I've been working all day."

"Yep."

"I haven't showered."

"Ah-huh."

"Are you sure you want to . . ."

"Yes, now be quiet or I'll gag you."

Holy shit. He sure knew how to romance a girl.

And are you complaining?

No, she was not.

Then his face was between her legs. He brushed her hand out of the way to run his tongue along her slick lips and a moan escaped her. It was so loud that she worried about whether the next-door neighbors could hear her.

Eh, it wasn't like she hadn't heard plenty of things through their thin walls that she wished she hadn't. Like the fact that her neighbor sounded like a squealing pig when he came.

Yeah, that had been enough to make her invest in some ear plugs.

A thick finger slid inside her, stealing all thoughts of her neighbors. All she could think about was him. The way he tongued her clit, flicking it then circling it. His finger pushing in and out of her passage. Arousal flowed through her, pushing her higher and higher.

Her sharp pants filled the room, her body shaking.

God. How was she so close already?

"I can't . . . I can't . . ." Could she come like this? He might be down on his knees, but she felt like the one in a vulnerable position. Naked. Spread. Needing him.

He drew back and she wanted to reach for him. To demand that he push her over that edge.

"Get into the armchair, legs over the arms and your butt at the edge of the seat. I want access to your ass."

"W-why?"

"Why do you think?" he countered. "Do you have any lube?"

"N-no," she said in a high-pitched voice that made her wince. "I, uh, I've never . . ."

"You've never had someone play with your ass?" he asked, looking incredulous. "Why not? Is that something you don't want to explore? Do you not want me to touch you there?"

"I . . . I . . . it's been something I've thought about trying. But the truth is, I've barely done anything. I've only experienced oral sex a few times. The guys I was with before—"

He let out a low growl that had her staring down at him in shock. Cold fury filled his face. "We won't talk of them."

"W-what?"

"There were no guys before me."

She stared at him in confusion. "But I'm not a virgin."

"I don't care that you're not a virgin. But I don't want to hear about you with other men. I don't want to think about it, imagine it. From now on, there's only me. There was no before. Understand?"

And she kind of did, because she felt more than a little murderous at the idea of him with another woman.

"Yeah, I understand."

"So anal play is a yes?"

"Yes," she whispered.

"That's my good girl. Don't worry, you'll like it. No lube?"

"I think I might have some. I . . . I'll be back." She hurried into her bedroom. There was an ancient packet of condoms in her top drawer.

How long did condoms last before they expired?

She needed to check. But she was certain that there had been a sample pack of lube in there.

"Ah-huh!"

She held it up triumphantly.

Chill. Don't need to get so excited about lube. It's a bit odd.

Walking back into the room, she had to resist the urge to try and cover herself. "Here it is."

He took the lube without a word. Then he wrapped his hand around the back of her neck and drew her close to kiss her. "Good. Now get into position."

Lord, this position was worse than the last one. She felt like her tummy was a sea of rolls and her ass and pussy were even more on display.

And then he crouched down, his gaze eating her up and her breath caught in a hitch. Some of her insecurities melted away. She was certain they would be back. But right now, she felt desirable and beautiful.

"Fuck, baby. You are so damn sexy. You're going to come on my tongue while my finger is in your ass, aren't you?"

"Yes, yes," she moaned.

His mouth returned to her pussy. Damn, he was good at that. His tongue touched her with just the right amount of pressure, and all too soon, she could feel herself getting closer and closer to that edge.

"That's my good girl," he murmured. "Just relax."

Relax? Was he insane? Then he opened the packet of lube and placed some on her back hole.

Holy crap. That was cold.

"Sorry, baby. I should have warmed it first."

"No, no. It feels kind of good."

"That's a good girl. Remember, just relax. We're going to take it slow."

His thumb ran over her back hole as he pressed a finger from his other hand into her pussy.

Another finger was added to the first and she clenched down around him, so close to coming. His thumb continued to tease her back hole. The tip pressed slightly inside her. Then he flicked at her clit with his tongue until she was driven over the edge with a scream. It was the most intense orgasm she'd ever had.

The pulses of pleasure just didn't want to stop. She stopped breathing, her body locked up and a tendril of panic moved through her.

"Breathe, baby. Look at me. It's all right. I know it's intense. But I'm going to need you to fucking breathe." Victor placed his hand on her chest, between her breasts, then he moved her, so she was sitting up.

"Breathe. Just breathe."

She took one gasping breath then another.

"That's it. Good girl. That's my good girl." He stared down at her in worry. "Why didn't you tell me your orgasms were so intense?"

"I didn't . . . I've never . . . I just . . ." She reached for him, floundering, and he gathered her into his lap as he kneeled on the floor, holding her tightly.

"Shh. Close your eyes."

Turning, he settled back on his ass with her pressed against him. He held her against him, keeping her safe.

"I'm here. I'm not going anywhere."

"I'm so sorry," she said eventually.

"Look at me, Gracen."

She tilted her head back, staring up into his gorgeous face. "There is nothing to be sorry for. It's damn flattering to know that I made you come that hard."

"I've never . . . it's never been like that before. It was almost too much, you know."

"But we found a way to bring you back down. And it might never happen again. Hold onto me, let me help you, then everything will be all right."

She nodded. She still felt a bit embarrassed. Who acted like that after an orgasm? Maybe she needed to start making herself come more regularly. Perhaps it had just been too long since she'd last come.

That had to be it.

"Tired, baby?"

"Yeah." She yawned. "Sorry."

He kissed the top of her head. "Come on. I'm going to get you in the bath, then you can go to bed."

Somehow, he managed to stand while holding her in his arms. Shit, he was strong. She should probably tell him to put her down. No doubt he was going to hurt himself. But she just wasn't ready to be out of his arms.

He walked into her bedroom first and grabbed a blanket off the end of the bed. Then he moved into the bathroom and set her on her feet. He wrapped the blanket securely around her before lifting her onto the counter.

"You shouldn't pick me up like that," she whispered to him as he washed his hands in the sink.

Right, because he'd just had his thumb in her ass. Well, maybe not all the way in, but still . . . yikes.

"You don't want to finish that sentence, little bit," he told her sternly. "I have no qualms about spanking your ass again. And this time, it will be twenty."

Yikes. Even with the blanket as padding her butt was tender. She didn't need a further spanking on top of the one she'd just had.

"No, no, I'm good," she told him. "I'm shutting my mouth right now." She mimicked locking her mouth and throwing away the key.

"Good." He put the plug in the bath then turned on the taps. "You got any bath shit?"

"Bath shit?"

"Yeah, my sister had a heap of it. You got any?"

"Uh, yeah, there's some bubble bath under the sink." She blushed as she remembered that she'd bought some kids' stuff. It had been cheaper, and it made much better bubbles.

"I can get it," she told him, trying to wriggle her way off the counter. But he held a hand up, stopping her.

"Stay there," he commanded.

She knew she had to be bright red as he drew out the bottle. But he didn't even give it a second look. Instead, he poured a healthy amount into the water and swirled it around with his hand before putting it away again.

"So, you have a sister?"

"I do. She doesn't live with us now, though. The house is kind of quiet without her. Not that Lottie was ever loud. But she made it feel more like a home and less like a mausoleum."

"I'm sorry. Did she move away?"

"Yeah, to New York state." He studied her intently. "You feeling okay?"

She shifted around on the counter, wishing the bath would fill quicker. She was grateful this tiny apartment actually had a tub. Even if it was avocado green.

"I'm all right."

"Gracen," he said in a warning voice, cupping her face between his rough hands. "You don't ever lie to me."

"I'm not. I'm all right. A bit tender from being spanked and a little embarrassed from the way I reacted. But I'm all right."

"There's no need to be embarrassed." He ran a finger along her lower lip. "I have no problem taking care of you in whatever way you need."

Her breath hitched.

"But I do think we'll hold off on trying to edge you. That might be too much."

Yikes.

"I think so."

Bending down to her height, he looked her in the eyes. "You need to know this, though. You're fucking stunning when you come, and I want to do that to you all the time. Not to mention you taste like the sweetest candy. It could become addictive. I'm going to want to eat you over and over and over again. "

"I don't think I have a problem with that."

His lips twitched, and he moved back to the bath, turning off the taps. She tried to wriggle off the counter again, but he held his hand up. "I didn't say you could move."

She froze. He checked the water temperature, then turned to lift her down. When he unwrapped the blanket from around her, she finally clued on that he wasn't going to leave and let her bathe alone.

"I, uh, are you going to have a bath too?"

He stared down at the tub. "Even if I could get myself in that thing, I'm pretty sure I wouldn't be able to get back out."

She glanced from the narrow bath to his wide shoulders. "Good point."

"I've got a huge tub at my place. One day, I'll take you there and we can bathe together. Come on, in you go." He held her hand and helped her balance as she climbed into the steaming water.

She sank down, the bubbles covering her. It was the perfect temperature and her eyes drifted shut.

"Good?"

"Better than good."

She startled when she felt him brush a washcloth over her arm. Damn, had she been falling asleep?

"I can do that."

"Shh. I'm taking care of you. Just close your eyes and relax. If you fall asleep, it's all right. I'm here. I'll look after you."

Yeah, of that she had no doubts. He washed one arm and she sighed happily. She'd never had someone wash her. Well, not since her mom was alive, she guessed.

Certainly, none of the guys she'd dated had done this for her.

"Just going to wash your legs," he murmured. He raised one leg up onto the side of the bath and she could feel herself blushing. She hoped he just thought she was flushed because of the heat from the bath.

He moved the cloth over her lower leg, then her thigh, getting higher and higher until he reached her pussy. Then he drew back and proceeded to do the other leg. Again, he went higher and higher then pulled back.

She groaned in frustration.

"Poor baby. What's wrong? What do you need?"

She couldn't believe her body was stirring again. But then he drew the cloth over her nipples, and she moaned with pleasure.

"Do you need to come again?"

"I don't think I can." She stared up at him with a mix of chagrin and need.

"Have you ever come just from having your nipples played with?"

"N-no. I don't think that's possible."

"Hmm." He cleaned her breasts and chest, then had her lean forward so he could wash her back.

When she lay back once more, he put both of her legs back up on the edge of the bath so he could wash between her thighs. The cloth brushed against her sensitive clit, and she whimpered.

"Too much?"

"Yes. No. I don't know."

"Trust me?"

"Yes, of course."

"Put your legs back in the water," he commanded.

She wasn't sure how she felt about another orgasm. She was spent and the last one had left her hyper-sensitive.

"It's all right. I'm not going to do anything that you don't want. Understand?"

"Yes, Victor."

"Cup your breast, hold it up."

She cupped the breast closest to him, holding it above the water. He grabbed a cup from beside the sink, filled it, and then poured some cool water over her tight nub.

She gasped as the sensation. "Hey! Mean."

"Shh." He leaned in and sucked her nipple into his mouth. And dear Lord, the sensation of going from cold to hot . . . it was indescribable. Her pleasure rose again.

"Other nipple," he told her huskily, picking up the cup of water again. This time, when he sucked on her nipple, he used the heel of his hand to press against her clit.

She moaned. She couldn't do it. She wasn't sure she wanted to. But as he sucked then tongued her nipple, his hand pressing down on her clit but not actually coming into contact with her clit, she felt herself dive over the edge into bliss.

It was a far less intense orgasm. And she actually felt a lot better after, knowing that she wasn't always going to experience an orgasm like the previous one.

And she guessed he might have known that. Might have realized that she needed to have a less intense orgasm.

Damn, it was kind of scary how in-tune with her he was.

"Good girl," he whispered. "Just relax back. I'm going to get your pajamas. Where are they?"

"Oh, um, in the middle drawer of my dresser."

She drifted in the bath, feeling sleepy and satisfied.

"Come on, baby. Out you go."

"Don't want to."

"Tough."

"You can be such a meanie."

"That's better than you calling me kind," he said dryly as he pulled her out of the bath. She shivered but he quickly dried her off. "This towel is thin and tiny."

She cringed. Yeah, it didn't feel that great against her skin either—a bit like sandpaper.

"Let's get you dressed." He grabbed a pair of panties and then crouched in front of her. "Hands on my shoulders then lift your left foot."

"I can get dressed on my own."

"Assumed so since you don't walk around naked. Hands on my shoulders. Lift your foot."

Damn, he was so stubborn.

He slid her panties on. Next went on her pajama pants, then her top. They had images of cupcakes all over them.

"Anita bought me these for my birthday." And she loved them. But she also felt a bit childish in front of this sexy, sophisticated man.

"They're adorable." He cleared his throat as though he hadn't meant to say that. "Pee. I'll be back in a moment," he told her.

Good of him to give her some privacy to pee on her own. But also, she kind of missed him as soon as he left.

So silly.

After she used the toilet, she brushed her teeth. She was just rinsing when he walked back in and took hold of her hand.

He ushered her into her bedroom, and she noticed with some amazement that he'd already pulled back the covers and drawn the curtains. The only light on was the one beside her bed.

"Wow. How the heck are you single?" she asked as he tucked her into bed.

"I was waiting for you."

Oh, man. That was so sweet. She really hoped he meant it.

He kissed her forehead. "Do you need anything else to sleep?"

She reached out and took hold of his hand. "Would you stay? I mean, you don't have to. If you don't want to. I just thought maybe . . ."

"Stay as long as I can, but I may have to go take care of some things. Don't worry if you wake up and I'm not here. I'll be back tomorrow to take you to get your car. And I'll leave you my phone number. All right?"

"Yes, okay."

He stepped back and took off his shoes, then his shirt. She stared at his chest in amazement. Boy, he was ripped. She didn't know why she'd worried that he'd hurt himself lifting her. He looked like he could bench press a car.

His chest was covered in dark hair, and she wanted to lay her head on it, to listen to his heartbeat. To feel his arms around her, keeping her safe.

"Scoot over, baby."

"But this is my side."

"It's the side closest to the door."

"Oh, in case you have to leave in a hurry? Are you a doctor?"

"No, if anyone comes in here to attack you, they'll have to get through me first. And no one will get through me to harm you."

A rush of surprise and happiness filled her.

What had she ever done to deserve this man?

9

She was moping.

Even though he'd warned her that he'd likely have to leave, she'd hoped he'd still be there when she woke up.

Instead, she'd woken up to a cold, empty bed.

So now she was sulking on her one day off. But at least he'd left his phone number.

He still hasn't told you what he does, though.

No. And she got the feeling that was because it was nothing good.

She wasn't sure how to feel about that.

Thoughts of Ice and his friends who were part of the Ventura gang ran through her head. Could that be it?

What would she do if he was some criminal kingpin? Would she still be interested in being with him?

The fact was, she wasn't certain at this stage that she could be without him. Just look at her now. It had been a few hours and she was ready to get out the ice cream she was feeling so down.

Stupid girl.

It had only been a few hours. This was ridiculous.

Sitting on the couch, she picked up her coffee and brought her legs up, tucking her oversized sweatshirt over her knees. Then she switched the television on to watch a home improvement show. She loved these shows.

A knock on the door came a few minutes later. She frowned over at it, but untucked her legs and walked over, looking through the peephole.

Victor.

Her heart raced. She glanced down at herself. Holy. Shit.

Why hadn't she dressed in something better? She hadn't even done her hair.

"Gracen? You in there?"

Oh, crap. Oh, crap. She frantically gazed around the room. For what, she had no idea.

"Gracen!" His voice was growing increasingly agitated.

"Yes, I'm here."

"You going to open the door?"

"Not yet."

"What? Gracen, open the door. What's wrong? Is someone in there with you?"

"What? No, no. I just . . . I'm not decent."

"I don't care if you're decent or not. Just unlock the door. Now."

There was no way she could ignore the command in his voice. Taking a deep breath, she opened the door and stared up into his hard face. His gaze took in the room, searching for something before he stared down at her.

Rage filled his face making her eyes widen. What was it? Why was he so upset? She glanced down at herself and around the apartment. Was it because she'd taken a couple of minutes to answer the door? But he hadn't seemed mad until he'd seen her.

"Whose sweatshirt is that?" he asked in a voice filled with possessive intent.

"Huh? Oh, uh, it was my brother's. Why? Is there something wrong with it?"

"Ahh, no. Can I come in?"

"Sure, come in." She shut the door behind him. He had a tray with two coffees as well as a bag all in one hand.

"Aren't you going to lock the door?"

"What? It will be fine."

"Gracen, lock the door," he commanded.

"Okay," she said slowly. He was in a very grouchy mood this morning. "Did you not get enough sleep?"

"I got enough. I don't need a lot, why?" He put the tray and the bag on her small table. It only had seating for two, which was fine since she was the only one who ever sat at it. And most of the time she ate while sitting on the couch and watching TV. That's if she even managed to find the time to sit and eat.

"You just seem a bit grumpy this morning."

He moved toward her, staring down at the sweatshirt. "Your brother's? He gave it to you?"

"Yeah, he, uh, he died a few years back. And I stole this out of his closet. It makes me feel close to him when I wear it."

He closed his eyes and let out a long sigh. "Shit."

"What is it?"

"I was going to tell you that I didn't want you wearing any man's clothing, except mine, not even your brother's. But now that would make me a complete asshole."

"Yeah, it really would. It makes you uncomfortable?" She wasn't quite sure why it would.

"Not uncomfortable, no. It's just if I see you in any man's clothing I want it to be mine."

"Hmm, don't take this the wrong way, but I don't think we're the same size." She winked at him.

He cupped his hand around the side of her face. "No. But I like our size difference."

She ran her gaze over him. "Me too. I'll go get changed." And that would give her a chance to comb her hair and brush her teeth.

"No, I . . . I want you to have that connection to your brother. I'm sorry he died."

"Me too."

He sighed. "I'm close to my brothers and sister, I couldn't ever imagine losing one of them." He crouched down to look directly into her eyes. "Keep the sweatshirt on. Okay?"

"Okay," she whispered.

"Seems I've started the morning off wrong. What I should have said was good morning, beautiful."

Dear Lord.

How was he so perfect?

And how the heck could he think she looked beautiful? Especially right now?

"Have you had your eyesight checked lately?" she blurted out without thinking about it.

His eyes narrowed and he straightened. Grabbing hold of her chin, he gently tilted her head back. "Are we going to start the morning off with a spanking?"

"What? No. Nope. That does not sound like a good way to start the day. I just . . . well, I haven't brushed my hair or washed my face or . . ."

"I don't care about any of that." Leaning down, he kissed her lips.

"Brushed my teeth," she finished. "And you just kissed me."

"Come on, sit down. You can get ready after you've eaten. Unless you've had breakfast?"

"I've had two cups of coffee. Does that count?"

"It does not," he replied firmly. He pulled out her chair for her to sit. Out of the bag, he produced some bagels along with little pots of various types of cream cheese.

"Oh, yum. Bagels. I'll get some knives."

"I'll get them. See if your coffee is to your liking." He checked the lids of the cups, then handed her one.

She sipped at it then moaned. Whoops. That was embarrassing.

"Good?" he asked, sounding amused.

"So good."

He returned with two knives, then took a seat in her other chair. It wobbled and he quickly stood.

"Oh, shoot! I don't sit very much at the table, and I forgot one of the chairs is broken. Are you all right?" she asked worriedly.

"One of your chairs is broken?"

"Well, not completely broken." She stood and came around. "You just have to sit on the very edge of it. Here, I'll swap with you. The other chair is all good."

He gave her an incredulous look. "You are not sitting in a broken chair. What if it collapses under you?"

"It will be fine. I've fallen off it before."

He shook his head, then picked up the chair and put it by the door. "We'll put it in the dumpster on the way out."

"But then I've only got one chair. I suppose we can eat while sitting on the sofa." She had been meaning to get rid of that chair. It wasn't like anyone ever used it.

Walking back over to her, he held out his hand. She slid hers into his. Damn, she loved the feel of his hands. They might be her favorite part of him. Although after seeing his chest last night they had a close contender.

After helping her up, he sat in her chair. That was a bit rude, but she guessed he was the guest.

She stepped toward the sofa, letting out a loud gasp as he wrapped an arm around her waist and deposited her onto his lap.

"Victor!"

"Where do you think you're going?"

"To sit on the sofa." She squirmed on his lap.

"Too far away."

"I can't eat breakfast while sitting on your lap."

"Why is that?" His voice was a soft cajole, tempting her to spill her every thought.

"Um, well, I . . . you won't be able to eat very easily."

"I can eat just fine. And I like you close to me. Keeps you out of trouble."

She gasped, turning to look at him. "I never get in trouble."

"I've got a feeling your mouth is going to get you into plenty of trouble."

"No, it won't. Well, okay, maybe it will. Could it also get me out of trouble?" She waggled her eyebrows.

He gave her a small grin and shook his head. "Eat your bagel. Before you end up over my knee in an entirely different position."

She sliced up both bagels and loaded them up after asking how he liked his. After eating one half, she held the other piece up for him. "Want this?"

"You eat it, baby."

"I'm full."

He gave her a skeptical look.

"Promise. I don't eat a lot for breakfast."

He polished off the rest of the food, then held his finger up, showing her a smidgen of cream cheese clinging to it. He ran his finger along her lower lip.

"Open."

Oh, hell yes. She opened her mouth, and he slowly pushed his finger between her lips.

"Clean me up."

She hummed as she sucked on his finger. Drawing his hand away, he wrapped his hands around her waist and turned her, so she straddled his lap. She gave a shocked gasp. She didn't know if she'd ever get used to how easily he maneuvered her.

His big hands rested on her thighs, and she squirmed as she remembered the two orgasms he'd given her last night. She'd been kind of selfish, hadn't she? She wondered if she could do something in return for him . . .

"What are you thinking about?"

"I was just thinking that last night I was pretty selfish. I got to come twice, and you didn't get anything." Guilt swirled in her stomach. Jacob would complain for weeks if she didn't take care of him.

He wrapped his hand around the back of her neck. "Not keeping a tally here, baby. There's no tit for tat. I got exactly what I wanted last night, got me?"

"I . . . yes. I guess so. Are you sure?"

"I'm sure. If I want something, I'll tell you. Going down on you, bringing you to orgasm is something I'll always want."

"Really?"

"Really." He kissed her forehead. "Thank you for letting me pleasure you."

"Ah, well, it was a hardship, but I guess I can give you that . . . if it's something you really need."

His eyes warmed with amusement. "It is."

"I wasn't sure if you were really coming back this morning. I kind of thought last night might have been a dream."

"Never been considered a dream. A nightmare, but not a dream."

She scowled. "Who called you a nightmare? I want a name."

"Oh, yeah? What you going to do, little bit?" he asked with clear amusement.

Folding her arms over her chest, she gave him her best stern look. "You don't want to know. Plausible deniability and all that."

He grinned. "You planning on killing someone, baby?"

"Anyone who speaks badly about you has to answer to me."

She thumped her chest with her fist. "And I can be damn scary when I want to be."

"Sure you can. But I don't need you to fight my battles."

Maybe he didn't think he did. But everyone needed someone to stick up for them, to be on their side no matter what. To be their ride or die.

"Thank you." He tilted her head back with his finger under her chin then kissed her.

She melted into him, wrapping her arms around his neck. And it wasn't until he drew back that her brain came back online.

Crap! She still hadn't brushed her teeth. How did he make her forget everything? She squirmed on his lap, trying to get off.

"Where do you think you're going?" he asked.

"To brush my teeth."

To her shock, he lifted her off him without argument. "Go get ready then. We'll get your car and bring it back here, then I'm taking you out."

"You are? Where?"

"It's a surprise."

A surprise? When was the last time someone had surprised her? She couldn't even remember.

"What do I need to bring? How do I dress?" And did she have enough makeup to cover the bruise on her cheek? At least the swelling had gone down and she could easily see out of her eye. She'd woken up with a bit of a headache, but she'd caved and taken some painkillers and it had disappeared.

"Casually."

Her mind raced as she thought about her wardrobe. There was barely anything in it. What if he was taking her out to another nice restaurant? She'd prefer to be halfway decently dressed. And have some cash. Shoot. She needed to raid her emergency stash.

Standing, he turned her toward her bedroom door. "Go get

ready. Or I'll get you ready myself." A slap on her ass sent her scampering into her bedroom.

Damn, that smack had her entire body tingling.

Twenty minutes later, after about ten changes of clothes, she stepped out in a flowing sundress. She'd finally managed to brush her teeth and hair. She'd even managed to cover up some of the bruises with the tiny bit of makeup she owned.

Heat filled his eyes as he ran his gaze over her.

"Fuck, baby. You look gorgeous. Come here." He crooked a finger at her.

She moved over to him, her heart racing. Did he really think she was gorgeous? She wasn't sure she would ever tire from hearing him say it.

Wrapping a hand around the back of her neck, he drew her into him. "So fucking lucky that you want to be seen with my ugly mug."

That was absolutely ridiculous. Ugly? And if anyone was lucky, it was her.

After kissing her until her insides melted, he took her hand in his and led her down to his truck.

She didn't even bother to try and get in by herself. This had become his thing, lifting her in and doing up her seatbelt.

"So, you're not going to tell me anything about where we're going?"

"Nope."

She bit her lip. "But what if you're taking me to do something that I'm allergic to?"

He glanced over at her as he downshifted and turned into the parking lot she indicated.

Great. There was her car. Part of her had hoped it might get stolen. Then she could at least claim insurance.

She sighed. Not that what it was insured for would get her much. But could it be much worse than what she had?

"You got any allergies?" he asked.

"Um, no."

"Then I think we're safe. This yours?" He eyed her vehicle critically.

Gracen felt herself shrinking back into her seat. It got her from point A to point B, and that was the nicest thing she could say about her beaten-up, rusty old car.

"Yeah."

She waited for him to comment on how crappy it looked, but he just nodded. "Will you be all right driving it back to your place? I'll drive behind you. Unless you want to drive my truck?"

"Uh, no, I really, really don't want to drive your truck." Knowing her luck, she'd wreck the darn thing.

He raised an eyebrow at the vehemence in her voice but didn't say anything. Getting out, he walked around and opened her door. After lifting her down, he walked over with her to her car. She unlocked the door and he helped her inside, fastening her seatbelt. As if he was worried she wouldn't do it up on her own.

Still, it was kind of sweet.

"Meet you there." He closed her door.

She started up the car, wincing at the loud noise it made. Frowning, he knocked on her window, and indicated that she should lower it.

There was just one problem with that . . .

She opened her door. "Sorry, my window doesn't open."

"Your . . . your what?"

"My window doesn't open," she said louder, thinking he couldn't hear her over the noise her car was making.

"Your window doesn't open," he said slowly. "You can't drive a car when the window doesn't open."

"Um, well, technically, you can. It's really okay, the others work."

He rubbed his hand over his face.

"Are you feeling all right?" she asked with concern. He looked a bit gray.

"Not sure. Have you had that noise looked at?"

"What noise? Oh, the car. No, I haven't had a chance to take it to a mechanic yet."

"We need to get onto that. Don't drive too fast, follow all the laws."

"I always do."

He gave her a very skeptical look.

When she got back to her apartment, she climbed out and locked up. Although why she bothered locking it, she didn't know. She was pretty sure that no one would steal the heap of junk.

Victor lifted her into his truck, and they set off.

"Did you have to leave last night for work?" she asked.

"Yeah."

"Was it an emergency?" she asked.

"No."

"You still haven't told me what you do."

"Thought you were guessing."

"Hmm, good point. You're sure you're not a doctor?" She stared around curiously as they drove out of the city. Where were they going?

"Pretty sure."

"Vet?"

"Nope."

"I know, an orthodontist."

"An orthodontist? What sort of orthodontist works at night?" he asked.

"I don't know. There might have been a tooth emergency. Maybe you're an orthodontist to movie stars or something."

"Movie stars have orthodontists?"

"They have teeth problems too." She grinned over at him. Then she clicked her fingers. "I have it!"

"Really don't think you do."

"You're a hairdresser. There, totally nailed it."

"Not a hairdresser."

"Hmm. Beard model?"

He huffed out a laugh, and her insides danced with happiness as he pulled into what looked to be a private airport. Were they flying somewhere?

He parked next to a large hangar.

"Are we going flying?" she asked, turning to stare at him in shock.

"We're going out in a chopper," he replied.

"A chopper? A helicopter? Really?"

"Yes. That all right?"

"I . . . I've never even flown in a plane. Is it safe?"

Undoing their belts, he reached over and gently took hold of her chin. "Do you think I would ever put you at risk?"

She took in a deep breath. "No. I know you wouldn't. I've just never done anything like this."

"Trust me?"

"Yes." It was something she felt deep inside her. This innate feeling of trust in him. Knowing he wouldn't allow harm to come to her.

"Wait there." Climbing out, he moved over to the helicopter where a man who she assumed was their pilot, waited. To her surprise, though, the other man just nodded and walked off.

Who was going to pilot the helicopter? Victor climbed into the chopper and disappeared from sight for a moment. Her nerves started to build, and she grabbed out her phone, tapping a message to Sammy.

GRACEN: *If I die today, I love you and I'll haunt you forever. Try to look out for Anita.*

Sammy: *Die? You can't die. What's wrong? Do you need me?*

Gracen: *No. Just being dramatic. I'm good.*

Sammy. *Thank fuck. Because there is no way I want to be saddled with your niece.*

Gracen: *Wouldn't do that to you.*

Sammy: *How is your eye?*

GRACEN STUDIED her reflection in the small mirror attached to the back of the sun visor. The makeup helped, but it wasn't enough to completely conceal the bruise.

She sent Sammy a selfie.

SAMMY: *Ouch. Still love me?*

Gracen: *Always.*

THE PASSENGER DOOR OPENED, and Victor stood there. Right. Time to do this.

Yikes.

10

Victor could tell she was nervous.

And he liked the way she clung to him as he led her to the chopper. He'd always take care of her.

While he'd been checking over the helicopter, he'd sent a message to one of his guys. Isaac would grab her car today and take it to his workshop to check it over and fix what he could.

Sure, he probably should tell Gracen what he was doing. Isaac was essentially stealing her car.

But he knew she'd argue with him. And he didn't want their day to start off with tension. Today was about having fun. Something she didn't seem to have much of.

They had that in common.

He helped her up into the chopper, then pulled her seatbelt over her, settling her handbag between her feet. Then he shut her door and walked around to the other side.

"Victor? Who's going to drive this thing?" she asked, staring around.

"Fly, baby."

"What?"

"You fly a chopper." He winked at her.

"Argh, yeah. That was a dumb thing to say. I'm such an idiot."

No. That wasn't happening.

"Hey, look at me," he said in a deep voice, waiting for her to glance over at him. "No putting yourself down, remember? You don't want your first helicopter flight to be with you sitting on a warm ass, do you?"

"Ah, nope. Definitely not." She stared over at him with wide eyes.

He really didn't like what she thought about herself. It wasn't okay. And she seemed to have trouble realizing that.

"To answer your question, I'm flying it."

"You?"

"Yep. That a problem?"

She shook her head, letting out a big breath. "No, the opposite, actually. I feel better knowing you're in charge. I know it's silly, you're not infallible or anything. But I just know that if something goes wrong, you'll take care of it."

"I will. Just like I'll take care of you. Always."

SHE COULDN'T HELP her nerves as they took off into the air. She let out a small squeal, hoping he didn't hear that through the mic and headphones they both wore. The worried look he shot her told her that was a fruitless hope.

But as they flew along, her nerves started to fade, and excitement took its place.

Holy. Hell.

The view from up here was magnificent. She started to recognize landmarks, pointing them out to him even though he'd likely seen them all before.

He grinned over at her. There seemed something lighter about him. As though some tension had lifted from his shoulders.

"Enjoying yourself?" he asked through the mic.

"This is amazing!"

"Good, baby. We're going to land soon. I have something else set up for you."

"Nothing is going to top this."

"We'll see."

Soon, they were landing in a flat area of the countryside. She couldn't see anything else around but shrugged. Whatever he'd set up, she'd enjoy it.

When he lifted her down, she wrapped her arms around him, kissing him enthusiastically. "That was amazing! Thank you so much! I'll never forget that as long as I live."

"Glad you enjoyed it, baby. Told you I'd keep you safe."

"I know," she replied huskily. Then her stomach gurgled, and she gasped in horror, putting her hand over it. "Sorry."

"Come on, a short walk and then we'll be there."

"Be where? Is there somewhere to eat around here?" She glanced around, unsure where they even were. She loved New Orleans, but she had to admit that it was nice to get out of the city.

"It's so beautiful here," she commented, glancing around at enormous trees ahead of them.

"Come on. Just down here." He led her along a path in the trees until they came out next to the bayou.

It was an idyllic spot. She let out a gasp as she spotted a picnic already set up on the grassy bank.

"We're having a picnic?"

"Yep."

"Who? Where? What?"

"I got someone to set it up while I flew you here."

She stared at him. "Victor, you're a big romantic under all that gruffness, aren't you?"

"Don't tell anyone." He tapped his finger against his lips.

She grinned at him. "Your secret is safe with me. Although I may have to use it as a bribe to get out of punishment."

"You can try." Keeping a tight hold of her hand, he led her over to where a checked white and red blanket had been laid out. There was a huge wicker basket as well as an ice bucket with two bottles in it.

"Two bottles?"

"One is sparkling grape juice. I don't drink and fly."

"I'm happy with grape juice." She settled onto the blanket and stared around her. The sun beat down on her face and she was grateful she'd chosen a sundress.

Victor started unpacking the basket.

"Can I help?"

"No, you just rest, baby."

"I haven't exactly exerted myself today," she protested.

"You're still tired looking. You need more rest. And besides, you'll exert yourself plenty later."

A flush of pleasure filled her. He poured them both a glass of sparkling grape juice and handed her one.

Seeing his big hand wrapped around a tiny, delicate wine glass amused her. It also made her realize that there were so many sides to this man. How many men would set up something like this?

"Is it odd I don't know your last name?" she asked as he picked up a plate. There were several different kinds of sandwiches, potato salad, and a loaf of French bread.

Yum.

She decided to let him get what he liked first. He had to be hungry.

"You want to guess it as well?"

"I do like guessing games. Is it Smith?"

"Uh, no."

"Huh, Smith is a very common name. Although you're not a very common man," she added hastily.

"Good to know. What would you like to eat?"

"Oh, I'll just have a turkey sandwich and some potato salad."

He picked up two sandwiches and two big scoops of salad, then handed her the plate.

It was for her? Here she'd thought he was getting his own lunch.

"Thank you." She stared down at the huge plate of food, wondering how she'd eat it all.

He put twice as much food on his plate, and they sat peacefully for a few moments, eating. She kind of wished she'd brought a sunhat with her, though. She had skin that easily burned.

But she wasn't complaining. Nope.

"You've finished?" he asked when she set her plate down.

"Yes, I'm sorry. I can't eat anymore."

"It was good?"

"More than good," she told him. "This whole day has been magical."

He packed everything up, then set the basket aside. To her surprise, he stood and then held out his hand to her.

Oh, they had to go back already? That was a shame.

"Are we headed back?"

"No, we have to move into the shade. Should have brought sunscreen and a hat for you. I'll remember next time."

There would be a next time? Happiness filled her. She didn't care if she got a bit sunburned. It was worth it.

She helped him settle the rug under the shade of a big tree. She tried to guess his name and occupation several times as they worked.

"Chin? You think my last name could be Chin?" he asked incredulously.

"No? Hmm. I'll get it. I mean, I already figured out that you're a beard model."

"I'm not a beard model."

She sighed. "Well, that is a huge disappointment. I really don't know if I can be seen with you anymore."

He reached over and tickled her until she gave in breathlessly. "Mercy! Mercy! I take it back. I'll be seen with you, even if you shave your beard off and you're all pale underneath. You'll have a two-toned face, but I'll still kiss you!"

"Good to know. A two-toned face, really?"

"It could happen, right?"

"Are you wearing a bra?" he asked suddenly.

That was out of left field.

"Ah, yes. You saw my boobs last night. There's no way I can get away with free-boobing."

"Free-boobing?"

"Yep, like free-balling. But the boob version. I made it up."

"Clever."

"I thought so."

"Take your bra off," he said in a low, commanding voice.

"Here? Right now?"

"Yes, here. Right now."

"But is there anyone else here? What if someone walks along?" she asked, staring around.

"This is my property, and there are no neighbors for miles. And the people who set this picnic up left before we got arrived. No one will see you."

Okay, then.

It wasn't easy but she managed to undo and take off her bra while keeping her dress covering everything.

"And now your panties." She reached underneath and took off her panties. He held out his hand for both and she gave them to him.

"I don't suppose you saw where my panties went from last night?" she asked. She hadn't been able to find them this morning when she'd tidied up.

"Yep, in my pocket."

He slid these panties into his pocket as well.

"Hey, I'm going to need those back! I don't have an endless supply of panties."

"I'll replace them."

"I don't need them replaced. I just need for you to stop stealing my old ones," she grumbled.

"Come here. Lie on your back." He lay on his side, patting the blanket in front of him.

Nerves flooded her tummy along with excitement.

She lay next to him on her back, staring up at him. He ran a finger along her cleavage. Her dress was stretchy, and it tightened under her breasts before flaring out loosely.

He pushed the dress away from her globe, baring it to his gaze. A low moan escaped her as he sucked her nipple into his mouth. This felt wanton and crazy and like nothing she'd done before.

She seemed to be experiencing a lot of firsts with him.

"You taste so good. All I could think of last night was getting your taste on my tongue again."

Her heart raced as she stared up at him. He bared her other breast before leaning over to lick the tight nub until she was moaning, wriggling on the blanket as waves of arousal flooded her.

He blew out a breath over the bud before flicking it with his tongue.

"Victor!" she cried out.

"You're sensitive, aren't you, baby?" he murmured. "My poor girl. If you still had panties on, no doubt you'd have made a mess of them."

Dear. Lord.

The things he said.

"Bring the bottom of your dress up to your waist, then spread your legs. I want to see how wet you are."

With hands that shook, she did as ordered. She prayed he was right about no one coming along and seeing her like this.

Then again, did she really care? This was his land after all.

Wait, he owned this land?

"This is your property?" she asked breathlessly as his hand moved up her thigh toward her slick pussy.

"That's what you're thinking about? Obviously, I'm not doing a very good job if you can still think."

She flushed. "Sorry. You are, you're very good at this. I just . . . you own this beautiful land?"

"Yep." He cupped her pussy, squeezing it lightly. She raised her hips, wanting more, seeking his touch. "I do. The plan was to build a place to live out here one day, but my family needs me right now."

"It would be a beautiful place to live. You wouldn't miss the city?"

He shrugged. "Too many people. I'm not a people person. There are about eleven people I like. That number can go down and up on any given day."

"Am I one of them?"

"Yeah, baby. Right now, you're number one on the list."

"Ooh, number one. Go me!"

"Hmm, and to stay number one you have to do exactly as I say, understand?"

"You're lying," she teased. "I'll be number one even if I don't do what you say."

"You will," he admitted. "But you'll be number one with a hot ass."

She sucked in a sharp breath as he ran two fingers through her slick lips.

"Please. Please. Please." She wrapped her arms around his neck. She wanted more. Craved it.

She didn't know how she could be so needy when she'd come twice last night. She should have been well satisfied.

Turns out, his touch just made her hungrier.

"What do you want, baby?"

"I need to come. I want to feel you inside me."

"Not yet. We're not there yet."

Really? He was rejecting her? Her hands dropped away from him.

Suddenly, he moved over her, his hands on the blanket on either side of her head. He was careful not to lean too much of his weight on her.

"That was not me rejecting you."

"You don't want to fuck me?" she whispered.

"I want to fuck you, little bit. I want to fuck you every minute of every hour that I'm awake. Even when I'm asleep, I dream of fucking you."

Although she knew that couldn't be true, it still made her flush with pleasure.

"But we're already moving faster than I thought we would. Because I can't resist your taste, the sounds you make when you come, the satisfaction that comes from knowing I pleasured you. But I also want you to know how much you mean to me. This isn't just about sex."

"I know," she whispered. And part of her actually appreciated what he was doing. Most men would've jumped at the chance to finally have sex.

"That was naughty of you to assume that I was rejecting you."

"Sorry, Victor." He wouldn't deny her an orgasm as punishment, would he? His eyes were twinkling so she didn't think he was too serious.

"You're going to have to be punished for that. Put your hands above your head and keep them there."

That was it?

She'd gotten off easy. And she wasn't going to complain.

Raising her hands over her head, she stared up at him. He moved back to his side next to her.

"I want you to lie nice and still. If you move, I stop touching you."

Oh, crap. That was going to be far harder.

He ran the tips of his fingers along her slick lips, then pushed them into her passage. "My baby is very wet. Poor girl." He pumped his fingers in and out of her pussy and she tried to stay still, she really did.

But it was impossible.

She rocked her hips up to meet his touch. Her clit throbbed, begging for his touch.

Suddenly, he pulled his fingers free.

"No, please!"

"What did I say would happen if you moved?" he murmured.

"I'm sorry! I won't move again."

"Somehow, I think you will." He shook his head in mock disappointment. "Naughty girl."

"I promise. I'll be good."

"Hmm, I suppose I can try again if you think you can be good."

She nodded. "I can. I will. Promise."

"Clean me off first." He held the fingers to her lips and she opened them. He pushed his fingers into her mouth and she sucked on them happily.

"That's my good girl," he murmured as he removed his fingers, pushing them back inside her pussy. "That's my very good girl. You liked the taste of yourself on my fingers, didn't you?"

She didn't answer.

"You best answer me, little bit," he growled, stilling.

"Yes! Yes, I liked my taste on your fingers."

"That's better. Remember, you have to always answer me."

"Sorry," she said breathlessly. "It's hard to think with your fingers in my pussy."

Whoa. Did she just say that?

"Is it? Well, you'll need to get used to it. Because I intend to do this often."

Oh, hell.

She might be in real trouble here. He moved his mouth down to her nipple once more, sucking on it as he fucked her steadily with his fingers.

She gasped for breath, focusing on not moving. Because she really, really didn't want him to stop. When he drew his fingers out of her, she whimpered in response.

"I didn't move!"

"Shh, I know. You're doing such a good job of obeying me. I just want to taste you." He sucked his fingers into his mouth with a hum of pleasure.

Damn. She thought she might come just from watching the delight fill his face as he tasted her.

"Delicious."

Reaching over, he grabbed the ice bucket.

She really hoped he didn't plan to pour grape juice over her and lick it up. Because that was not her jam, she'd get all sticky and she didn't have spare clothes . . .

But instead, he grabbed some ice and popped it into his mouth. Then his cool fingers flicked at her clit while he placed his mouth around her nipple.

The shocking cold of the ice had her gasping and she had to concentrate hard on staying still.

Killing. Her.

He did it again. Grabbing some more ice, he put it in his mouth before taking her other nipple into his mouth.

He drove his fingers into her pussy at the same time his lips circled her nipple and she cried out in shock, waves of pleasure washing through her as she came. He continued to suckle on her nipple as he slid his fingers free, running his thumb over her clit. Then he cupped her pussy as he kissed her.

"Oh. Oh. Ohhh," she moaned as she started to come down from her high. For a moment, she'd felt like she was going to spiral.

Victor rolled onto his back, taking her with him. He secured her on top of him, her cheek pressed to his chest, her breathing coming in small, raspy gasps.

His arms were tight bands around her. Holding her in place and allowing her time to come firmly back into her skin.

He ran his fingers over her lips and she sucked on the tips. She was all right. That wasn't as intense as last night, not even close. But she liked being held by him like this. Knowing that he had her and wouldn't let her go until he made certain she was all right.

When she felt a breeze on her ass, she realized that the hem of her dress was up over her bottom. Wriggling, she reached back to lower it, only to have her butt cheek lightly slapped.

"Leave it." He cupped her ass in his hands, squeezing and massaging.

She moaned in pleasure.

"You like that, huh?"

"Yes." He spread her cheeks slightly, then pushed them together once more. Damn, who knew a butt massage could feel so amazing.

There was a hardness against her stomach. She wriggled, getting up on her knees between his legs.

"Can I do something for you?"

He raised his eyebrows. "Something for me?"

She nodded. She reached for her dress, intending to pull it up over her breasts as she realized they were bare. But he brushed her hands away.

"Leave your breasts out," he ordered. "What would you like to do for me, little bit?"

"I want to make you come. Please?"

"How will you do that?"

Shoot. He'd never struck her as talkative. But it seemed when it came to sex, he couldn't shut up. Well, not quite. But she wasn't used to talking about sex.

"I thought I'd take you into my mouth."

"Did you? Then what?"

"Then I was going to suck you until you came." She bit her lip worriedly. "I might not be any good, though."

He narrowed his gaze then sat up. "And what makes you think that?"

"My ex. He kept telling me I needed practice. But usually I was so tired that I wanted it to be over, so I did it as quickly as possible so I could sleep."

He let out a low, growling noise of displeasure.

"But that's not how I feel about you," she said hastily. "I want to suck you off. I just . . . don't know how good I'll be at it. And I don't want you to be disappointed in me."

He pulled her onto his lap and ran a finger over her nipple. "First, I could never be disappointed in you. Ever."

She wasn't sure that was true, but it was nice to hear.

"Second, if there is ever a time you feel pressured to do something you don't want to do, I want you to tell me. If I don't listen, you're to walk away. Understand? You don't put up with that sort of shit. Not from anyone."

She wrapped her arms around his neck, pressing against him. "You're a good man Victor Johnson."

"Nope. Good try, though."

She leaned back so she could look up at him. Licking her lips, she gave him her best puppy dog eyes. "So can I touch you? Suck on you?"

He eyed her. "Maybe not today, little bit."

Oh, shit. She'd ruined things by being honest. Crap, she should have just kept that to herself.

"Hey, what is it? What's wrong?"

"I was just wishing I hadn't told you that."

"You're to tell me anything that worries or upsets you."

"Even when it stops you from doing something that we both want. Or that I want and hope you do—"

He placed his lips against hers, silencing her. "You're sure?"

"Yes. Please. I really, really want to take you into my mouth."

"Damn, baby. You beg so prettily. I think you should beg every time you want my dick in your mouth."

If it got her what she wanted, then she wasn't above begging.

"Please say yes." She clasped her hands together.

He ran his fingers through her hair. "Christ. Not sure I'll ever be able to say no to you."

"I'll remember that."

He grasped her chin. "Unless it's something that will put you in danger. I'll never allow that."

A shiver ran up her spine at the promise in his words. She believed him. And she loved how he kept her safe.

"I'll try not to ever put myself in danger."

"Good girl," he said in a rumble of approval. "Don't want you to be . . . intimidated by me."

What did that mean?

"I won't be. You don't scare me."

He grunted but didn't look convinced. "Move back onto your knees where you were before."

She slid back, kneeling between his legs.

He slid onto his back once more. "Undo my belt."

Fingers shaking with excitement, she followed his order.

"Now, my pants."

She undid the button and zipper, then waited for more instruction. She might be the one about to pleasure him. But there was no mistaking who was in charge.

And it definitely wasn't her.

He lifted his hips and pushed his pants and boxers down, revealing his thick long cock.

Holy. Shit.

She'd had some idea of his size. But it seemed her imagination didn't live up to the reality. Is this what he'd meant by intimidating her?

Yeah, he was huge.

And yeah, she wasn't entirely sure how he'd fit inside her.

But that didn't mean she was turned off or scared of him. Not at all.

"You worried about my size, baby?"

"I'd be lying if I didn't say that you're definitely large. Far bigger than my ex—"

He interrupted her with a low growl of displeasure. "I thought we'd agreed not to talk about that bastard."

"Sorry," she said hastily.

Reaching down, he ran his hand up and down his monster dick.

Shit. Shit. Shit.

"You're scared?"

"No."

"Don't lie to me. That will never be acceptable. If you're worried or frightened or whatever, I want to know."

She licked her lips. "It's slightly intimidating, but I'm not scared."

He gave her a skeptical look. But when he went to say something, she leaned forward and placed her fingers over his lips. "I know that you will never hurt me, that you'll take care of me. And so, I'm not scared."

"Your trust is so fucking sexy. Come here."

She rested her hands on either side of his head, then leaned in to kiss him. He didn't let her lead, of course. Even though she was in the more dominant position, she wasn't in charge.

And she wouldn't have it any other way.

He wrapped his hand around the back of her neck, his other hand drifting down to her ass. He gave her a sharp smack, and she moaned as her clit throbbed.

He was turning her into this sex-driven fiend.

And she was so down for that.

He massaged away the burn, then slapped her other cheek.

"Get that gorgeous mouth around my dick," he told her. "I want you to suck me. You're going to make me come and you're going to swallow every drop aren't you, baby?"

She slid down his body, undoing his shirt button by button and kissing each inch of skin that she revealed. She moaned as she flicked her tongue over his nipple.

"Fuck, baby." Placing his hand around the back of her head, he guided her to his other nipple. "Suck."

She put her lips around his nipple, flicking the tip of her tongue over the tight nub.

Smack!

His other hand landed on her ass. She moaned. Was he trying to make her come again?

"Do as you were told," he commanded.

As she was told? Oh, right. Yep, she'd get right onto that. She sucked on his nipple before moving down his stomach. It was toned. He was so strong and big. Every part of him. When she came to his dick, she licked her way along the shaft to the head, taking it into her mouth. She ran her tongue along the tip, delighting in his moan.

"Fuck, baby. Your ex was an idiot if he thought you weren't any good at this."

Happiness filled her. She moved her tongue back down his cock. Then she ran it over his balls as she used her hand to jack him. She couldn't even get her fingers all the way around his girth.

"Baby, get your mouth around my dick," he ordered.

She smiled to herself at the gruff command. She liked having some power over him, knowing that she could affect him, could drive him nuts the same way he did her.

She slid back up, taking as much of him into her mouth as she could. It was a stretch and she had to move back up, gasping in a deep breath.

Keeping her hand around the base of him, she moved her mouth up and down his shaft.

"Yes, baby. Good girl. That's it. Now run your tongue over the head. Yes. Fuck."

The taste of him zinged along her tongue, and she moaned in delight.

"Fuck. Fuck."

He grew tense as she wrapped both hands around him, moving them up and down his shaft while she sucked on the tip.

"Take me as deep as you can. Now."

She moved one hand away and took as much of him as she could manage without gagging.

"Yes. Fuck. Yes. Again."

She pulled back up, then ran her tongue around his head before taking him inside her once more. She kept up the same movements, hearing his breathing grow faster, his entire body trembled with need.

"I'm going to come, baby. Make sure you drink all of it down." He rested his hand lightly on the back of her head and she moaned in pleasure as he came in her mouth.

She swallowed, making sure she didn't miss any of it. Wow,

that was hot, and she couldn't wait to do it again. In fact, she might just stay here for a moment. Keeping his cock in her mouth, she maneuvered herself so she lay half on top of him. She suckled on his softening dick.

She kind of expected him to pull her off, but he just ran his fingers through her hair.

"You like that, baby?" he murmured.

"Hmm." Damn, she could almost fall asleep like this.

"Don't fall asleep on me. Come here. I know you were enjoying yourself. But it's nearly time to go, and I want to hold you."

She ended up lying on top of him again while he held her.

She could really get used to this.

11

*G*ood morning, baby. I won't be coming into the bakery this morning, but I'll see you later. Behave.

HUH. She always behaved.

Well, mostly.

She ran her finger over the note he'd left on her bedside table with a smile. It was kind of sweet that he'd taken the time to write this, rather than just sending her a text message.

They'd spent all of yesterday together, but he'd had to leave around ten last night. He didn't go into details, and she knew she was burying her head in the sand when it came to what it was that he did. If it were anything simple, something normal, then he would have just told her.

And she couldn't think of any reasonable explanation for him having jobs to do at ten on a Sunday night.

But she wanted to ignore whatever it was he was hiding for a while longer. To just have him to herself for a bit without any drama or worries.

Leaving the note, she headed out of the apartment. She climbed into her car with a sigh. It was early and cold. Her coat wasn't much protection against the chill in the air. She started her car, knowing it never started easily on cooler mornings.

To her shock, it started up right away.

Where was that horrible whining noise? That was strange. It couldn't have just disappeared, could it? She didn't have that sort of luck.

Well, maybe it had. Which would be amazing.

She headed toward the bakery, yawning, and sipping on her coffee to keep herself warm and awake. She glanced down at her gas gauge.

Huh. That couldn't be right, could it?

She could have sworn that her tank had less than a quarter left when she'd driven it home yesterday. How could it be full?

"All right, I'm obviously losing my mind." Or there was something wrong with her gas gauge. Shit. That was probably it. Now what was she going to do? The last thing she wanted was to get stranded with no gas because her gauge was showing it was full.

She'd get some gas after work today or tomorrow.

Pulling into her parking space, she hauled her tired body out and walked to her shop. Yesterday had been amazing. Victor had simultaneously treated her like a princess while doing filthy things to her body and mind.

With a sigh, she drifted through all her opening jobs. Even Anita arriving twenty minutes late couldn't mess with her good mood.

"What's up with you?" Anita asked, frowning.

"Nothing. Why would you say that?"

"I don't know. You're singing and shit. You seem happier or

something. And I don't get why since that sexy hunk hasn't been back. I think you scared him away."

Gracen knew that Anita was trying to hurt her. It hurt that Anita felt the need to try and bring her down. Their relationship was growing more and more strained the more time Anita spent with Ice.

"Actually, I saw him yesterday."

"What? Seriously."

"Yes, seriously. We went on a date together." Maybe she was being stupid. She should probably keep Victor to herself.

"Aunty G, do you know—"

"There's a customer," she interrupted.

"But—"

"Customer, Anita!"

Anita let out an irritated huff before stomping off to the front counter.

Nothing was bringing her down today.

GRACEN SIGHED as she walked into the back of the bakery after turning the closed sign around. She'd sent Anita home earlier, unable to take her icy stares and the silent treatment.

"What's wrong?"

She screamed. Jumping into the air, she dropped the bowl she'd been holding. It shattered on the floor as she turned to see Victor emerging from the shadows.

"Holy shit. You scared the crap out of me."

He grimaced. "Sorry, baby. I thought you knew I was back here."

"What? How would I know that?"

"I made plenty of noise."

"We might have different ideas of what plenty of noise means." She sighed, glancing down at the bowl which lay in pieces on the floor. Crouching, she started picking up the bigger pieces, yelping as a shard cut into her finger.

"What are you doing? Leave that." He stomped over and picked her up, setting her on the counter. "Where are you hurt?"

"It's fine." She stuck her finger into her mouth to suck on it.

"Show me."

She shook her head.

"Gracen," he said in a warning voice. "Show. Me."

She pulled her finger out, showing him the minuscule cut.

"Fuck."

"It's all right. Look, it's barely even bleeding."

He shook his head. "Have you got a first aid kit?"

"Uh, yeah, in the cabinet under the sink. But it's fine, Victor." She sighed as he ignored her.

Stubborn man.

He returned with the kit, opening it and drawing out a Band-Aid. He carefully wrapped it around her finger, his big hands gentle.

Then to her shock, he brought her finger to his lips and kissed it. "Good?"

"Uh, yes. Thank you."

He placed his finger under her chin, raising her face. "What's the matter?"

"Nothing."

"Gracen," he said warningly.

"It's just my niece. She's been giving me the silent treatment all day. Nothing important."

"Hmm. Not very mature, is she?"

"Most nineteen-year-olds are the same, I'm sure. I better tidy this up. I thought you'd meet me at the apartment."

"I'll clean it up. You stay there. You have a broom and dustpan?"

"Uh, yeah. Over in the cupboard." She gestured to where the cleaning supplies were. "But I can do it."

"Stay. You're tired. And it's my fault you dropped the bowl. I'll replace it."

"You don't have to."

"I do. I got you a gift."

He moved to where he'd been standing and picked up two bags. One was pink and white striped with Victoria's Secret written along the front. The other was plain brown.

"Victor, you didn't have to buy me anything."

He shrugged, placing them beside her on the counter. "I wanted to."

She opened the Victoria's Secret bag first, her mouth dropping in shock as she took in the pile of panties and bras. There had to be ten matching sets—as well as two baby doll nighties.

"Victor! This is way too much."

"You don't like them?"

"Of course I like them. But you shouldn't spend so much on me."

He dumped the shards of the bowl into the garbage can, and after putting everything away, walked over to her. Spreading her legs, he moved between them and leaned his hands on the counter on either side of her.

"You're worth it. And more."

Oh. Lord.

She licked her lips.

"I don't know what to say."

"Say, thank you, Victor."

"Thank you, Victor." She put her arms around his neck and kissed him gently. "I love them."

"Good. Open your other gift."

"You're spoiling me."

He didn't reply, just watched as she opened the next bag and pulled out the object. It was red and small with a silver tip at one end.

"It's a safety hammer," he explained. "Keep it in your car in case you have to break the window."

"Oh, that's so awesome. Thank you!" She kind of loved it more than the underwear. He was always doing whatever he could to keep her safe.

What had she ever done to deserve this man?

"I HAVE NEWS."

Gracen looked up from where she was frowning down at an invoice from one of her suppliers. Why was it so big? Shit. Everything had gone up in price. She'd known it was coming, but somehow she'd naively thought she'd still be able to cover everything. Only thing was, her earnings were also down. What was going on?

"What? Have you cleaned up the kitchen?" Gracen asked. She'd holed herself up in the small office in an attempt to pay some bills. It had been a quiet Thursday afternoon and she'd figured Anita could handle everything.

That might have been a mistake.

Everything else in her life was amazing at the moment. She couldn't ask for a better boyfriend than Victor. Not that they'd declared anything to each other. But he was thoughtful, protective, and kind.

And, also, secretive, stubborn and bossy.

She still didn't know who he really was.

She pushed aside that nagging worry.

Sammy was away for work all week, so they couldn't meet up tomorrow night. Which was too bad because she could really use a watered-down daiquiri.

Anita frowned at her. "You never listen to me anymore, Aunty G. All you care about is your own life. Don't you care about what's going on with me, anymore?"

She sighed quietly. Anita didn't seem to get that she had a thousand things to worry about. But she knew that she was still a teenager, and everything seemed oh-so very important.

"I'm sorry. What was it that you wanted to tell me? Wait, is the shop empty?"

"Yes, the shop is empty. Aunty G, you care more about the bakery than you do me."

She took off her reading glasses, pinching the top of her nose. She had a headache pounding in her temples, money worries out the wazoo, and she still hadn't found the time to get someone to check her gas gauge.

The one good thing in her life at the moment was Victor.

But she needed more than amazing orgasms and cuddles to pay her bills and keep her afloat. She still couldn't believe he'd bought her all that lingerie. And he'd replaced the bowl she'd dropped with a gorgeous bowl that had to have cost ten times what the old one had.

"That's not true. I love you. I was just making sure that our customers were taken care of."

"What customers? I swear we get fewer people in each day. You should really think about selling."

"This bakery has been in our family for three generations, I can't just sell it."

"Yeah, but it's not like you have someone to hand it down to, right? I mean, I'm your only relative, and I don't want to do this all my life. Me and Ice have plans. Fact is, if you died tomorrow, I'd sell it."

Great. That made her feel so good.

Why are you working so hard? You're going to send yourself into an early grave to keep a bakery afloat that your niece doesn't care about.

"Anyway, back to my news, even though you didn't ask."

"I'm sorry. What's going on in your life," she said woodenly.

Her headache was getting worse. How long was it until closing? She wanted to go home, have a bath, then go to sleep.

"Ice got a job!"

Okay. That wasn't what she'd been expecting Anita to say. As far as she could tell, Ice was a career gangster wannabe, so this was a shock.

"A job? Anita, that's great. Doing what? Is he going to train for a trade or work in a store or . . ." she trailed off as Anita cracked up.

"Oh, Aunty G, you're hilarious. Is he going to work in a store? That's so funny."

"All right," she said, feeling irritated. "What did he get a job doing?"

Anita leaned in and that was when she figured out that this was not something she was going to want to hear. "He got a job working for Carlos Santiago."

Oh. Shit.

She rubbed her chest. Was she still breathing?

"Carlos Santiago? Damn it, Anita. That's so stupid. Why would he work for him? It's dangerous!"

Anita scowled. "Should have known you wouldn't understand. You don't get it, Aunty G."

"Then tell me."

"This is our ticket out of this hellhole. Ice starts working for Santiago, he works his way up the food chain and then we get the fancy house, the money, the cars. God, you're so short-sighted. And a hypocrite."

"How am I a hypocrite?"

Anita's eyes widened. "Oh my God, you still don't know, do you? That's hilarious."

"Know what?" She was starting to wish she kept alcohol back here.

"Who it is that you're seeing. If you're still seeing him, that is. I've noticed he hasn't been around."

"Are you talking about Victor?" she asked, a bad feeling coming over her.

"Yeah, Victor. Don't you know who he is?"

"What do you mean? Who is he?" She licked her suddenly dry lips.

"He's Victor Malone," Anita said with glee.

"How do you know his last name?" she asked. Darn, she hadn't even come close to guessing that.

"Oh, God, Aunty G! Will you pay attention to something besides the bakery! I can't believe you've been seeing a criminal without even knowing it. That's hilarious."

"What do you mean? A criminal?"

She shouldn't be shocked. She'd known it. Deep down, she'd known he couldn't be involved in anything good. The odd hours. His reluctance to admit what he did for a living. Hell, just the way people looked at him when they were out. Not that they'd really gone out together since that dinner.

Maybe because he didn't want anyone to recognize him?

"Look, I didn't know who he was either," Anita said, obviously seeing Gracen's shock. "I just heard one of the customers wondering why a Malone was here. Then I mentioned it to Ice the other day and he got all excited. Regent Malone is the head of the biggest criminal syndicate in the city."

Regent? Was that a relative? One of his brothers?

"But surely everyone would know who he was."

"The Malones are very secretive. They're an old family with

ties to the city and people mostly ignore their criminal ties because they give lots of money to charities and stuff."

"I . . . I don't even know what to say."

"Apparently, Victor is like his brother's enforcer or something. He's well known in the underground fighting rings for being vicious and brutal. Ice said people call him the beast of New Orleans. So, can I go early?"

Gracen's mind was whirling. "Uh, yes. But lock the door and turn the sign first." She felt numb. And ill. She needed a moment to think about all of this.

As soon as Anita left, she turned on her ancient computer. Using the search engine, she put in Victor's name.

Nothing much came up. That was odd. She thought there would be something. There were results for Regent Malone. But they were all society articles about him attending charity functions. And there were other things about a Jardin Malone, who was an attorney. Most of the articles were about Maxim Malone. He owned some nightclubs and he also seemed to have a different woman on his arm each weekend.

But nothing about Victor.

She closed down her computer, then leaned her forehead on her hands. Her elbows were bent and resting on the desk. This time she heard him come through the back.

He no longer came into the bakery in the mornings, but she always saved him a sticky bun. Now, she was starting to wonder if that was because he didn't want anyone to see him with her.

To protect her?

Or himself?

"Baby? You okay?"

She heaved in a breath.

Be brave, Gracen.

Only, this might be the last time she saw him, and she wasn't sure she could handle that.

He'd kept this from her.

But she'd known. Deep down, she'd known, so she couldn't be angry.

"Hey, what is it? Is it Anita?" She heard him moving but wasn't able to stop her flinch as he touched her back. "What's happened? Has someone hurt you?" His voice was filled with protective intensity. "Gracen, look at me."

Unable to stop herself, she turned, moving her hand so she could see him.

Would this be the last time? Did he really want to be with her or was she just convenient? Gullible and naive?

"Hello, Victor Malone."

The flare of his eyes was the only sign that she'd surprised him. Then he sighed. "Fuck. I should have told you."

"Yes, you should have."

"How'd you find out?"

"Anita. One of the customers mentioned your last name, and she must have said something to Ice, her boyfriend."

"The gangster wannabe. You need to get her away from him."

She huffed out a laugh. "You think I haven't tried? And she just mentioned to me how much of a hypocrite I am putting Ice down when I'm dating you. I mean, is that what we're doing? Because we haven't really talked about it."

"You're mad."

She rubbed her hand over her face. "Maybe I should be. I don't know. I'm so confused. I knew there was something going on, how could I not? Yet, I chose to ignore the signs, so that's on me. I can't be angry with you about that. How bad is it? What you do? I mean, I know that's a stupid question. Breaking the law is still breaking the law so it's all bad, right? But you . . . you treat me so well. I've never been with someone like you. And it's so hard to try to merge the two sides of you together."

"Calm down, baby. You're going to give yourself a bad headache."

"How can I want you when you're . . . you're . . ."

"A bad person?" he offered.

She shook her head, then winced in pain. "But you're not a bad person. I know that."

"I do bad things. I've done terrible things. Some of them I regret, some of them I don't. I'm my brother's enforcer, the guy who stands between him and danger. And that means I've had to get my hands dirty. And I don't blame you for not wanting them to touch you." He stared down at his hands. "I don't think they'll ever be clean again."

"Victor," she whispered hoarsely, hating the look of loathing that crossed his face. The pain in his voice.

She didn't want that for him. Or for her.

God, did she . . . did she love this man?

But she hadn't known him long enough for that. Right?

And he hadn't been truthful with her. But she hadn't pressed him for answers.

She reached for him, and he drew back, breathing heavily.

"This is it, Gracen."

"What? You mean . . . it's over? Just like that?" A sob broke free from her mouth.

"Baby." He closed his eyes, looking pained. Then he opened them, piercing her with the sorrow and resolve she saw looking back at her. "It's a crossroads. Where you decide which path to take."

She wiped at the tears leaking down her cheeks. "What path?"

"You have to decide whether you can be with me or not. My life is dangerous and it's wrong, but I can't turn away from it. This is who I am. Who I'm always going to be. I didn't tell you because I was selfish. Because I wanted you to be mine, but being mine won't be easy. Not that I know how to walk away from you. Fuck. But I should give you this one chance to leave."

Her tears were coming faster, and she reached for a tissue with a shaky hand.

"If you were mine, Gracen, I would always be in charge of your safety. There would be things in place to keep you protected. I wouldn't ever be able to share everything. And there's no leaving this life once you're in. Once I claim you, you'd have to live with it. Not only that, but you have to fucking thrive. Because I wouldn't have it any other way. I'd cherish you. I'd protect you. I'd fucking adore and love you. I'd do whatever it took to stop the darkness from touching you. But I'm never leaving it, understand?"

Not really. But she nodded anyway.

"If you said yes to being mine, I would never let you go. I would fucking own you. Do you get that, Gracen?"

"Would I own you?"

"Baby. You already do."

She took a shuddering breath.

"Going to go now. I'm going to give you one chance. If you want me, then you know how to get in touch. But, baby, I'm always there in the shadows watching over you. Because you're a part of me now."

He stepped back and walked out.

She just sat there, trying to remember how to breathe. Had he really just left after laying that on her? How could he do that?

And could she really let him go?

Because she already felt ill at the thought of never seeing him again. A sob worked its way out of her.

She wanted to race after him, tell him that she wanted to be with him. But she knew he was giving her a chance to think and she should take it. Because there would be no leaving once she was in.

She got the feeling he didn't give many people these sorts of chances. And she would do a disservice to both of them not to take some time to think this through.

All she knew, though, was that she couldn't imagine her life without him in it.

As intense as he was, she would never have someone desire her like he did. Want her as much as he did.

Be as utterly dedicated to her happiness and safety as he was.

And she wanted to be his.

Forever.

12

Gracen mopped the floor.

Damn it. This was Anita's job. She was supposed to do it before she left. It was Saturday evening and she had better things to do than deep clean the bakery.

No, you don't.

She wished Sammy was in town so she could meet up with her. She really needed to talk about what happened with Victor.

And at the same time, she couldn't talk to anyone. Sammy wouldn't really get it. She wouldn't get how Gracen could have feelings for a criminal who had obviously done bad things. And yet, she still wanted him in her life.

Because he was the best thing that had ever happened to her.

Because all she thought about was him. Day in and day out.

Sammy would remind her that he'd basically deceived her. That he was keeping things from her.

But that wasn't all on him.

God, she didn't know what to do.

Setting the mop down, she closed her eyes and took a deep breath.

What it really came down to was whether she wanted to be with Victor or not. Whether she could live with his other side.

And perhaps it made her a terrible person or a selfish one, but she still wanted him.

Opening her eyes, she took a deep breath.

He'd told her it was forever. And that's what she wanted.

Because she loved him. She wouldn't feel this awful, this torn and sick if she didn't.

The thought of living without him was worse than anything else.

Decision made, she grabbed the garbage bag and hauled it to the dumpster in the alley out the back.

A bad feeling rolled over her. It was dark already, she'd been here longer than she'd intended. That's what happened when you paused every few minutes to think.

Shaking it off, she walked back into the bakery. That's when she heard voices from the front.

Oh, God! Someone was here! But who? She looked around for a weapon. Why the hell didn't she keep a bat or something in here?

Just leave. Get out the back and run.

Smart idea.

This place wasn't worth getting hurt over, and it wasn't like she had much money on the premises.

Turning, she stepped toward the back door.

"Going somewhere?" a voice asked from behind her.

Shit. Should have moved faster.

She turned, her heart racing. Nausea bubbled in her stomach as she took in the two scruffy guys standing there. They were younger than her. Likely in their early twenties. Both of them wore dark T-shirts and ripped jeans. One was completely bald while the other one had long, dark hair.

And both of them made her skin crawl.

"If you're after money, just take it and go. I won't call the cops."

Baldy grinned. "We know you won't call the cops. Because that would be a very stupid thing to do, and you're not stupid, are you?"

Her gaze flickered between them. "What do you want?"

"I thought there'd be some goodies around here to eat," the other one complained, moving around and opening cupboards and the fridge. He drew out a carton of milk and started drinking straight from it. It was then that she got a look at the tattoo on his forearm.

A large V with a viper swirling around the letter.

Ventura gang. She'd never had issues with them before, but she knew Ice hung out with some of them. Anita had made it sound like Ice was planning to join the gang one day.

"Are you looking for Ice? He's not here."

"Who's Ice?" Baldy asked. "He your boyfriend? He shouldn't let a cute little thing like you stay here on your own, should he? Bad things could happen to you."

The other guy let out a loud burp, making her cringe. Then he threw the carton of milk toward the garbage can that she'd just emptied. He obviously didn't drink all of it as milk sprayed everywhere.

She stared at the floors that she'd just mopped in dismay.

Dirty floors are the least of your worries right now.

"What do you want then?"

"We're here to offer you a really good deal. It's something all your neighbors are getting too."

"What sort of deal?" she asked. This wasn't going to be anything good.

"Why, our protection. See, crime in this city is at an all-time high. Terrible, really."

"What else you got in here?" Burpy demanded, searching around for food.

"Yeah, terrible," she agreed, ignoring Burpy. "What has that got to do with me?"

"You're one of the lucky ones we're offering our protection to."

Protection? When they were the ones probably causing most of the increase in crime? What the hell?

"And why would I want your protection?"

"Because we'll keep you and your business safe. Don't you want to be safe? From all these criminals?"

"Criminals like you?" she whispered, then wished she hadn't. What was she doing? She needed to get them to leave, not antagonize them.

"Criminals like us? We aren't no criminals are we, Badger?" Baldy said.

Badger? Seriously?

"Nope," Burpy replied. He let out another belch as he gorged himself on her leftover cream buns and cupcakes.

Asshole.

"What do you want in return?" she asked.

"Why, just a small monetary donation."

Oh, God. She got it now. They wanted protection money.

"And if I don't pay you?"

"Then you don't get our protection." Baldy smiled at her, but it wasn't a pleasant smile. No, he looked like a shark about to take a bite. From her. "And that wouldn't be good. For you. So, we'll be here first of every month. Have our money waiting. Got it?"

"How much?"

"Ah, six hundred a month should cover it."

Six hundred a month? They were going to bankrupt her. She didn't even have her head above water now. She'd had to dip into her emergency stash just to make rent this month.

"You'll put me out of business."

"Don't worry, sweetie," Baldy said, moving in closer to her.

Fuck. Fuck.

Her heart raced in fear as he backed her up against a wall. He ran a finger down her cheek. God, he smelled awful. Like rotten garbage. He leaned in, his breath fanning across her face, nearly making her gag.

"If you got problems paying, I'm sure we can come to some arrangement." He grabbed her breast with his hand, squeezing it.

She shoved him back then placed an arm over her chest protectively. "Get away from me asshole! I wouldn't touch your disease-ridden dick if it was the last one on the planet."

He raised his hand, and she flinched, ready for another black eye. But Burpy reached out and grabbed his arm. "Chill, man."

"Fuck, fine." Baldy straightened his clothes. "Frigid bitch. Be seeing you in a week. Have the money." Baldy slapped Burpy's back, making the other guy belch again. She was starting to think he had digestion issues.

Not that she cared.

Once they'd left she made sure the doors were all locked. She thought Anita had locked them on her way out.

"Doesn't matter. Unimportant. Shit. Shit." She slumped to the ground behind her counter, pulling her legs up to her chest.

What the hell was she going to do?

"We need to be careful," Regent said as he climbed into the backseat of the car. "We don't know whether Santiago is working with Patrick, but this could be a setup."

Victor just grunted. He glanced down at his phone.

Still no message. No missed calls.

Fuck.

Just take a peek at her.

He'd been able to get some cameras into her apartment when he'd been there. But he was trying not to check on her too often.

And failing miserably.

He'd never be able to let her go. Not fully. He could step into the shadows and watch her like he had before, but he'd always be there.

When he touched her, he felt at peace. That was something that not even fighting gave him. She kept the demons at bay.

How could he live without her?

He opened the app to check her apartment. He frowned. She wasn't in the living room, kitchen, or bedroom. Maybe she was in the bathroom.

"Did you hear me? Victor? You seem distracted, and I need you to have your head in the game."

"My head's in the game." He set his phone aside. "You sure going to this meet with Santiago is a good idea? Could be a trap."

"Which is why I need you with me and not with her."

Victor shot his brother a look. "You know about her?"

"Course I do. Can't believe you thought I wouldn't. You took her to Matteo's."

Matteo, the owner of the restaurant he'd taken her to for dinner was also friends with Maxim.

"You wanted me to know," Regent claimed.

"Guess I did." Subconsciously.

"If you want her, then you need to protect her, Victor."

He stiffened. "You think Santiago will try to take us on?"

"I don't know if it's him or if there's someone else in the shadows. Ever since we got that tip that Patrick was hiding out under Santiago's protection, I've been working on turning one of his men to my side. But that could be why Santiago has called this meeting. Wants to feel us out, figure out what we want."

Victor grunted. He didn't like it. He had a bad feeling about all of this shit.

Regent got out his phone. "If it's just about sex, I get it. But I've never known you to keep going back to the same person. Or take someone out for dinner. So, if she's something more, get her secured, Victor."

"I gave her a choice. A chance to back out. I think she's decided she can't stomach being with me."

"You're going to let her choose?" Regent gaped at him. "Who are you? This isn't you. Aren't you the one who often argues that we need to protect the women in our lives no matter what their views are?"

Yeah. And if Gracen agreed to be his, he knew that his protective instincts were going to roar loud and clear.

"I know, I just—"

An engine revved loudly then something smashed into the side of them, sending the car spinning. It rolled and someone yelled. The world shook around him. Screams of pain. The screech of metal.

And then something hit his head.

And he knew no more.

13

Gracen paced up and down the small living room.

She glanced over at the clock. It was eleven at night.

She'd texted Victor over an hour ago, asking him to come see her.

Nothing. She chewed her lip.

Had he given up on her? Did he no longer want her? He wouldn't be asleep. He was a night owl.

And he always had his phone on him. Always.

Okay, this didn't have to mean anything. He would get back to her. Or he'd turn up here. She just had to wait.

Her stomach roiled, and she knew she should eat something, but she wouldn't be able to stomach it.

Was she going to tell him about her visit from Baldy and Burpy?

How could she not tell him? But maybe not tonight. Tonight would be about them. She'd mention it before they were supposed to come back, though.

Because she needed help, and she wasn't ashamed to admit it.

She just didn't want him to think that the only reason she'd contacted him was for his protection.

It wasn't.

Sitting, she turned on the television and decided to wait.

WHERE WAS HE?

Worry flooded her. This wasn't like him. If he didn't want to be with her anymore, surely he'd have the gumption to tell her.

She stared at her phone. It was nearly ten in the morning. Over twelve hours since she'd messaged him.

Maybe he didn't get her message. Who knew with her crappy phone?

And you should have called him.

Maybe she should give him a bit longer.

No. Screw it.

Before she could talk herself out of it, she hit his name on her contact list. It rang and went to voicemail.

She hung up, not ready to leave a message. Maybe she should, though.

And say what?

God, she hated being so indecisive. Before she could figure out what to do, her phone buzzed in her hand.

Victor.

Thank God.

"Victor," she said quickly. "I wasn't sure whether to leave a message or not. And I texted you last night, but you didn't reply. Can you come over? Please?"

Yikes. That probably sounded really desperate.

Then again, she was kind of desperate.

"Hello," a voice who wasn't Victor said. "As you can probably tell, I'm not Victor. But I have his phone."

She ended the call abruptly. Who would have his phone? Had something happened to him? Oh God, what if whoever had his phone had hurt him?

She didn't even have a clue how to get in touch with his family. What was she going to do?

Her phone buzzed, he was ringing back. But she shouldn't answer, right? If she didn't though, how would she know what had happened?

A message came through.

PLEASE ANSWER MY CALL. *This is Maxim. Victor's brother.*

HE COULD BE LYING. Or maybe he wasn't.

Fuck.

Deciding to take a chance because she didn't have any other options, she answered the next call.

"Thank you for answering my call, Gracen," Maxim told her.

"How do you know my name? Are you really Victor's brother? What if you're someone who kidnapped him and now you're calling me pretending to be his brother?"

"Uh, well. I know your name because it's typed into his phone. As for proving I'm his brother, I could tell you his middle name."

"I don't know his middle name, though."

"You don't? Well, it's Guillaume."

"What? Really?"

"Yes, really. Poor guy. He got teased mercilessly when he was younger."

"He did?" It was hard to believe anyone having the courage to tease Victor.

"Yes, by me."

"What's your middle name, then?" she asked him.

"Gracen, I think we better keep some secrets between us, yeah? Keep the mystery alive."

Even though he was making an attempt to joke, she thought he sounded tired and stressed.

"It's going to be hard to prove I am who I say. But I am Victor's brother."

"All right," she whispered. "What's going on, Maxim?" She had no reason not to believe him. But it was odd he had Victor's phone. If he wasn't really Maxim, if he'd hurt Victor, then she needed to know where to find him.

So she could kill him painfully and slowly.

"You're close to Victor?" Maxim asked.

"I love him. I haven't told him that yet, though, so don't say anything to him, please. He and I . . . it's complicated, I guess."

"The best things usually are. Fuck. Victor would kill me for giving up personal information. So would Regent."

"What personal information? Maxim, you're really starting to worry me. Where is Victor?"

"He's been in a car accident."

SHE RUSHED into the private hospital.

She'd never been here before, so she paused for a moment, looking around. A security guard stepped up to her.

"Ma'am, can I help you?" He was giving her a skeptical look, like he couldn't understand why she'd be here.

She peered down at herself. Oh, crap. She was dressed in her brother's sweatshirt, a pair of worn denim shorts, which you couldn't really see under the long top, and flip-flops.

Yeah, she didn't look like she should be here. What was more, she wasn't sure if she was supposed to ask for Victor or not. When

Maxim had told her what hospital to come to, she'd just hung up and raced out of there.

"I . . . I . . . I'm looking for . . ."

"Gracen?"

She glanced over, recognizing Maxim from the images she'd seen online. Although he wasn't looking as polished right now. His hair was sticking up on end, and there were dark bags under his eyes.

"Maxim!" She rushed forward. "Where is he? Is he all right?"

"She's with me, Jack," he said to the guard.

She turned to see the other man nod respectfully. "Sorry, ma'am."

"It . . . it's okay. I don't . . . I don't really look like I belong here."

"Nobody cares what you're wearing. Come with me." Maxim led her through a maze of corridors. Her heart raced so hard she felt ill. Another man followed behind them, but Maxim didn't introduce them.

She looked back at him once, but he never looked her way and Maxim urged her forward.

Another guy in a suit stood in front of a door. Were they all here to guard Victor? Why?

When they approached, the man moved with a respectful nod. They walked into a waiting room.

"Wait. I thought you were taking me to Victor." She whirled toward Maxim.

Maxim grimaced. "I'm sorry, Gracen. I can't take you to him yet."

"Why not? Is he not allowed visitors?"

"I've tightened security. Only Jardin and I are allowed in to see either of my brothers."

"I . . . I can't see him?" But she had to see him. Her breath came in short bursts and the room started spinning.

"Please, sit." He offered her a chair. She sat, shocked to find it was comfortable. Not her experience with hospitals.

Maxim sat across from her. "Victor is a secretive guy, and he's never, uh, well . . . mentioned you."

"Oh. Right." She twisted her fingers together. "So, you don't want to let me see him?"

Maxim blew out a breath. "I probably shouldn't. But I also know that if I had a girl that was special, I'd likely want to keep her to myself too. About a week or so ago, Victor took a woman out to dinner at my friend Matteo's restaurant. I'm thinking that was you."

"Yes. I ordered the filet mignon well-done, and the chef got upset."

"That would be Roger. Yeah, he's an ass."

"He sure is."

"Never known Victor to take a girl on a date."

"Really?"

"Like I said, he's secretive. But damn it, he should have told us about you. What if something happened to him and you . . . well, something did happen."

"Will you . . . is he going to be okay . . ."

Please let him be okay.

What would she do if he wasn't?

"I hope so. He's got a concussion. The MRI showed some brain swelling. So far, he hasn't woken up."

"Oh God. Was anyone else hurt?"

"Yeah, their driver suffered a ruptured spleen, he's in the operating room. My oldest brother, Regent, was in the back with Victor. He's also in surgery. Jardin left two days ago to take his family on vacation, so that leaves me. I'm not supposed to be left in charge, Gracen." He shook his head. "Don't know what the right fucking thing to do is."

"It . . . it's all right. I can . . . I can wait here until he's awake. I don't want to put you under more stress." It was obvious he was just trying to look after his brothers.

"You're a sweetheart, aren't you?" He studied her. "Where'd he find you?"

"At *Make It Sweet* bakery. I own it."

"Do you? Do you know how to make mocha brownies?"

"Of course. That's your favorite? I can make that for you."

"Thank you, doll. How about this? Why don't we go in and see him together? I don't think Victor would want you to be alone right now."

And he could keep an eye on her. Not that she cared if he wanted to watch her. She wanted Victor taken care of and protected.

"Was it . . . was it an accident?" she asked as Maxim stood.

His face shut down, growing impassive. "Well, that's the big question, isn't it?"

She pondered those words as he led her through to another room. This one had a guard on the outside and the inside. But as soon as she stepped in, she forgot about the man who left the room when they entered. Her whole attention was on the big man lying in the hospital bed.

It wasn't that he looked fragile or even ill. Victor was still huge and strong. But the tube in his mouth, the IV line, and all the equipment keeping track of his vitals hit her hard. She stood there, her hand over her mouth as tears streamed down her face.

"Gracen? If it's too much, we can leave." Maxim's hand landed gently on the small of her back.

Pull yourself together, Gracen. He needs you.

"No. No." She moved slowly forward. She didn't know where to touch him. She ran her gaze over him, but she couldn't see any visible effects from the accident.

"He's got some bruised ribs, probably from the seatbelt. Thank God they were both wearing them," Maxim told her. "Regent broke his leg. They're hoping the swelling in Victor's brain will go down quickly." His phone rang. "Shoot. I have to take this, it's my sister. I'll go into the bathroom."

He disappeared into the attached bathroom but he didn't shut the door.

That was okay. She reached out to brush her hand over Victor's arm. Then she slid her hand into his. She didn't know how long she stood there, staring down at him. But she jumped in fright as Maxim moved up next to her.

"Here, doll. Sit down. You need to rest."

She sat back in the chair he'd pulled over. Then he sat next to her. He had to keep taking calls, but she sat there, watching Victor breathe.

"I have to go see Regent, he's out of surgery."

"Oh." She didn't want to leave. She had this awful feeling that something would happen to him if she wasn't here.

"Why don't I get someone to take you home?"

"I . . . can't I stay? In the waiting room? Please? I can't . . . I can't leave him."

He gave her a worried look. "Stay in here. I'll send Aero back in to stay with you. Tell him or Mickey if you want something, all right?"

She nodded, thankful he was letting her stay.

"All right, I'll be back soon."

"GRACEN? HEY, GRACEN?"

She turned to look at Maxim, who was crouching beside her.

"Hey, there. You all right?"

"Oh, yes. What . . . what's going on?"

"It's getting late, doll. It's nearly ten at night."

"It is? How is Regent doing?" He'd come out of surgery several hours ago.

"He's actually doing really well. He's lucid. And he's been asking about Victor. And you."

"Me? Why?"

"He knew about you. I don't know how. Maybe Victor told him. Anyway, he wants you to have a permanent guard on you right now."

"What? Why? Am I in danger? It wasn't an accident?"

"We're still trying to sort that out. The driver of the other vehicle ran a red light, but he died at the scene. Could have been drunk or high. Regent wants to be careful, and he knows you're special to Victor."

"I . . . I don't think I need anyone."

Maxim gave her a small smile. "I'm sorry, doll. But in this family, Regent is in charge and what he says goes."

"But I'm not part of the family."

"At the moment, think of yourself as an honorary member. It comes with pros and cons. If it makes you feel any better, our sister, Lottie wants to come home but Regent has forbidden it."

What kind of power did Regent have?

"Jardin should be here tomorrow, he left Carrick, Thea, and the boys in California."

"Carrick and Thea?"

"Oh, you don't know about them? Uh, well." He shrugged and sat on the chair next to her. "Let's see, how to explain this? Jardin is with Thea, who he loves and Carrick, who he also loves. The three of them all love each other."

"You mean, they're in a permanent ménage relationship?"

"Uh, yes. you took that surprisingly well."

She had to smile. "Apparently, my great-grandma was in a similar sort of relationship with two men years ago. But it was taboo to talk about it, so one of the men had to pretend to be the butler."

"Wow. Okay. Lottie also has two husbands, they all got married to each other a few months ago in this weird town called Haven."

"Is it something in the water at your house," she joked.

"Seems like it, doesn't it?"

"I'm not sure that I could handle more than one Malone."

"Well, to be fair, there's only one Malone in each of those relationships. Although two of my cousins are in a relationship with one girl. Poor thing. And that's the Texas Malones. They're wild. I wouldn't want to date them."

She actually found herself smiling.

"Let me send someone home with you, all right? Make me feel better and I won't have to lie to Regent. He'll kick my ass if I go against him. You don't want to see me cry, do you?"

She shook her head. "Lord forbid. That would look truly pathetic."

"It really would."

"But I'm not going anywhere. Not until Victor wakes up."

"Gracen—"

"I can't. Please."

He let out a loud sigh. Then he ran a hand over his face. He looked as exhausted as she felt.

"Damn, doll. Victor is going to kill me."

"I can't leave. I'll just worry about him."

"All right. Here's the deal. You can stay until he wakes up, but you have to sleep on a cot I'll have brought in. Understand? And you need to try and eat."

"I'll try, but my stomach is tied in knots."

"I get it. I really do. And I'll try to get you some things to make it more comfortable."

"Thanks, Maxim. I really appreciate it."

14

She watched the doctor like a hawk, aware that Maxim was doing the same thing from beside her.

Victor had woken a few times yesterday but hadn't been very coherent. This morning, though, he'd managed to open his eyes, say her name, and he'd asked her for some water. Then he'd frowned at her, telling her to get some more rest before falling back asleep.

She'd actually wept in relief.

They'd just taken him for another MRI and she was praying for some good news. She dropped her hand, slipping it around Maxim's. Over the last few days, they'd become close.

Jardin had arrived yesterday. He had been surprised by her presence but accepting once Maxim explained everything. He was currently sitting with Regent, who was apparently driving everyone nuts from his bed.

"The swelling has gone down considerably," the doctor finally said.

She let out a deep breath. The room spun slightly, and she

tightened her hold on Maxim. She had barely slept these past few days. Or eaten. All of her energy had been focused on Victor.

"I would expect him to become more and more coherent."

She nodded, then regretted it as nausea washed through her. Turning, she buried her face in Maxim's arm.

"Hey, he's going to be all right. Gracen?"

"I'm just relieved."

"I know, me too. Soon, he'll be awake and bossing us all around. Come on, I have to tell Regent and Jardin the good news."

She nodded. "All right." She turned back to Victor, running her hand down his arm.

"No, doll. I want you to come with me."

"With you?" She gave him an alarmed look. "To see Regent?"

Maxim grinned at her. "He's not that scary."

She just stared at him.

"All right, he is. But he'll be nice to you. I promise. Well, maybe not nice, but he's not going to hurt you."

"Wow, that really makes me want to go see him. I can't wait."

"Come on."

"I can't leave Victor." What if he woke up?

"Gracen, you haven't left this room since you arrived. Just ten minutes. Aero will watch him closely."

She looked over at Aero who nodded solemnly.

"Five minutes," she told him.

He took her hand and led her out of the room. She'd decided to close the bakery while she was here. Frankly, she didn't care if the thing went under. Not when Victor needed her. Maybe Anita was right, it was time to give up. She wasn't making any money, and now she had the Ventura gang wanting her to pay for their protection?

Yeah, it was all too much. Especially at the moment.

So, she'd told Anita to put a sign in the window and stayed at the hospital with Victor, which is where she belonged.

She followed Maxim down the hall to another door. "I didn't realize they were so close."

"We actually have this whole floor," Maxim told her. "Only certain people have clearance to be on this floor."

They did seem to be really paranoid about security. But she guessed they had good reason to be.

He led her into a room. She saw Jardin sitting across the room next to the bed, which held a handsome, commanding-looking man. None of the other brothers were as big as Victor, but Regent was definitely more intimidating. There was just something about him that made her stomach drop and her heart race.

She stilled and tightened her hold on Maxim's hand. Regent's eyes narrowed at the move.

"Hey, how's Vic?" Jardin asked.

"Better. The swelling is down, they expect him to get more and more coherent," Maxim replied.

"You know, I still want to hear how you two met," Jardin said. "Victor has been keeping you a secret. I'm surprised he didn't lock you up in his room and keep you there."

"I'm sure he was tempted," Maxim said.

"Victor wouldn't do that," she protested.

All three men gave her skeptical looks.

"I'm shocked you've left his side," Jardin said as he stretched.

"She didn't want to," Maxim replied.

"She needs to go home," Regent said.

She stiffened, and Maxim let out a sigh.

"Regent . . ."

"She looks terrible. He'll be pissed when he wakes up and sees the state she's in."

Jardin stood and winked at her. "I'll go sit with him."

She glanced down at herself. She'd taken a quick shower this morning. And Maxim had gotten her some clean clothes. She didn't think she looked that bad. All of the bruising had faded from her face. They should have seen her a week ago.

"Regent, for fucks sake, no wonder you're single." Maxim glared at him. "Don't listen to him, doll. You're beautiful as always."

"She's pale with dark bags under her eyes. Has she been eating? Sleeping? If she ends up in the hospital from dehydration and exhaustion, he's going to lose his mind. Then he'll come after us."

"Um, I don't . . . I don't think Victor will blame you if I'm, uh, tired."

Both men stared at her in disbelief.

"Actually, yeah, he will, Gracen," Maxim told her. "He'll kick my butt in particular since I'm in charge while he and Regent are out of action."

"I'm not out. I am temporarily stuck in this fucking bed. But I'm leaving as soon as Victor can."

He was?

"The doctor said you can leave?" she asked.

Regent just stared at her. "No. I said that. And the doctors and nurses here do as I say since I pay their wages."

"You've got weeks of rehab for your leg," Maxim told him.

"I'll be fine."

Maxim muttered something. She thought she caught the words stubborn and goat.

She couldn't help the giggle that crossed her lips.

"You think that's funny, Gracen?" Regent asked coolly. "That he refers to me as a stubborn goat?"

"Oh, I, uh . . . no?"

"Regent," Maxim snapped.

Regent sighed. "I apologize. I'm like a lion with a sore paw. Irritable and looking to take my irritation out on others. Which is unacceptable. And I sincerely apologize yet again."

"It's all right," she said quietly. She knew how hard it could be to apologize. "I get what it's like to feel trapped. I'm sure you're not used to lying around and doing nothing. Plus, you're probably in pain."

"Well, yes." He looked a bit surprised. "I'm sorry we had to meet under these circumstances. Victor was keeping you to himself, not that we blame him."

"Nope," Maxim said. "I'd likely do the same."

"We haven't known each other long. Well, not really. He's been coming in for my sticky buns for a few months now."

"Your sticky buns?" Regent asked.

"Oh, I own a bakery."

"Yes, I know," Regent said smoothly. "I had you investigated."

"You did?" she whispered.

"Regent, damn it. Did you need to tell her that?"

"Of course I did. She deserves the truth if she's going to be part of this family. Are you?"

Was she?

She'd made up her mind, hadn't she?

And there was no way she wanted to be separated from Victor. No. Nope. Not happening.

But still . . .

"Why did you have me investigated?"

"Because I protect my family. No matter what, they come first. And everything I do is for them."

She took in a deep breath. "Then yes, I'm going to become family, provided Victor still wants me."

Regent smiled at her. "Somehow, I don't think that will be a problem."

VICTOR FORCED HIS EYES OPEN. He felt foggy, disorientated.

His mouth was dry, and he had no idea where he was.

Panic started to flow through him. What the fuck had happened?

He turned his head. Shit. That hurt. Then his gaze landed on white-blond hair. That belonged to a body he knew well.

Relief flooded him.

Gracen. She was here. She was all right.

Suddenly, she raised her head from the bed. Why did she look so terrible? Like she hadn't been sleeping?

"Gracen? What's wrong, baby?"

"Victor," she breathed out with relief. "You're awake. Do you know where you are?"

He glanced around in confusion.

"It doesn't matter. Don't worry. I'll get a nurse. Wait there. Oh, you can't go anywhere. Aero, he's awake."

"I'll call someone."

He tried to raise his hand to her face but fell short. And then darkness flooded over him once more.

Gracen . . . come back to me.

GRACEN COULD FEEL her eyelids growing heavier.

Victor had been far more lucid that last time and she wanted to stay awake, to be there in case he woke up. He might need her.

Her head drooped, and she forced it back.

"Gracen, you're falling asleep," Maxim said in a scolding tone as he entered the room. He was carrying two cups of coffee.

"Ooh, coffee. Gimme." She held up her hand.

"No way. This isn't for you. You're going to sleep."

"I don't need to sleep."

"You definitely need to sleep. Don't think I didn't catch you nearly nodding off just now. The last thing you need is caffeine."

"Maxim, don't be mean to me. Give me the coffee." She gave him her best puppy dog eyes.

"Nope."

"Maxim."

"Maxim, give her what she wants."

They both turned to stare at Victor. He was frowning up at them. "And why're you in my bedroom, brother?"

"Hey there, brother," Maxim said. He sat the coffee down on the nightstand and moved up next to her. She'd stood and was leaning over Victor, her hand on his.

"Victor? How are you feeling? Are you in pain? Shall I get the nurse?"

"Why the fuck would I want a nurse?" He stared up at her, then his frown deepened. "Are you ill? Are we in the hospital? Baby?"

"It's all right," she told him soothingly. "There was a car accident, and you hit your head pretty badly. You're going to be fine, though."

He frowned at her. Then glanced up at Maxim. "The truth."

"If you didn't have a hard head, you'd likely be dead, you asshole. Don't ever fucking do that to me again."

"Maxim," she scolded. "You can't talk to him like that."

"Why not?" Victor asked. "It's how he always talks to me."

"What? Why? I thought you guys were close?"

"So did I, baby. So did I," Victor said in a sad voice.

She turned to glare at Maxim for upsetting Victor. She admitted she was feeling overly protective of him at the moment.

She could have lost him.

No, don't think of that right now.

But instead of appearing chagrined, Maxim was gaping down at Victor in shock. "Are you . . . are you joking around? Jesus, the doctor said you might have some fuzziness and cognitive issues, but he didn't say you'd have a complete lobotomy."

"Maxim!" she scolded again. "What is wrong with you?"

"Not as much as is wrong with him."

Victor stared at her, hard. "Why don't you look well? Maxim?" There was growing alarm in his voice, and she reached out to lightly grab his arm.

"Victor, I'm fine. There's nothing wrong with me."

"Then why do you look like this?"

"I really look that bad?" She stared up at Maxim.

The other man shrugged. "I've been trying to tell you that he wouldn't be happy that you haven't been taking care of yourself when he woke up."

She ground her teeth together. He was giving Victor more ammunition.

"What?" Victor growled.

She ran her hand up and down his arm. "Maxim, stop upsetting him. He's supposed to be kept quiet."

"Who said that?" Victor asked, then he coughed, wincing

She jumped up, trying to ignore the way the room spun, then reached for a cup. Only she managed to knock it off the nightstand.

"Drat. Sorry. I'll get it." She bent down and grabbed the cup.

But she didn't remember trying to stand back up.

She awoke to a loud roaring noise.

"Why did she faint? What's wrong with her?"

"Mr. Malone. You have to calm down. You've got a head injury."

"I don't give a fuck about me. Put her on the bed with me."

"We can't put her on the bed with you, sir. It's against policy."

"Don't we own this fucking hospital? Maxim?"

"We do," Maxim said in the coldest voice imaginable. "And you are to treat her as well as you do us."

"Better," Victor snarled.

"Better," Maxim agreed. "Go and get a spare bed and bring it in here for her."

She then became aware of being placed next to a warm body. Arms that she knew well surrounded her, drawing her close.

"Baby," Victor whispered in a broken voice. "Wake up."

"I'm okay," she told him, patting his chest and forcing herself to open her eyes. "Just tired. Need that coffee."

"No coffee," Maxim said in a firm voice. "You need sleep."

"He's being mean to me, Victor," she complained, burying her face into his chest.

"No, he's trying to take care of you. Something you clearly need."

"You both need sleep," Maxim told them. "And someone to look after you. Can't say it's my strong suit, but for now, it's me. So, both of you go to sleep. Got me?"

And for once, she decided to do what he said without an argument.

SHE WOKE UP WITH A CRY. Sitting up in bed as her heart raced. The door knocking back into the wall made her scream again.

"It's all right," Victor said calmly, sitting as well. "She was having a nightmare."

She had been?

Then it rushed back at her. Victor had been in a car accident. Turning to him, she hugged him as the door to their room shut and the guard disappeared. Poor guy, she'd probably scared him when she'd screamed.

"I'm sorry. I'm sorry."

Victor drew her back with him so they were lying on the bed once more. "You have nothing to be sorry for."

She heaved for breath, trying to calm her racing heartbeat.

"What was it about?"

"Losing you," she whispered. "It was about me losing you."

He rolled onto his back, pulling her to lie on top of him. His arms held her tightly. And gradually, she started to relax.

"You'll never lose me, baby. I'm right here. I'm not going anywhere." He ran his hand up and down her back.

Her heart started to slow. Turning her face, she kissed his chest. "I was so scared."

"I know, I'm sorry for scaring you."

"Then don't do it again, you hear me, Victor Malone?"

"Yes, ma'am."

15

She opened her eyes.

Damn, why did she feel so bad? Her entire body ached. She glanced around, seeing that she lay on one side of a double bed. It was a strange bed, though. Kind of hard and it smelled like a hospital.

She gasped and turned, searching out Victor. Where was he? Where was Aero? Why was she alone?

"Victor! Victor!"

She climbed off the bed. But she only managed a few steps before her legs gave way beneath her as the room spun.

"Ouch!"

"Gracen?"

She glanced up through tear-filled eyes and there he was. He looked kind of gray and had bags under his eyes, but he was there.

She tried to get onto her feet. He reached out and placed his hands under her arms, hauling her up.

"Victor, you can't lift me. Be careful."

"I'm fine."

But he wasn't. She could tell. He stumbled slightly once he had her on her feet. Worry filled her. She was used to him being so strong and in charge.

"You shouldn't be up. What were you doing?" she asked.

"I needed the bathroom. Not peeing in a bag or a pan."

She sighed. Men. She managed to get her arm around his back. "Come on, lean on me, let's get you back to bed."

"Baby." He shot her an incredulous look. "If you think I'm going to lean on you, then maybe we should get your head looked at."

"That's not very nice. I can take your weight. I'm stronger than I look."

"If you could see yourself right now, you wouldn't say you looked strong." He cupped her face between his hands, staring down at her. "Baby, why did you run yourself ragged sitting by my bedside? If I can't do it, I need you to take care of yourself. I didn't have a heart before you. You are my heart and I can't lose you. I don't care if you need to walk away. Not fucking letting you go. Where you go, I go."

She rubbed her cheek against his palm like a contented cat. "That's good. Because I feel the same. Before I got the call from Maxim about you being hurt, I had sent you a message asking you to come see me." She stared up at him. "Because I love you, Victor Malone and I want to be yours. No matter what."

He closed his eyes, swaying slightly. "Thank fuck. I love you, Gracen." He opened his eyes staring down at her intently. "And I promise I'm going to take care of you."

"I know you will. But right now, you need to get back to bed. Did they take out your IV? How long have I been out?"

"Nearly twenty hours," he told her.

"What? Yikes. No wonder I really have to pee. Come on, bed. Then I'm going to the toilet."

"I'll go with you."

"Uh, no you won't. Bed, mister. I do not need any help peeing."

He didn't look happy, but thankfully, he didn't try to follow her into the bathroom. She quickly took care of business then washed her hands, yelping as she glanced in the mirror.

The door slammed open, and she cried out again.

"What is it? What happened?"

"Victor." She put her hand over her chest, trying to calm her racing heart. Then she glared at him. "Were you outside the door, listening?"

"You cried out. What happened?"

"Nothing." A quick glance in the mirror told her that she was bright red.

"Gracen, don't lie."

"I just caught a look at myself in the mirror. I look terrible."

"Yeah, you do."

Awesome.

"But you're still so beautiful. You just need a bit of care. Come on, back to bed."

She sighed and moved out to where he was, letting him shuffle her back to bed because she figured that was the only way she would get him to lie down.

"Is this how it's always going to be? You bossing me around?"

"Yep." He hauled her into his arms, settling her on top of his chest.

"Victor, I can't lie like this!"

"Sure you can. I need to keep you close so I can keep an eye on you."

"You don't need to keep an eye on me! You're the one who was injured."

"You fainted and then slept for twenty hours. You haven't been sleeping or eating properly lately. As far as I can see, you need closer watching. And it's my job to provide what you need."

"You won't always get your way."

"We'll see." Reaching down, he patted her ass. "Now, quiet. I need some sleep. Gotta build up my strength so I can see to your discipline later."

"What? Why?"

"Because you're in big trouble, that's why."

"Victor, you can't talk like that in here. We're surrounded by people. What if someone hears?"

"Then they'll know just how much I care about you."

Damn, how could she be upset with him when he said things like that?

GRACEN STARED up at the house in amazement. Well, it wasn't a house. It was a mansion.

It had been a week since she'd gotten that terrible phone call from Maxim. Since her world had been rocked. Since she'd realized that Victor wasn't invincible. She'd barely been able to let him out of her sight. It had been tempting to follow him into the bathroom.

And it seemed he was feeling the same way.

But Victor's headaches had finally eased up and he'd been given the all clear to return home. Regent was returning home as well today. They were both supposed to take it easy still. But she wasn't sure how much of that would happen.

Regent was barely mobile. He'd been sent home with a wheelchair, but she could tell he was going to be an asshole about using it.

She'd grown close with all the Malone brothers. Although she hadn't seen much of Jardin as he'd gone back to where his family was vacationing. But he'd told her that Thea wanted to meet her soon.

Nerves rattled her at the thought.

Victor had been making her rest, but she still felt off. And she thought it was going to take more than a few meals and some good sleep to make her feel better.

She'd nearly lost him.

She tightened her hold on his hand. This was something she was going to have to get over. Because he was always going to be at risk. She still felt ill every time she thought of losing him.

"Baby? You all right?"

"This place is enormous. This is really where you live?"

"Yeah. It's where we all grew up." His face was pensive. "Regent has an attachment to the place. It has mixed memories for me. Our mother died when Lottie was around eight. Our father, he was always distant, but he became more so. He only really had time for Regent. Spent most of my time trying to get him to notice me."

"Oh, Victor. I'm sorry. My brother and I lost our parents when we were young. But Grandpa was amazing. He taught me to bake. And it became like a refuge for me. A way to escape."

"It was a long time ago, baby."

Didn't mean it still didn't hurt.

"Are you sure it's all right for me to stay with you?" she asked, not for the first time.

"Gracen," Victor said in a low voice.

She stared up at him.

"It's just a house."

Right. Just a house. He'd said that about his truck too.

"I want you with me. Do you want to be with me?"

"Yes." It would kill her to leave him.

"Good. So just try leaving me and see what happens," he warned in a low voice that had her rolling her eyes.

"Bossy," she grumbled without meaning it.

"Come on, need to get you inside so you can rest. And I'm going to have to help Maxim with Regent. He's going to be a real asshole to put up with over the next few weeks while he recovers."

"*He's* going to be an asshole, huh?" she said dryly.

"Yeah, he's not used to having to accept help. Don't know how we're going to get help for him either, because he doesn't trust anyone out of the family and his closest men. Not after . . ."

"Not after what?"

Victor sighed. "He was poisoned a while ago. By someone who worked for us."

"What? Oh my God!"

"Now the only person allowed to cook for him is Gerald. But he's away at the moment. He's been with us for years."

The car came to a stop at the bottom of the stairs leading to the house. Regent and Maxim were in the car behind them. They'd had cars in front and behind them as they traveled. Regent had been taking no chances with their safety.

Which told her what she needed to know about whether the accident had really been an accident.

Not that anyone would tell her anything. Seemed that all the Malone men could be secretive and stubborn. And bossy. Really bossy.

Like you'd have them any other way.

Victor's door opened at the same time as hers did. She glanced up into Aero's face. He was kind of growing on her. If someone who never spoke and never showed any facial expression except menace could grow on you.

"No," Victor said, reaching for her as she went to get out her door. "You come out my side."

She sighed but didn't complain.

She was beginning to figure out that it was pointless to argue. The old adage, that it was better to ask for forgiveness than permission kept running through her mind. She'd just have to find a way to get around him if she really wanted to do something he didn't approve of.

But she knew that he only wanted to keep her safe, and at the moment, she wanted to lessen all of his worries.

So, she slid out his side of the car, taking his hand as he hauled her up. She stared up at the stairs then over at Regent who was leaning heavily on his crutches. Maxim held his wheelchair behind him.

"Um, how is Regent going to get up those stairs?"

"Regent is going to climb them," the man replied. He turned to scowl at Maxim. "Get that chair the fuck away."

"Brother, there's no way you can get up those stairs," Victor said quietly. He glanced around at their men who were all poised and watchful. "All of you can go except Jose."

The men all slid away except for the large bodyguard Regent seemed to favor.

Victor stared down at his brother. "Now I can carry you."

"Dude, head injury, remember?" Maxim pointed out. "You can't carry anyone."

"No one is carrying me anywhere, you assholes," Regent said grouchily.

Oh, yeah, he was going to be a problem while he recovered.

"Maybe Maxim and I could carry you in the chair?" she said equally as quietly.

Everyone gaped at her.

"How do you want to do this, boss?" Jose asked.

"Fuck. I'll sit in the chair. You take the back. Maxim, you take the front. Don't fucking drop me. Victor, get Gracen inside. She looks pale and tired. She's not taking care of herself."

She sighed, but didn't say anything. If Regent needed to grumble at her in order to feel better about his injuries, then she could handle it.

Victor turned to study her. "He's right. We need to get you inside. Lean on me."

Maxim shot her a wink. "Get used to it, little sister. We're all going to be fussing over you now. Just ask Lottie how that went for her."

Regent sat and his big bodyguard and Maxim carried him up the stairs.

Whoa. Maxim was stronger than he looked. He was the slightest of all the brothers, but he wasn't lacking in muscle, that was for sure.

"If you continue to look at my brother like that, I will turn you over my knee right here," Victor said to her, wrapping a tight arm around her waist as they followed them up the stairs.

"What? I wasn't. Sheesh. I was just thinking he's stronger than he looks."

"Thanks, doll," Maxim called back. "I don't even work out. I'm just naturally this buff and good-looking. Definitely the best looking among my brothers."

Regent huffed out a breath. "Dream on."

Victor grumbled, tightening his arm around her. She looked up in worry, concerned that he was actually upset. But he sent her a wink.

She froze as a scream came from in the house.

16

Victor tensed then sighed. "It's all right, baby. It's Lottie."

"Lottie? Your sister? She's here?"

Great. She looked awful. And she was going to meet their beloved baby sister?

Freaking fantastic.

When they walked into the huge foyer, her mouth dropped open. She'd known the place was going to be something else. But this was . . . this was gorgeous. And overwhelming. The staircase was a masterpiece, curling its way upstairs. The flooring looked to be real marble while the walls were painted dark blue.

Finally, she pulled her attention away from the house. She glanced over to find Regent who was still sitting in his wheelchair with a slight, dark-haired woman kneeling in front of him, her face buried against his thigh.

Jose seemed to have disappeared. Regent was murmuring something to the woman while another man with dark hair kneeled behind her. He glanced up and she sucked in a sharp breath as she recognized him.

Nico Carmichael.

The singer.

Holy. Crap. He'd just shot up the charts with a hit song recently. She loved his singing so much. What was he doing here?

"Careful, doll. You have a bit of drool there." Maxim tapped her chin with a grin, and she scowled at him.

"I do not."

Victor stared down at her. "Why were you staring at Nico?"

"I wasn't."

She totally had been.

Another man moved from the shadows to join Nico. This man was blond-haired and muscular. And utterly terrifying.

She stepped into Victor, who held her securely.

"Lottie, darling," Regent said in the softest voice she'd heard him use. His hand rested lightly on Lottie's back. "I'm all right, darling. I promise."

She glanced up and Gracen's eyes widened as she took in the fierce look on the other woman's face. "Damn it, Regent! You should be better protected. How did this happen? Nothing is supposed to happen to you guys. That's it. We're moving back." She got to her feet with the help of the blond-haired man.

"We're not moving back," the scary man said, wrapping his arm around Lottie's tiny waist. Dear Lord, she was gorgeous.

Great. Now she felt fat, frumpy, and ugly next to this beautiful woman.

"Yes, we are. My brothers need me."

"You're not moving back, Lottie," Regent told her in a firmer voice.

"But look at you. You're going to need someone to take care of you. And we can't trust just anyone. Gerald's not here. I'll have to cook for you all."

Everyone stared at her in shock.

"Uh, Lottie, you can't cook," Nico said to her.

"You can help me."

"Darling," Regent told her, taking her hand. "It's not safe to stay here. You can't stay."

"But we just got here. We're not going anywhere. Wait, where's Vicky?" She turned around, spotting Victor.

"Vicky?" Gracen murmured.

"I knew I forgot to tell you something." Maxim grinned at her, clicking his fingers together.

"Oh, hello," Lottie said, suddenly looking shy.

Nico wrapped his arm around her waist, much like Victor was doing with her.

"Lottie, Nico, Liam, this is Gracen. Baby, my sister and her two men. Liam's the big, blond one, and this is Nico." Victor frowned at Nico, who looked back at him quizzically.

"Um . . . I . . . well, hello."

Great job, Gracen. Well done on making a good first impression.

"You . . . who . . . what . . ." Lottie looked from her to Victor, then back. "I'm sorry, who are you?"

"She's mine," Victor said.

Lottie's mouth dropped open in shock. Was it so unbelievable? Gracen tugged at her top, which was something Maxim had bought for her and was probably worth more than her entire wardrobe combined. But she still felt out of place with this gorgeous woman.

"Oh my God! That's amazing!" Lottie rushed toward them, but Nico held her back.

"Whoa, baby. I don't know that Victor is ready for you to tackle him."

Lottie gasped, her hand coming to her mouth. "I forgot. Vicky, are you all right? Your poor head."

"He looks fine," Liam said, pulling her against him, so she was sandwiched between the two men.

Wow. Gracen wondered how she dealt with two men. Gracen could barely handle just Victor and his protective instincts.

"He's got a hard head," Nico agreed.

"Liam, why did you bring her here?" Regent grumbled. "It's not safe, you know that."

"She was making herself sick with worry," the blond-haired man shot back. "Would you deny her something she needed to make her feel better?"

"I would if it kept her safe."

"Hey, you two. I'm right here." Lottie glared at them both.

Gracen stared at her in shock. Lottie was tiny, but she seemed to have no problem sticking up for herself.

"I'm sorry, darling," Regent told her. "But it will be safer for you to be far away from me right now."

"And why is that? What's going on? Was that accident not an accident?"

"No," Regent said quietly. "I don't think it was. And I think things are going to get very nasty and I don't want you here. Which is why you're going home. Liam, you can join us in my office."

Lottie huffed out a breath. Liam kissed the top of her head and whispered something that made her smile.

"I set up a downstairs bedroom for you, Reggie," Lottie told him.

Regent frowned but nodded, before heading toward a door that she guessed led to his office.

"I've got to go put Gracen to bed," Victor stated. "Then I'll be in."

She glared up at him. "If anyone should be in bed, it's you. And Regent."

"No time for that," Regent called back.

"You need to rest," Victor said.

"No, what I need is to bake." She needed to ease some of this stress.

"You bake?" Nico asked, patting his stomach. "Do you make cinnamon rolls?"

He stared right at her, and she had to work hard to find her voice. "Yes, of course."

"Oh, thank God. I'm starved."

"She's not here to feed you," Victor growled. "And if she's going to bake anything, it will be sticky buns."

"Victor loves my sticky buns," she stated.

"I'll just bet he does," Liam drawled.

Crap.

"Liam!" Lottie scolded, but she looked like she was about to burst into laughter.

"Are you all coming?" Regent snapped. "Nico, watch over Lottie and Gracen."

Nico saluted Regent. "On it, boss."

Liam eyed her suspiciously.

"Don't worry, Liam. Gracen is family."

She glanced over at Regent, warmed by his words.

"What's your favorite baked item?" she asked him.

He gave her a surprised look. "I don't eat sweet things."

"Hmm, I'll find something you like."

TWO HOURS LATER, she pulled a batch of cinnamon rolls from the oven for Nico, who was clapping his hands in excitement. The longer she spent with Nico, the less awed she became. Not in a bad way, but because he was so normal.

She'd had to take a moment to tell him how much she loved his music, though. To her shock, he'd blushed and started stammering until Lottie hugged him, telling Gracen that she had good taste.

They'd pestered her with questions about her and Victor. She'd told them everything about how they'd met and they seemed genuinely excited about their relationship.

Thankfully, the kitchen was amazingly stocked. She'd found a heap of frozen meals that Gerald had obviously made before he'd left. But she'd decided to cook chili.

"Wow, I can't believe Victor was coming into your bakery for months," Lottie said. "That's so romantic."

"Not exactly a word I would have used to describe Victor," Nico said, picking up a roll and biting into it. "Oh, hot, hot."

Lottie rolled her eyes but got him a glass of water.

"To be honest, I'm surprised he didn't move you in here straight away," Lottie said.

"Uh, well, I suppose we're still getting to know each other," she said shyly.

"Didn't think Victor would care much about that," Nico commented.

"Nico!" Lottie chided. "I think it's sweet that Victor is taking his time with you."

Well, she wasn't sure that was true. They'd moved pretty fast in some ways. But then, it also felt like they'd known each other forever.

"Victor is sweet," she said.

Nico gaped at her, then grinned. "Jesus, how did he find the one woman in the world that would think he's sweet?"

"Hey, I think he can be sweet," Lottie protested.

"Yeah, but you're his sister. He loves you. To everyone else, he's the boogeyman your parents warn you about. The savage beast of New Orleans. And he's been tamed by a beauty and her sticky buns."

Her cheeks went red. She was starting to regret telling them how they'd met. "He's not savage or a beast or a boogeyman."

Nico held his hands up. "Sorry, sweetheart. Just telling you what other people think. Not me. Nope. Vicky and I are best buds."

Lottie rolled her eyes, then moved closer to Gracen. "It's not always easy being part of this family. Are you sure you know what you're getting into?"

"Are you trying to warn me away from your brother?"

"No, not at all. I'm so pleased he has you. But bad things happen in our world, and I just want you to be really sure because Victor has never shown interest in a woman before. Not serious interest. And I just . . . I don't want to see either of you hurt."

"It's all right, Lottie. I know it's a dangerous world you all live in. But the truth is, my world would be nothing without Victor. So, I'm willing to risk everything just to be with him."

Lottie wrapped her arms around her. "Thank you. Thank you for loving him."

"You don't ever have to thank me for that." They both smiled at each other.

"Everything okay in here?"

She jumped then looked over as Liam walked in. She gave him a wary look. There was something so intimidating about him. But Lottie's face lit up as she saw him. She went to him immediately, cuddling up to his side.

"Of course. Is everything all right? Is there a threat?"

Liam sighed. "Regent thinks Patrick's making trouble again."

"Patrick?" Nico asked. "I thought Regent took care of him."

"We never found Patrick," Victor said, entering the room. He moved over to her, gathering her in tight.

"Yum, cinnamon rolls." Maxim walked in and grabbed one.

"Don't eat too much. I'm making chili for dinner. I mean, if that's all right. I was just doing something simple." They were probably used to really posh food, but she didn't know how to make any of that.

"It's been ages since we had chili," Maxim told her with a smile.

"Oh, good," she replied shyly. "And mocha brownies for dessert."

Maxim suddenly dropped to his knees and shuffled over to her, his hands up in a prayer. "Gracen, marry me. Please."

She blushed. Lord, he was an idiot.

"Mine," Victor growled.

Maxim pouted. "Fine. I guess having her as a sister-in-law will have to do."

"Maxim, Vicky hasn't proposed yet. Although, it won't be far away, I'm sure," Lottie suggested slyly.

"Baby," Liam warned.

Lottie just grinned. Then she sobered as Regent used his crutches to enter the room. "Regent! You shouldn't be out of the wheelchair." She fussed over him as he moved to sit at the small breakfast table.

"I'm fine, Lottie."

He didn't look fine, though. She poured him a cup of coffee and put a roll on a plate then walked it over to him.

He stared down at the roll and coffee then up at her. "Thank you, Gracen."

"You're welcome." She moved quickly back to Victor, who led her to another chair. He sat and pulled her onto his lap.

"I've got things to do," she told him, trying to wriggle off.

"No, you don't. You look pale. Sit."

Well, she supposed if it meant he would sit, she would. After all, he needed to rest.

"So, what's this about Patrick?" Lottie asked, sitting next to them with Nico on her other side.

Maxim grabbed some coffee for them all. She itched to do that. She glanced over at the fridge, she should get the creamer and the rest of the rolls.

"Relax, baby. Maxim has it sorted." Victor placed his hand on her thigh, and she sucked in a breath as a wave of arousal washed over her. Completely inappropriate timing.

"You don't need to worry about Patrick," Regent told her,

sipping on his coffee. He didn't touch the roll. She needed to find something he couldn't resist. Unless he didn't trust her to cook for him. Victor said he only trusted Gerald, which she understood.

She tried to get up again, but Victor tightened his arm around her waist. He brushed his lips against her ear. "Try to move again and I'll spank your ass."

Holy. Heck.

She probably should be annoyed at his words. But another rush of arousal flooded her.

At this stage, she was going to need to change her panties.

"Regent, you can't keep this from us. What's going on? What happened?" Lottie asked.

They were answers she wanted as well. Regent glanced at Liam.

"She needs to know," Liam said. "Especially as you're intent on sending her away."

"Fine. The truth is, we were on our way for a meeting with Santiago when we were hit."

"Carlos Santiago?" she asked. Then she wished she hadn't spoken as everyone glanced over at her.

"You know him?" Victor asked.

"What? No. I've heard of him, though. He has a bad reputation." She tried not to look at anyone as she said that.

"We've all got bad reputations, doll," Maxim said as he placed a small plate with a roll on it in front of her. She had no appetite though. "But Santiago's rep is worse."

"Do you . . . own brothels?" Somehow that thought hadn't occurred to her.

"No," Regent said. "We don't sell flesh."

She flinched at the term, and Lottie looked slightly ill.

"You think Santiago did this?" Nico asked. "That he paid off that guy to crash into you?"

"Him or someone else, yes. The cops will rule it a drunk-driving incident, I'm sure. But it's too much of a coincidence. Santiago sent a message telling me he was sorry about the crash. And we didn't tell anyone what happened."

"Dumb bastard," Liam muttered.

"Yeah."

"Why would Santiago want to take you both out?" Nico asked. "You having issues with him?"

Regent sighed. "We got a tip that Patrick was seen back in the city at one of Santiago's clubs. We discovered someone boasting about what he was planning on doing to me. And when we, uh, questioned him, we found out that Patrick likes one of Santiago's dancers. It doesn't mean he's working with Santiago, but someone has to be helping him. Hiding him from me."

"So, what are you going to do?" Liam asked.

Regent shared a look at Victor. "We're going to fight back. I'm working on flipping one of his men. But this attack . . . it means we need to tighten security. That is why everyone is going on lockdown. You don't travel anywhere without guards. None of you. Liam, you're to take Lottie and Nico home. I told Jardin to keep his family far away for a while. He's not happy, but he's going to take them to Haven to see our cousins."

Victor tore off a small piece of the cinnamon roll and held it to her lips.

"I'm not hungry," she whispered.

"Eat."

Argh. Fine. She took the bite, but her tummy didn't react well.

"Maxim, this applies to you too. I want you to move back in here."

Maxim nodded. "Yeah, okay."

Regent turned to her. "Gracen, you'll be moving in here as well."

It wasn't said as a question. She narrowed her gaze at Regent. He didn't get to boss her around.

"We've already discussed this," Victor said with a frown at Regent. "Gracen is staying."

"Good. Now, about your work, we should be able to spare a couple of men to—"

"Don't worry about that," she interrupted Regent.

He raised one eyebrow. Whoops, he probably wasn't used to someone interrupting him.

"You need to be guarded," Victor told her, not unkindly. "I'm afraid you can't go to work or anywhere else alone. Having a bodyguard is part of being in this family."

"You don't have one," she pointed out.

"You're more important than me."

Oh, no, he didn't. She turned to scowl at him and prodded his chest with her finger. "What bullshit. You are just as important as anyone else in this room. Right?" She glared around at everyone, daring them to argue.

But they all nodded.

"Of course he is," Lottie said. "Vicky has always thought he needs to act the bodyguard for the rest of us, but the truth is we'd be lost if anything happened to him."

Victor shifted around on his seat, obviously uncomfortable, but she didn't care. He needed to hear this. She turned to Regent.

"Nothing will happen to any member of my family," Regent swore. "They all mean everything to me. And Victor has more importance than he knows."

Victor leaned in to whisper in her ear. "Brat. You'll pay for this."

Poor Victor, he was all embarrassed.

"And he doesn't have a bodyguard because he refuses to," Regent told her.

"That's going to change."

"Indeed," Regent replied. She thought she heard a hint of amusement in his voice.

"I like you even more now," Lottie told her. "You're exactly what Victor needs."

"Thank you." It was her turn to be embarrassed.

"So, about the bakery," Regent said. "I can spare two men."

"No, I didn't mean I don't want bodyguards. I'm saying that I don't think it's worth reopening at this point."

"But you love baking," Victor said.

"Well, it seems you guys need some help around here. I can cook and bake until Gerald gets back." She glanced at Regent. "If you want me to, that is."

"That would be very good of you. But I don't want you to feel obliged."

"I don't. I want to help out."

Victor turned her face up toward his. She stared up at him and shrugged, trying to fight tears.

"Little bit, why don't you want to go back?"

"It's not safe."

"It would be a risk," Regent said. "But I didn't expect you to be so agreeable about not going back."

"There are other reasons, aren't there?" Victor asked.

"Yes. It isn't doing well," she admitted to him. "I'm a great baker but a failure at accounts."

"We can help you with that," Maxim said. "I have a great accountant."

"Thank you, but it's not just that. I've been keeping the bakery open in my grandpa's memory, but I'm not sure I'm enjoying it anymore. That area of town has become so unsafe. And the other day . . ." she trailed off, unsure whether she should tell Victor this.

She let out a deep breath.

"The other day, what?" Victor asked.

"I had a visit from two members of the Ventura gang."

"What?" Victor's eyes widened. "And what did they want?"

"To offer me protection. For a fee."

17

Victor clenched his jaw together as the room went silent. He had to work hard to keep his rage from spilling over.

How the fuck had this happened? How had he not known? How long had she kept this from him?

"When?"

She eyed him cautiously. He never wanted her to be afraid of him, but he also wanted her to know that this wasn't acceptable.

"Saturday evening. They caught me at the bakery alone."

Right. So, she hadn't really been keeping it from him. A lot had gone on since then.

"I didn't text and ask you to come over because of that," she said hastily, obviously misreading his silence. "I'd decided before they came in that I wanted to be with you."

"I'm not upset with you, baby. I'm fucking furious that any of those assholes got close to you." He stared down at her. "Did they touch you? Hurt you?"

She swallowed heavily and looked away.

Mother. Fucker.

"Tell me," he said in a hoarse voice. He needed to destroy something. Kill it. A rage, unlike anything he'd ever felt before, filled him. The demons he needed to exorcise by pummeling some evil asshole in the ring had nothing on what now had hold of him.

Kill. Destroy.

Protect.

"What did they do?"

"Nothing that bad," she said hastily. "Really, it's not worth mentioning."

"Do. Not. Lie."

"Best tell him, doll," Maxim said quietly. "He's not going to harm you, but he needs to know."

"Of course I wouldn't harm her. Gracen knows that."

She nodded. "I should have mentioned it."

He let out a low noise of dissent. "You are never to keep things from me. Ever."

"I just . . . I don't want to upset you. Your head—"

"My head will be fine. Tell me."

"I, uh, I told them I didn't have the money to pay them. They wanted six hundred a month. I don't have that sort of money. And one of them pushed me back against the wall. He said . . . he said I could pay in other ways. And he, uh, he squeezed my breast."

The last part was said in a whisper.

He stood hastily with her in his arms. His chair slammed back on the floor, and she let out a startled yelp.

"Victor! Victor!" Regent said. "You cannot let the anger get ahold of you."

He breathed in and out heavily. He needed to punch something. The gym.

"Wait," Regent said. "If you're headed to destroy something, then leave Gracen here."

"No," he replied.

She held onto him.

"You cannot put her at risk," Maxim told him warily.

"Going to the gym."

There was a collective sigh of relief.

"The gym? You can't work out with your concussion, Victor," she told him. "You shouldn't be carrying me."

"She's right, Victor," Lottie said. "You could do yourself some damage. And who will protect Gracen if you're hurt?"

Fuck! Fuck!

But he had to have some way to let the rage out. Normally being with her calmed him . . . but this was different.

"If you still want to go," Regent said calmly, "then leave Gracen here. Lottie can show her to your room so she can rest."

"No." He wasn't letting her out of his sight. Not in the immediate future. Maybe never.

"I still have some things I need to ask," Regent said calmly.

Victor picked up his chair, setting it down before forcing himself to sit. But he was right on the edge, so Regent better be careful.

"What is it?"

"Did anyone know about the two of you? You went to Matteo's that time, but is that it? Is Santiago liable to know about Gracen?"

"I don't know. We kept things quiet. After that dinner, I tried to only come to her when there was no one around."

"Gracen?" Regent asked.

"Ah, my friend Sammy knows I'm seeing someone but not who he is. But my niece knows."

"Your niece?" Regent asked. "She works for you?

"Ah, yes. She came to live with me after her dad, my brother, died. But now she lives with her boyfriend, Ice."

"Ice?" Lottie asked. "That can't be his real name."

"I think it's Robert," she told him. "Actually, there's something else you need to know."

Fuck. He wasn't sure if he could handle anything else.

"A few times when I've gone to Anita's place, Ice had some friends over. They were members of the Ventura gang."

"What?" Victor snapped. "You were around them?"

"Yes, but they didn't pay me any mind."

"So, the gang that your niece's boyfriend belongs to, threatened you?" Nico asked incredulously.

"Ice isn't part of the gang. Not yet anyway. And the two guys who threatened me didn't seem to know who he was. But, uh, there's something else."

He groaned. She was killing him.

"I'm sorry, Victor. I wasn't trying to keep this from you. Really. I didn't know about your, uh, connection to Santiago. Or that those guys from the Ventura gang would come threaten me."

"It's all right, baby. Just tell us."

"Ice just got a new job. Working for Carlos Santiago."

Jesus.

Regent leaned forward. "Could he be persuaded to spy on him?"

"To work for you?" she asked. "I don't know. I honestly don't think you could trust him. Ice is shifty. I think he lies to my niece. I don't think it would be a good idea."

Regent nodded. "Thank you for telling us all of this. But I'm afraid you're right, going back to the bakery would be dangerous."

"When were they supposed to collect the money?" Victor asked her.

"Uh, they said the first of each month. Which is soon."

Victor shared a look with Regent, who nodded.

"Wait. What was that look about?" Gracen asked. "What are you guys planning on doing?"

"Come on, baby. You need to lie down."

"But I've got chili in the crockpot and I need to make cornbread to go with it."

"You're not here to cook for us," he grumbled at her. He stood with her held against his chest. "And you need to rest." He carried her out of the kitchen and toward the stairs.

"Victor, you need to set me down. You can't carry me up the stairs."

Of course he could.

Except, he was feeling weaker than he liked. What if he dropped her?

Reluctantly, he set her down on her feet and took hold of her hand.

"Victor?" she asked as he led her up the stairs. "Are you planning on doing something about Baldy and Burpy?"

"Who? Fuck, is there someone else threatening you?"

"No, no, that's what I nicknamed those two Ventura gang members. What are you planning?" she asked as he led her into his bedroom.

He winced at how stark it was. There was a bed, two nightstands, and that was it. His clothes were in the closet. There were no photos, no paintings, nothing that would soften the masculine feel.

"Sorry about my room," he told her as he led her to the bed.

"It's nice. It has gorgeous big windows and a huge bed."

"I'm a big guy." He closed the curtains and grabbed one of his T-shirts. Then he started stripping her clothes off.

"Victor, tell me."

"Go use the bathroom."

She sighed. "Tell me."

"I'm going to make them pay for putting their hands on you. For hurting and scaring you."

"And how do you plan to do that?" she asked.

"I figure I'll wait for them to come to the bakery, and then I'm going to make them hurt." And he was looking forward to it.

"I should be there. So that they don't get suspicious."

"Yeah, there's no way that's happening. Bathroom. Go." Turning her toward the door, he gave her a slap on the ass to get her moving.

She huffed at him but stomped off to the bathroom. He took a few deep, calming breaths. He needed to do something about this rage before it overwhelmed him. He palmed his stiff cock. All it took was having her close and he was hard as hell.

He waited until she came out, then he pulled back the covers. "In."

She looked tiny in his T-shirt. She was tiny. Delicate.

And his to protect.

Her mouth was turned down and he could see defeat in the slump of her shoulders.

Fuck. He hated that.

As she moved closer, he reached out and grabbed her hips, pulling her to him. "I will protect you no matter what. Even if it makes you angry with me."

"I just don't want you to get hurt, Victor. I want to take care of you too. You're important. To all of us."

He kissed her forehead. Yeah, he'd gotten that from what she'd instigated downstairs. "I've never had a real relationship. Never had someone I love the way I do you. So, you might have to be patient with me."

She slipped her arms around him. "You're coming to bed with me, right?"

"Baby, I've got to get rid of this rage riding me hard. I don't want it around you."

"You'd never hurt me."

Fuck, no, he wouldn't. He wrapped his arms around her, careful not to make his hold too tight.

"What do you usually do to get rid of it?"

"I get into the ring and beat some asshole. I always make sure he deserves it," he added hastily.

"I don't like the sound of that. It sounds self-destructive. What other things make you so angry?"

"Just old memories. The knowledge that my father never saw me as more than fodder to keep Regent safe."

"What?" she asked, leaning back. "That's not true! Regent doesn't see you that way."

"No, he doesn't. But he's not the problem. I am. Because that's what I've believed for the longest time. That I'm not worth anything more than to be my brother's bodyguard. To take the bullets. And it seems I've failed at that again since he was just hurt."

And that was riding him hard as well.

He needed to make someone pay.

"You listen to me, Victor Guillaume Malone. You could never be a failure. And you are worth far, far more than being cannon fodder. You are amazing, smart, and sometimes thoughtful but mostly stubborn and bossy. And I love you, so I'm going to need you to change your mindset quickly because I expect you to be around for a long, long time. Got me?"

"Yes, ma'am." He drew her against him.

"Tighter, Victor. I need to feel you."

He hated the shiver of fear in her voice. "Baby, I'm here."

"I could have lost you. I can't lose you."

"Shh, you won't."

"Please lie down with me."

"All right. I just need to go take a shower." And take care of something.

"You don't need a shower. You smell fine."

"Ah, well . . ."

"Oh." She pulled back, her cheeks red. Then she licked her lips and ran her hand over his erection. "I could help with that."

"You need rest."

"But I think I might need this more. Please."

He eyed her. "Only if I get to eat you out first."

"You know, I think I'd be okay with that."

To his shock, he almost felt like smiling. How had she calmed him so quickly and easily? Normally, that sort of rage would take several bloody fights. But Gracen had him feeling far calmer with a hug and a few words.

"Get naked."

He stripped as she took off the T-shirt and her panties. She stood and waited for his next direction.

"Kneel on the bed."

She climbed on the bed and kneeled. Fuck, she was beautiful. All soft curves. Delicious. He ran his hand up and down his thick dick, loving the way she licked her lips.

"You want my dick, baby?"

"Yes, Victor."

"You want it in your mouth? Your pussy?"

"Both, please."

"Not sure you're ready for my dick in your pussy. We might have to help you get there."

Plus, he didn't intend to take her while he still felt a bit off.

"I know," she agreed breathlessly, watching him move his hand up and down his dick. "I was thinking I might have to buy myself that vibrator, get myself ready for your monster dick."

He huffed out a short laugh. "Monster dick? Seriously?"

"If anyone can claim that title, it's you. But I can't wait to feel you inside me, taking me, stretching me. I want you, Victor. So badly."

Relief filled him. He'd hate for her to be scared.

"Going to take really good care of you."

"I know you will. Come here." She patted the mattress next to her.

"Who's in charge?"

She bit her lower lip, staring up at him. "You are, Victor."

"That's right. Turn away from me, then lean down on your forearms. You're getting the spanking you're owed for not taking care of yourself properly."

"Victor, nooo," she moaned. "You're not up to giving me a spanking."

Oh. Challenge. Accepted.

"Get into place, brat. Even once I'm old and gray, there will never be a time where I won't be able to take care of any discipline you need."

He watched her eyes widen and her breathing quicken.

She moved into position, pushing her ass out. He smacked his hand down on her butt, loving the way her skin turned pink. Several more slaps had her breath coming faster. She was enjoying this far too much. He increased the strength of his smacks until she groaned.

Then he eased off, rubbing the heat into her bottom before dipping his finger down to her pussy, running it along the slick lips.

"Someone enjoyed their spanking too much. She might need another one later."

"What? No!"

"No? You didn't enjoy it? Then how come your pussy is slick? Hmm?"

"That's from before. When you put your hand on my thigh while we were downstairs. And just from you being close to me."

His eyebrows rose at that revelation. "Really? That got you all hot and bothered, little bit?"

She wiggled her ass in the air. "Yes."

He climbed onto the bed and lay back. Damn it. He wasn't expecting to still feel so tired. Not after all the rest he'd had over this last week.

"Get over here. Put your pussy over my face."

"What?" she squealed, turning. "I can't do that."

He gave her a stern look. "Who is in charge?"

"You are, but—"

"And so, what should you be doing?"

"I've never done that before, though. What if I . . . what if I suffocate you?"

"Baby, you think you could suffocate me? Even if you did, I could easily move you. Trust me. Put your hands on the headboard to hold your balance and straddle my face."

HOLY. Heck.

She maneuvered herself into position. She didn't know if this was a good idea, though. He was still recovering from a concussion, and was covered in bruises. Not that he seemed to care about that when he was picking her up and carrying her places.

He thought he was indestructible.

But he wasn't, and that thought sobered her.

"Victor, slap my thigh if you want me to move," she told him as she stared down at him from where she knelt with her legs on either side of his head.

She blushed at the sight she must make.

"Fuck, baby. Come here. I'm hungry, and it's been too long since I had the taste of you on my tongue."

Holy. Heck. He was too much.

She lowered her pussy toward his mouth, gasping as he ran his tongue along her lips.

Shit. This was crazy. Intense.

He flicked his tongue around her clit, lazily toying with it until she was shaking, her thighs trembling as she tried to hold herself up.

Then he grabbed her hips, holding her steady as he devoured her. She couldn't do anything but attempt to breathe as he drove her higher and higher, closer to the edge.

His tongue thrust into her passage before moving up to her clit.

"Please, please, please." She just needed a bit more.

Then he drove her up and over, making her cry out as her body shook with her pleasure. It was too much. So intense. She couldn't stop it.

He quickly pulled her down his body, holding her firmly against him.

His weight soon penetrated her near-panic, helping her pull herself back into her skin. His hold, a claim of ownership that made her shiver even as that panic still clawed at her throat.

"You're all right, baby. I'm here. I'm right here."

"Hold me."

"You're okay, baby. You're fine. I have you."

She buried her face in his chest, reveling in the tight way he held her. He was always so careful when touching her. But she liked it best when he let go.

Moving her mouth, she sucked on his nipple and more of the panic faded. She turned her head, taking hold of the other nipple. She really needed him.

She tried to wriggle her way free of his firm hold.

"Stay where you are," he commanded.

"I want to move."

"No."

"I'm good now, Victor," she whispered, trying to slide down his body. "I need your dick in my mouth."

"What you need is rest. You spent the whole time I was in the hospital taking care of me. Now, I'm going to take care of you."

"Please. I really do need this." She managed to lean up, so she was looking down at him.

"Really?" He gave her a skeptical look. "My dick is something you really need?"

"Yes."

He loosened his hold, and she slid down his body, kissing his chest, his abs, down to his thick cock.

She licked her way along it then over the head, taking in the salty taste of him. She swore it could become addictive. She sucked on the head of his cock then drew more of him into her mouth.

God.

So good.

She took as much of him into her mouth as she could manage. It was a stretch and there was no way she could ever take all of him. She wrapped her hand around the base.

There was something about this that she loved. It enabled her to turn off everything in her head, everything around her, and just be in the moment. Maybe because it felt like he was always doing things for her, and it was a way she could feel more in control.

Whatever it was, she wasn't going to question it.

She moved her head faster, taking him deeper.

"Baby, I'm going to come soon." He rested his hand on the back of her head. She took him deep, sucking strongly and he came with a low moan, releasing in her mouth.

She drank all of him down. Then she kept her mouth on him as he grew smaller. He didn't ask if she was all right, didn't question her need. Instead, he just ran his fingers through her hair and talked to her quietly, telling her how beautiful she was.

Eventually, he pulled her up to lie in his tight embrace.

Where she belonged.

As she was drifting off, he spoke.

"Who the hell told you my middle name?"

She fell asleep with a smile on her face.

18

Gracen scrubbed at the kitchen counter.

It was spotless, but she needed something to do to distract herself from the nightmare that had just woken her up.

Luckily, she must have woken up before she started crying out in her sleep or thrashing around because Victor hadn't roused.

He was still recovering from a concussion, which is why she'd snuck out of the bed without waking him.

He needed his rest.

"Think that counter might be clean by now, baby."

She jumped with a cry, turning to glare at Victor, who stood leaning against the doorway, his arms over his thick chest. He'd put a pair of black pajama pants on. And damn, they looked good on him.

"Victor, you scared me. It's the middle of the night, you shouldn't be creeping around."

"I made plenty of noise. Thought I was going to wake up the whole household."

Guilt filled her. "I'm sorry I woke you up. You don't think I woke anyone else up, do you?"

Way to make a good impression, Gracen.

"No one else is awake," he reassured her. "And you've got it completely wrong."

"What do you mean?" She put the cloth down. Everyone had been very complimentary about the dinner she'd made last night.

It had been a bit odd, eating in a formal dining room. Growing up with her grandpa, they'd just sat in front of the TV to eat. They hadn't even had a table. So, it had been kind of intimidating. Luckily, Nico had made it all more lighthearted. At one stage he'd mock-whispered to her how the Queen of England probably had worse table manners than the Malones.

It could be true.

After dinner, she'd watched a movie with Victor before going up to bed a few hours ago. She'd probably gotten maybe an hour of sleep at most.

"Whenever you have a nightmare or can't sleep or you just need something, then you're to wake me up immediately. What you are not to do is sneak out of bed without telling me where you are."

She grimaced. "Were you worried when you woke up and I wasn't there?"

"Worried doesn't cover it, little bit." He prowled toward her, and she watched him warily.

He crowded her against the counter.

"I'm sorry," she told him. "You need your rest."

"So do you."

"I had an hour-long nap this afternoon, which is probably why I couldn't sleep tonight."

"Gracen," he warned. "That's not what happened. Do not lie."

She dropped her face, ashamed.

He cupped her chin, tilting her face back. "Nightmare?"

"Yes."

"What was it about?" he asked.

"Losing you."

He nodded solemnly. She thought he might tell her that nothing would ever happen to him. That her fears were silly. But instead, he lifted her onto the counter. She was only wearing panties and his T-shirt.

"Baby, you're freezing. Where are your pants? Socks? We need to get you some more clothes."

"I have clothes back at my apartment," she protested as he grabbed her feet. Stepping back, he shocked her by holding them to his tummy. He was boiling hot, and she gasped in surprise, trying to pull back as he rubbed his hands over them.

"Leave them there," he growled. "You're far too cold. You should have put more clothes on. What if one of my brothers had seen you like this?"

"It's just like wearing a dress." But he did have a point. "I need my clothes. Can we go get them?"

"I'll figure something out. We need to get all your stuff moved out and end your lease. How much time is left?"

"I don't know. But won't I need to move back into my apartment eventually?" She was only staying here while they were figuring out what had happened and whether Santiago was after them. Wasn't she?

"Baby, you live here now."

She gaped at him. "Permanently?"

He wrapped her legs around his waist, stepping up against her. His heat slid around her. Okay, she really had been cold.

"That's what being mine means. You live with me now. You're mine now. You wake me when you have nightmares. You tell me when you need something, like socks for instance. You let me know when you're cold, hot, tired, angry, sad, or happy. You getting this?"

"Yes, but I don't want it to be all one-sided." She never wanted him to think that she was using him.

"It's not. Trust me, I'm still getting the better deal out of this. Because I have you." He kissed her lightly, then lifted her into his arms.

"Victor you have to stop carrying me."

"If you say anything about being too heavy, I'm going to bend you over this counter and spank your ass with a wooden spoon."

Yikes.

"Um, I just meant because you're still recovering from a car accident."

"I'm fine." He carried her out of the kitchen.

"Wait, I was going to make some more cinnamon rolls for the morning."

"Not happening. You need sleep. You still look exhausted." He set her down by the stairs and led her up them.

"You keep trying to get me into bed. And you haven't even fucked me yet."

"Soon, baby. Soon."

Instead of putting her to bed, he led her into the bathroom and lifted her onto the counter. Then he turned the water on in the giant tub.

It really was big enough for the two of them.

He placed his hands on the counter on either side of her, watching her closely. She stared into his eyes, studying him back.

"You're scared of losing me. And I get why. I have the same fears. But I'm going to do everything I can to always come home safe to you. Understand?"

"Yes," she whispered.

He sighed and pulled her against him. "Know it's hard, baby. Know you're scared you'll lose me. But all I can promise is to be careful."

"I know." She hugged him.

"Is it still worth being mine? The worry and fears?" There was a note of vulnerability in his voice that floored her. It was something he rarely showed, and it proved just how much he trusted her.

Leaning back, she cupped his face between her hands. "You are worth that and more. There's nothing I wouldn't face or do to be yours, Victor Malone."

"Thank fuck for that." He kissed her gently, then pulled back to give her a stern look. "But the next time you sneak out of bed without waking me, I'm going to fry your ass."

Ah, there was her bossy man.

19

"Regent, I have something for you to try." Gracen walked into Regent's office with a cup of coffee and a small slice of coffee cake. He'd asked them all to join him in his office to discuss the plan to deal with Burpy and Baldy tomorrow when they came to collect their dues. There was something she wanted, so she'd decided to sweeten him up first.

"What's this?" he asked, turning away from his computer.

"Coffee cake."

Regent looked from the cake to her. "What are you after?"

Her eyes widened. "I'm insulted. Why would you think I'm after something?"

He just waited. And she quickly caved. Damn, he was good.

"I want to be there. When Victor takes care of Baldy and Burpy. The two Ventura gang guys."

Regent raised his eyebrows. "Isn't this something that you should bring to Victor?"

She pursed her lips. She had to word this correctly.

"Ah, I see. You asked, he said no, and you think I will override him. I won't. The answer is no."

"Why are you telling my girl no?" Victor grumbled as he stepped into the room. He frowned at Regent fiercely. Then drew her against him and kissed the top of her head. "Give her whatever she wants."

"What does Gracen want?" Maxim asked, walking in to sit on Regent's desk. The other man gave him a chilling look. With a grin, he slumped into a chair.

"She wants to be there when you take care of . . . what were their names?" he asked Gracen.

"Baldy and Burpy," she muttered. Drat. She hadn't thought through what would happen when Victor found out she'd gone to Regent.

Victor turned to her. "You came to ask Regent? I already said no."

"Everyone knows when Mom says no that you go ask Dad," Maxim said cheerfully, reaching over to pick up Regent's slice of cake.

"Hey, that was for Regent."

"But I'm the one on your side." Maxim pouted at her.

True.

"All right then."

He grinned and polished it off.

"You are not going to be there, and you're in big trouble for trying to go behind my back," Victor told her sternly.

Her bottom tingled at his words. Shoot.

"But what if they don't see me and back off? We'll lose our chance."

"She's got a point," Maxim replied.

It had been three days since she'd moved into the Malone mansion. Nico, Liam, and Lottie had returned home yesterday, and she was missing them. She'd sent them off with a bag of goodies which had Nico waxing poetic. Victor had started growling when she'd blushed at the gorgeous singer's words.

Silly Victor.

As if she could ever have eyes for anyone but him.

She'd thought it might take a while to get used to living here. The place was so huge for just the four of them. And Maxim didn't usually live here. But she loved the kitchen and she'd been baking up a storm. Luckily, all the men that worked for them enjoyed eating.

She'd cooked for them each night, even though they all said she didn't have to. She didn't know how to cook anything too fancy, but no one seemed worried. Last night, she'd made home-made pizza. They'd all eaten it with a knife and fork.

So strange.

Victor had been spending a lot of time with Regent in his office, and he'd been out every night, not coming back until the early hours of the morning. She knew whatever he was doing had something to do with Santiago and Patrick, but she didn't ask for details. She just wanted him to be safe.

Victor had spoken to her landlord about releasing her from her lease. She didn't know how much it had cost him, but she was relieved he'd taken over. Her landlord had never been easy to deal with. They were going to go pack up her personal belongings soon and let the rest go to charity.

Yesterday, she'd finally managed to get hold of Anita to tell her that the bakery was going to remain closed. All Anita had cared about was whether she was still going to pay her. She'd hung up when Gracen said she'd pay her for as long as she could. What her niece didn't seem to realize was that Gracen didn't have an endless supply of cash.

"I don't want you in any danger," Victor told her.

"But I won't be."

"These guys are dangerous," Regent told her.

"But Victor will be with me. He won't let anything happen to me."

"And what if they have guns? What if one of them shoots Victor? Or takes you hostage? They've got rap sheets as long as my arm."

She gaped at Regent, her heart racing.

"Damn it, Regent, what the fuck?" Victor snarled. Sitting, he reached over and lifted her onto his lap.

"If it's that dangerous then you shouldn't be doing anything. You should just not go," she cried.

"It's not that dangerous," Victor snarled. "I'm going to be just fine."

"I apologize, Gracen. I shouldn't have said that. I seem to be out of sorts at the moment."

She thought that was a big admission for the other man. And she knew he was struggling with his limited mobility. It was clear he hated having to rely on anyone for anything. She nodded, but there was still a tremble of fear inside her.

"But they'll likely have guns, right?" she asked.

"Yes, but they're not expecting me to be in there," Victor told her soothingly. "I'll go in, turn on some lights to make it look like you're in there. We have people watching both entrances and cameras inside. I can take care of two idiot gangsters."

"Wait, you have cameras inside? When were they put there?"

"Uh, I've had them in there for a while," he admitted.

"What? How?" She turned to look at him, shocked to find him looking chagrined.

"A while. I wanted to keep an eye on you."

She frowned. "Is this like the alarm you put into my apartment? You just set up cameras without telling me?"

"Something like that," he muttered.

Regent cleared his throat, drawing their attention back to him.

"Won't the gang retaliate?" she asked. "What if they figure out you guys were involved? Could they cause trouble for you all?"

Regent just stared at her. Then he smiled. Dark satisfaction filled his eyes. "The Ventura gang are very small fish in this ocean. I'm the shark."

"We're going to systematically destroy them," Victor said in a low voice. "And have fun doing it."

Holy hell.

"Damn, even I'm slightly scared of you guys right now," Maxim said.

"I still think I have a good point," she said. "What if Victor sneaks in the back before I enter, then I go in. If anyone's watching, they'll only see me. They might be suspicious because the bakery's been closed for days. Also, we don't even know when they'll come by. Victor could be in there for hours. I could be there, cleaning stuff out. And then when someone you have watching spots them approaching, I'll go out the back."

"I can go in as well and take her out into the alley," Maxim offered.

"I still don't like it," Victor said

She huffed out a breath. Stubborn man.

"But she has got a point. If they are watching and don't see her go in, they'll sense a trap and we'll never get them," Maxim said. "And you want these guys, right?"

She held her breath and waited for Victor's decision.

He turned her to face him. "You'll do exactly as I say."

"Yep."

"You don't and you'll be over my knee as soon as we get home."

She didn't dare look at Maxim or Regent. She was aware of Maxim coughing to cover a laugh.

Ass.

"I will do whatever you tell me, promise."

"As soon as they're spotted, you are out with Maxim."

"I promise."

"Damn, I don't think I would have volunteered for this if I'd realized it would be so boring," Maxim stated, putting his phone down. Both he and Victor were in the shadows to keep them hidden. Maxim had started complaining about an hour ago, and Victor kept frowning at her and telling her to stay away from the window and grumbling at her not to lift anything heavy and to rest.

She kept glaring at him every time she had to sit. She was still feeling the effects of the spanking he'd given her last night. Apparently, he really hadn't appreciated her going to Regent after he'd said no.

And she had felt bad about it. It had been a bit sneaky.

It had made her sad coming back to the bakery. It felt cold and empty. Seeing it now, after being away, she realized how rundown and old it felt. She'd emptied out the fridge, scrubbed everything, and now she was trying to figure out what to do with all of her equipment. Some of it she wanted to take to the Malone mansion, but she couldn't carry it out today. They'd have to come back for it.

"I don't think they're coming," she finally stated.

Victor and Maxim suddenly straightened.

"They've been spotted," Victor said, his finger going to the receiver in his ear. "They're coming from across the street. Nearly here." He nodded at her and Maxim.

"Victor," she said quietly, not wanting to leave him.

He shot her a fierce look. "Go. Now."

"Please be careful."

Maxim stepped forward and hauled her toward the back door just as a voice rang out.

"Hey, baker lady, we're back. You best have the cash for us."

Instead of heading out the back door, Maxim pulled her back to the side of the fridge. He placed a finger on her lips.

Yeah, she didn't need to be told twice.

"Yo, where are you, baker lady?" Baldy called out.

"She's not here," Victor said, stepping out of the shadows. "But I am."

Burpy yelled and Baldy fumbled for his gun at the small of his back.

She let out a squeak of warning, but Maxim turned her against him, pressing his hand to the back of her head. Then he moved his hands to her ears. But it couldn't fully muffle the noises. The thud of flesh hitting flesh. Moans and groans of pain. It sounded horrific, and the entire time, she was terrified that Victor was the one being beaten. But surely, Maxim wouldn't just stand here if that was the case.

At one stage, she tried to fight her way free of his hold, but he held onto her tighter, pulling her back further into the shadows.

Then there was nothing.

She trembled in Maxim's arms.

"Fuck," Maxim muttered as he removed his hands from her ears. But he kept her face pressed against his chest. "You completely annihilated them. I was totally ready to get in there, but you didn't need me."

"They're a pair of idiots," Victor said darkly. "They were no match for me."

"Here, you want Gracen?" Maxim offered.

"No. I'll get the car brought up outside the alley. Take her out there."

"No, Victor! I want you!" She tried to move, to get to him, but Maxim lifted her in his arms. She attempted to peer around Maxim. She couldn't see Victor, but she glimpsed a body lying on the floor. Her stomach turned and she shut her eyes. She didn't want to see that. She let out a low whimper. She felt ill, and all she wanted was Victor to hold her securely in his arms.

Maxim carried her out quickly. "He's just trying to keep you from seeing anything."

"But I want him."

"Soon, doll. Soon."

They exited into the alley, and she turned to see a dark car waiting there. Maxim's phone rang as soon as they were inside the vehicle.

He answered it with a frown, glancing over at her. "Sure? Gracen wants you."

She was trembling. She just needed to know he was all right. She just had to see him.

"All right. Fine." Maxim sighed and ended the call. Then he lowered the privacy screen. "Aero, take us home."

"What? No! Why?" she asked.

"Victor doesn't want you anywhere near here. He wants to get the bakery cleaned up. And make sure no one else was around. For that, he can't be worrying about you."

Or he didn't want to see her. She bit her lip. "Is he all right?"

"He's fine, doll. He has to take care of those idiots. Permanently. They won't be terrorizing anyone else."

It was hours later when she heard a car approach.

Regent was in his office, still set on destroying the entire Ventura gang. And she'd been pretending to watch a movie with Maxim. Jumping up, she rushed to the entrance. There he was. Whole. Unharmed.

But when he looked at her, she could tell that wasn't true. There was something in his gaze. Something cold and broken.

Should she go to him? Was that what he wanted? Or had he been staying away to avoid her? Were they over?

Screw it. If something had changed, he could damn well find the courage to tell her. What she needed right now was to hug him. So, she raced forward.

His eyes widened. "Gracen? What are you—*oomph*—" He caught her against his chest as she jumped.

She wrapped her arms around his neck and her legs around his waist and clung to him.

"Baby? What is it? What's wrong?" He rocked her back and forth. "Damn it, Maxim, I thought you were looking after her."

"I was trying," Maxim replied. "But she wanted you. She was worried about you."

"Baby, I'm fine."

"I needed to see you. To know for sure. You didn't even call. Where have you been?" She pushed back until he let go of her. Then she whacked him in the chest with the palm of her hand.

Which likely hurt her more than him. She shook her hand to ease the sting.

"What are you doing?" he barked. "You've hurt yourself."

"I'm fine. But I'm mad at you." She pointed at him to emphasize her point. Then turning, she stomped up the stairs. "I'm going to bed."

VICTOR WATCHED his girl as she raced up the stairs. He wanted to tell her to slow down, but he was still feeling speechless.

"She hit me. And then she stormed off . . . she's mad?" What was happening? When he'd come home, he'd been expecting an entirely different reaction.

He'd thought she would be scared of him, that she might try to hide from him. He hadn't expected that she'd throw herself at him, that she'd shake in his arms and tell him she was worried.

And he definitely hadn't expected her to stomp off, mad at him.

"You thought she'd be scared of you, huh?" Maxim guessed.

He rubbed his chest even though it didn't hurt.

"Vic, you miscalculated how much that girl loves you. She

adores you. All she wanted was to know you were safe, yet you sent her home without even checking in with her. Can you blame her for being mad?"

"I don't think I've ever seen her mad." And definitely not at him. It was a shock. And a turn-on.

Hell.

He needed to shower. He had to take care of the hard-on riding him. But mostly, he needed to make things up to his girl.

Because he didn't want her upset at him.

"I've got to go."

"Practice getting down on your knees," Maxim called out unhelpfully.

What he didn't know was that Victor would gladly spend his life on his knees if it meant he had her.

20

A rgh.

Had she really just done that? Whacked him in the chest, then stormed off?

Idiot. How old was she?

But it had just become too much. Her feelings had rapidly morphed from fear to blinding anger.

She stood in the shower, letting the water beat down on her. It wasn't hot enough, though. She was trembling, shaking with cold.

She turned the heat up.

Steam rose in the shower cubicle as tears trickled down her face. She was being stupid.

The door to the shower suddenly opened and she yelped, nearly slipping. Victor quickly grabbed hold of her. Then to her shock, he stepped into the shower in his clothes.

"Victor, what are you doing?"

Without a word, he slid onto his knees and wrapped his arms around her, kissing her tummy.

With a sigh, the last remnants of her anger fled. She ran her fingers through his dark hair.

She stood there for a long moment, then realized his clothes were all wet. Not to mention his knees had to be getting sore.

"Victor, stand up."

He leaned back to look up at her, wiping water off his face. She quickly turned the shower head away.

"I'm so sorry, baby. I made a mistake."

"Yeah, you did." She stared down at him solemnly. "I thought something was wrong. Maxim kept saying you were all right, but I just needed to know. Just to see you for a moment, and instead, you sent me home like an errant child."

"I'm so sorry, baby. You're right. I thought . . ." He shook his head. "I thought witnessing what I did to those guys would make you see me in a different light. I'm not a good man. I'm a violent man. I've done bad things and you're everything good in this world. I don't even deserve to touch you. Not with these hands."

He stared down at his hands in disgust. She placed her hands over his. Then she drew each one up to her mouth so she could kiss them. "You shut up, Victor Malone."

He gaped up at her.

"You are not a bad man, and I won't stand for such crap. I've told you before, I see the real you. Sure, some things you do aren't what everyone would agree with. But those assholes tonight were the bad guys. You saw their rap sheets. You took care of them. For me and everyone else, so we could all feel safe. And you did it despite knowing how it would affect you. And I know it does. Victor, I'm never turning away from you. Not ever."

He nuzzled her stomach. "I love you, baby."

"I love you too."

He ran his hands up her thighs, she saw that the knuckles were swollen and red, but the skin hadn't broken.

"Are you sure you want me touching you? Want these hands on you?" he whispered.

"I want nothing more. Make love to me, Victor. Please."

"I need to taste you. Lean back."

She rested back against the tile, moaning as he placed one leg over his shoulder and then spread her lips. He ate at her like he was starving. His tongue ran over her folds, swirling around her clit before he ran it over her entrance. All too soon, she was breathing heavily, her low moans filling the shower.

"Victor, stop. Stop."

He pulled back, looking up at her quizzically. "What's wrong?"

"I want you inside me tonight."

"You sure, baby?"

Sure? It was beyond time. She thought she'd been patient enough.

"Yes. God, yes. Please."

"All right. But I need to get you ready first. So, you're going to come for me while I eat you out. Then we'll finish showering and move to the bed."

Well, all right then.

He dove back between her thighs, using his tongue, lips, and teeth to drive her up into a spectacular orgasm. He licked at her clit with his tongue, his fingers toying with her nipples as the orgasm rocked her. Then he drew her down with him, settling her on his lap he held her firmly through the aftershocks. She reached for his shirt, undoing it with fingers that shook. She then lay kisses on his chest.

"Easy, baby. Easy," he murmured. She sucked on his skin where his neck and shoulder met, leaving a red mark.

Hmm, she liked marking him.

"Make you feel better?" he asked, staring down at her.

"A bit," she admitted.

"Because I like the idea of marking you too. Making sure everyone knows you're mine. Stand up."

He helped her stand, then he got out of the shower to strip.

Stepping back in, he washed them both thoroughly. She got a sharp smack on her wet ass when she attempted to help.

When he was finally finished and had dried them both, her skin felt like it was tingling. All her nerve endings were awake, and her nipples were hard buds.

Leaning down, he sucked on one, his finger dropping to circle her clit.

"Please, Victor, no more!" she cried. Her clit was getting so sensitive. She couldn't take much more, and she wanted to come again with his dick buried inside her.

"Lie on your back on the bed, legs spread, and arms above your head."

Her breath caught as she stared up at him.

"If you're a good girl and you do as you were told, you'll get my dick. Or you can be naughty and argue, and instead, I'll turn your ass red and send you to bed with nothing. What would you like?"

Damn, she loved when he talked dirty.

"I want your dick." She tried to say it in a sultry, sexy voice. Instead, she was certain she sounded ridiculous. But his eyes still lit up.

"Good girl. Now off you go."

He slapped her ass to get her moving.

DAMN.

That was a sight to walk in on. She was lying back on the bed, her hands above her head, her legs parted. He moved to the end of the bed, staring down at her.

Her lips were plump and pink. Her legs smooth and delicious.

"What a good girl you are," he murmured. He crawled his way up the bed and started kissing her. From the sole of her foot, up her leg to her knee, then up her thigh to her pussy. He gave her clit a fleeting kiss before continuing his way along her body to take one pink, plump nipple into his mouth.

He sucked on it. She raised her chest with a moan. After lightly biting the pert bud, he soothed it with his tongue.

"That's a good girl. Let me hear you moan for me. You're going to take my dick, aren't you?"

"Yes. Yes," she moaned.

He moved to her other nipple, sucking it then flicking it with his tongue. He sat back on his knees and stared down at her. "My beautiful girl. Now get onto your knees. Spread your legs, then lean your chest down on the bed, arms out in front of you."

He grabbed the lube from the nightstand as she got into position. He spread her ass cheeks, putting some lube on her hole before he worked his thumb inside her.

Her breathy moans filled the room.

"That's it, baby. Take my thumb. Fuck, that's sexy. Good girl. Just stay nice and relaxed. Such a good baby." He leaned down, keeping his thumb in her ass to lick at the entrance to her pussy, then he thrust his tongue deep inside her.

Drawing back, he lightly smacked her bottom. "You taste delicious." He was so hard that it hurt, his balls were tight as hell, and he wanted nothing more than to press his way inside her. But he knew he couldn't go hard and fast. Not this first time. Maybe not for a while.

But that was fine with him. Whatever she needed, he'd provide.

He moved two fingers to her entrance, slowly finger-fucking her. She pulsed around him. Damn, she was tight. He moved up to a third finger, paying attention to her body language. But she was thrusting back at him, her moans of pleasure filling the room.

She was so freaking gorgeous.

He pulled his fingers from her. He couldn't take much more. But he knew he had to make certain she was ready for him.

Rolling onto his back, he moved beneath her until his mouth was just below her pussy. Grabbing her hips, he drew her down to his mouth to tease and suck and lick until her moans filled the room. Her body shaking above his.

"Please. Please. Please."

Fuck it. He couldn't hold back any longer. He slid out from under her.

"Stay right where you are, I'll be right back." They'd already agreed that condoms weren't necessary since they'd both been checked not that long ago, and she was on birth control to help regulate her periods.

He went to the bathroom to wash his hands. Then he walked back into the bedroom and picked up the bottle of lube. He coated his dick in it as he took in the sight of her.

"Baby, you're going to have me coming so quickly, it'll be embarrassing."

"I don't care," she told him. "I just want to make you happy."

"Come here."

He waited until she turned to lean in, so they were at the same eye level. "Didn't know what happiness was until the day I met you."

She gave him the sweetest smile. He climbed onto the bed and leaned back against the pillows. "Now, straddle my hips."

He helped her move over him, holding his dick as she slowly lowered herself.

"Easy," he told her as she let out a loud breath. "Just take it nice and slow. You don't have to take all of me right now. That's it. Up and down. There's no rush, no expectation. Fuck, just feeling you around the head of my cock is like heaven. Look at you, taking my dick so well. Good girl. Are you all right? Do you feel okay?"

"I feel better than okay," she told him. "I want more."

"Just go slow."

"No. Noo."

He smacked his hand on her bottom. "Yes. Who is in charge?"

SHE STARED down at him breathlessly. His face was filled with determination, his gaze stern as he stared up at her.

"You are."

"That's right," he told her. "So, you're going to do as I say."

But she didn't want to. She wanted to sink herself down on him. Only, she was part way down and she could already feel the stretch. It was starting to burn, and she knew he had a good point.

Laying her hands on his firm chest, she pulled herself up then slowly drove down. With each movement she tried to take more of him. They were both breathing heavily, and she could see the strain in his face.

Neither of them could hold back more. She pushed down further.

"That's enough for tonight."

"Victor!"

"I said enough." He lifted her off him, rolled her onto her side and spooned her from behind.

"Victor, please." She needed him so badly. He wasn't stopping, right?

"Sh." He pushed her top leg back over his then pushed his cock inside her pussy.

Oh, it felt so good. This angle meant penetration was shallower, which was the point. For all she knew, he'd looked up best sex positions when you had a big dick.

She knew she had.

He took her with short, fast thrusts. Her breathing was harsh and fast. Reaching around, he played with her nipple as he placed small bites along her neck.

Then his hand slid down to her clit. She gasped as he circled it slowly.

"You feel so damn good, baby. You're doing such a good job at taking my cock. That's it. Good girl." His finger moved faster as pleasure flooded her, making her clench down on his dick.

He drove her higher and higher as he moved his finger with firm flicks over her swollen bud until finally, she came with a scream, clenching down around him. So good. Holy. Hell.

"Baby. God. Damn." He moaned as he found his own release. His arm was a tight band around her, holding her close to his chest as the orgasm rocked her, threatening to send her out of her own skin.

"Fuck, baby. Fuck. You have no idea how good you feel." He moaned as she continued to pulsate around his cock.

They were still breathing heavily as he pulled free. She held in a wince, not wanting him to blame himself for causing her discomfort.

"Gracen? Does it hurt?"

Drat. She should have known he would notice that wince.

"I'm fine. Honest. Maybe it hurts a tiny bit," she added when he made a noise of disbelief. "But it's nothing bad."

He climbed from the bed. "Stay right there." He moved into the bathroom.

She sighed. Now he was going to get all fussy over her. Like when she'd gotten a tiny bit worn out taking care of him.

And she loved him for it. Because no one had ever worried over her like he did.

She heard water splashing and guessed he was filling the bath. He walked back in and picked her up.

"I'm fine, Victor."

"Good. But I want you to be better than fine. You can take a bath and I'll get you an ice pack and a heating pad."

Ice pack and heating pad? Was he hedging his bets? He set her down next to the bath.

"Wasn't sure if I should put in some bubble bath or not." He drew a container of bubble bath from under the sink. Her eyes widened as she saw the cartoon image on the front.

"You like the same bubble bath as me?" she asked.

"What? Uh no. I don't use bubble bath mixture. Got this for you."

"Aw, that's so sweet. Um, well, I chose that one because it's not filled with a lot of crap that can, uh, irritate me. So, I think a bit will be all right."

He poured some in, then checked the temperature before adjusting the water coming through the taps. She leaned over his back, hugging him.

"Thank you, Victor. I love you so much."

"Love you too, little bit. Come on, let's get you in the bath."

He helped her in then brushed her hair off her face. "I'm going to take another quick shower. Then I'll get the other stuff. You want anything else? Cocoa?"

"Ooh, that would be amazing, please."

She lay back, almost falling asleep as she listened to him in the shower.

"Baby, don't fall asleep before I'm back. That's dangerous."

"Uh-huh," she murmured.

Fingers lightly twisted her nipple, making her gasp and glare up into his grinning face.

"Hey, not nice!"

"Just checking that you were listening. And that you were going to do as you were told."

She sighed. "I won't fall asleep."

He returned about fifteen minutes later and got her out, drying her off. Then taking her hand, he led her into the bedroom. There were some pajamas laid out on the bed for her with images of donuts all over them. She loved them.

"You bought me pajamas?" she asked.

"Yes. Do you like them?"

"I love them." She reached for the top.

"Wait, before you put them on, I want to check you."

Check her?

"Lie on your back and spread your legs."

"Victor! I'm fine."

He crossed his arms over his chest and gave her a stern look.

Honestly, the man was insane! But she had to be more insane since she did as he'd ordered.

Parting her lower lips, he checked her. She lay there, her arm over her eyes as she died of embarrassment.

"A bit red. But not too bad."

Well, thank you, doctor.

She didn't say that out loud, though.

Grabbing some panties, he pulled them over one foot then the other before taking them up her legs and over her hips.

"I can dress myself."

"I know. But I want to do it."

He worked in silence to get her dressed then settled her on her side of the bed. Which was, of course, the furthest from the door.

"Do you want this?" He held up the ice pack. "Or this?" He showed her the heating pad.

"Uh, maybe the heating pad."

She sipped on her cocoa, giggling at the movie he'd put on while snuggling into his side.

It was perfect.

21

Gracen answered her phone just as Aero pulled up outside her apartment. She and Victor were going to pack up her personal belongings today. Aero was driving while Brax rode shotgun. One would stay downstairs while the other stood outside the apartment while they worked.

She thought it was overkill, but Regent still insisted that everyone be careful. And since he and Victor were busy stirring things up with the Ventura gang and trying to systematically destroy them, she guessed it was smart.

She frowned as she looked for her car. That was odd. Had someone stolen it? She'd been planning to bring it back to the Malone mansion. She kind of wanted to see Regent's face when she parked it outside.

Her phone rang. The name of the person calling nearly made her drop her phone. "Hello? Anita?"

"Hey, Aunty G."

"Anita, I've been trying to get ahold of you and you haven't been answering my calls. I've been worried."

"Whoa, Aunty G, chill. I talked to you just the other day. You're so needy. I'm fine. It's not like I'm living with you anymore. Don't have a curfew I need to keep."

She'd never kept to her curfew when she'd lived with Gracen anyway.

"Anita, I need to talk to you again about the bakery."

"Yeah, that's why I'm calling. You stopped paying me. I need that money."

"Anita, I told you during our last call that I was closing the bakery."

"Well, you said you were going to keep paying me."

Gracen was aware of Victor studying her intently. She closed her eyes briefly. "I said that I would while I could afford to. But I can no longer pay you, Anita. You'll need to find a new job."

"What the fuck! Aunty G, you can't do that to me."

"I'm sorry, Anita. The bakery is never going to re-open." She didn't go into details. Truth was, she hadn't felt close to her niece since her brother died. But she also felt awful that she was almost giving up on her.

"Well, this just fucking sucks! It's got to be against the law for you to just stop paying me!"

"I'm sorry. But you can get unemployment while you look for another job."

"But unemployment isn't as much as I was earning. I need that money! Sorry isn't good enough. Some aunt you are. Daddy would be horrified by the way you've treated me."

"Anita—"

Her niece ended the call, and Gracen put her phone down, aware that her hands were shaking.

"What is it? What happened?" Victor asked, turning to face her.

"Uh, she's not happy that I'm not paying her any longer even though the bakery is shut, and she told me . . . she told me that my brother would be ashamed of the way I'm treating her."

A sob escaped from her.

"Baby, you know that's not true." Reaching over, he undid her belt then pulled her onto his lap, holding her tightly.

"I know, but it . . . it hurts. I tried so hard with her, but no matter what I did, it was never enough. I turned the other cheek over all the things she did or said, but I . . . I can't keep going on. I'm out of money. I can't keep paying her."

"Sounds to me like she needs to learn to stand on her own two feet. And not be so selfish. I would be happy to go and set her straight."

She wiped at her cheeks. "No, don't. Honestly, you getting involved would make everything worse."

"All right." He brushed her hair off her face. "We can come back and do this later if you're not feeling up to it."

She blew out a breath. "No, we're here now. I'm not going to let her words get to me. I know she's upset. Hopefully, she'll cool down."

After studying her for a moment longer, he nodded before he knocked on the privacy screen. He set her back on her seat as his door opened. Stepping out, he held a hand out for her.

Aero and Brax were both vigilant, watching their surroundings. Funny, it felt so long since she'd been here. They walked through the building toward her apartment.

Victor had the key out, opening it and letting Aero go in first to check through it.

They'd brought some flattened boxes, which Victor held under one arm.

"All clear, I'll wait out here," Aero told them.

The apartment smelled even worse after not being aired out for two weeks.

"Argh, it smells awful in here."

"Let's just move quickly," Victor said, opening up windows.

"Oh, I just remembered! My car isn't out the front. Do you think someone stole it?"

Why would anyone steal that heap of junk, though?

"Uh, no. I had it towed."

"Towed? Where? To your place? I would have driven it."

"It's your house now as well," he gently corrected. "And no, you wouldn't have driven it. You're never driving it again. It's been crushed."

"It's what?" She had to have heard him wrong.

"Baby, it was worth more as scrap metal than a car. I've got the money they gave me for it. I'll give it to you when we get home."

"Victor! You can't just turn my car into scrap metal without consulting me!"

"Would you have tried to keep driving it?"

"Well, yes, because I can't afford to get a new one. What will I do now?"

"There's a twelve-bay garage at home filled with cars. Choose one."

Her mouth opened then closed. "I can't just choose one."

"Gracen," he said seriously. "Everything I own is now yours. You can have anything you want, all you have to do is ask. But what I can't allow you to do is drive around in an unsafe vehicle. That car was falling apart."

That was the truth.

"You still should have told me."

"I apologize."

Huh. Seemed he might subscribe to the adage that it was better to ask for forgiveness than permission too.

"I'd just gotten rid of that noise. Although I think the gas gauge was out, it was showing full when I swear it was close to empty."

He rubbed his hand over the back of his neck, looking surprisingly sheepish.

"Victor," she said in a warning voice.

"Uh, that might have been me."

"What do you mean, it might have been you?"

"While I took you out in the helicopter, I had someone I know check your car over, fix what they could and put more gas in it."

"Oh my God! Victor!"

"I was just taking care of you."

"That doesn't make it okay. So that's why the noise disappeared. I feel like such an idiot!" She groaned.

"You're not an idiot," he told her firmly.

She didn't know what to think. This was so high-handed of him. But also, she wouldn't expect anything else from him.

This is who Victor was. And he was unapologetic about it.

"Damn, I had a hairy fairy godfather, and I didn't even know it."

He pointed at her sternly. "You are not to call me that."

"The hairy fairy. Yep, it's perfect."

"Gracen!"

He chased her around the room as she giggled and sang silly songs about the hairy fairy.

Capturing hold of her, he threw her over his shoulder and smacked her ass until she yelled for mercy. Putting her on her feet, he gave her bottom one final smack.

"Get packing."

"You got it, HFG."

He just shook his head, muttering to himself about sassy brats. Poor Victor.

An hour later, she stretched out her back and looked around. Everything she really wanted was packed away. There were some things at the bakery she needed, but they could wait.

Gracen checked her phone as it beeped, smiling. "Sammy wants to meet you. She's also not happy that we haven't gone out for daiquiris in ages." Gracen had told her that she was dating the sticky buns guy but not who he was. That was going to take a few daiquiris first to build up her courage.

"You realize those daiquiris are completely watered-down, right?" he asked as he checked around the room for anything they'd missed.

She gazed over at him curiously. "Yes, I am. But how do you know that?"

He froze, and a look of such intense guilt filled his face that it caught her by surprise.

"Victor, what did you do?"

He cleared his throat. "I'm going to remind you that you said you'd never leave me."

"So, it's bad. Spit it out."

"I followed you."

"Followed me? To the bar one night? Why?"

"Not just to the bar one night. Every night. I used to watch you leave your apartment building each morning. Then I'd drive quickly to get to the parking lot before you got there. I'd watch you leave your car and walk to the bakery. Then at night, I'd do the same."

What. The. Hell?

"You were stalking me?"

He crossed his arms over his chest and nodded. "Yes." He stared at her warily, but he wasn't stumbling over his words. He was just waiting for her reaction.

What was her reaction?

"How did I never see you?"

"If I don't want to be seen, you won't see me. Plus, you are very unaware of your surroundings. It's something we need to work on."

"Yes, in case I need it for the next stalker! Victor! What the hell? Did you . . . did you watch me in my apartment?"

"What! No! I couldn't get cameras in here without too much risk of being caught. At least not until you invited me in."

"Oh my God! So, wait . . . there are also some cameras in my apartment?"

"Yes. I'll need to retrieve them, actually."

She tugged at her hair. She didn't know what to do. She paced back and forth. "I . . . you . . . what . . . that's so creepy."

"I'm aware." His face was closed down and he was tense. As though he was expecting some sort of blow.

"Why?"

"Because I didn't want anything to happen to you."

Oh hell.

There had to be something wrong with her. Because with those words, he'd totally taken the wind out of her sails.

"Have you ever done this to anyone else?" she asked.

"What? No! Why would I want to? Gracen, from the moment I saw you, I knew you were the one. I knew it wasn't right, but I couldn't sleep at night worrying about you and when I saw you walking around in the dark on your own . . . I couldn't allow it to continue. I once stopped someone who was creeping up behind you, preparing to attack you."

Nausea bubbled, and she placed her hand over her stomach. "What? Really?"

"Yes, baby. You were so unaware that it terrified me. I didn't do it to watch you undress or shower or whatever. That wasn't the point. I just wanted to keep you safe."

She let out a deep breath. Someone had nearly attacked her? And she'd had no idea? That was scary.

"That's why you put the cameras in the bakery and my apartment?"

"Yes. That's why."

She let out a deep breath. "All right, I can live with that. But is there anything else you need to tell me? Because I've had a lot of shocks today and I'm starting to feel a bit faint."

He drew her against him. "Nothing else. All I've ever wanted is you to be safe. Having you as my woman, it felt completely out of reach. And now, with you in my arms, I consider myself the luckiest person on the planet."

"You sweet talker you."

22

"Baby, wake up."

She grumbled as someone shook her. She'd been having such a nice sleep. She wasn't ready to wake up. "I don't wanna go to work."

"Baby, I need you to wake up. It's about the bakery."

Who was that? It didn't sound like her grandpa. The bakery? What about it?

"Little bit? Can you hear me?"

Wait. That definitely wasn't her grandpa.

She sat up, narrowly missing smashing her head into Victor's chin.

"Easy, baby. It's all right. I'm sorry to wake you up."

"What is it? What's going on? What's wrong?" She glanced around, trying to get her bearings.

She was in Victor's bedroom. Well, their bedroom. Now that she'd moved some of her things in here, it really was beginning to feel like home.

"What time is it?" she asked huskily. It was still dark.

"Two in the morning. Baby, it's the bakery. We just got a notification from one of our guys who was doing a drive-by. Baby, I'm so sorry."

"What is it? What's going on?" Her heart raced with panic, making her feel nauseous.

"The bakery is on fire."

SHE STARED out at the flames the firefighters were battling in numb disbelief. How had this happened? Everything had been turned off. How could it be on fire? She just . . . she couldn't understand it.

Victor wouldn't let her leave the car, so they just sat here and watched. The two buildings on either side of her bakery had quickly gone up in flames as well, making the firefighter's jobs that much harder.

There it went. Her grandpa's bakery. All of her things that she'd left in there.

But they were just things. She couldn't get upset. As long as no one was hurt, that was the important thing.

Maxim opened the car door and slid in next to them. Regent still wasn't mobile enough to be out and about comfortably, so he'd stayed home with warnings to keep him up-to-date.

"I tried to talk to someone, but all I got out of anyone is that the bakery went up first. And that they won't be able to determine more until later."

"We should just go home then," Victor said, rubbing his hand up and down her thigh. For once, it wasn't turning her on. "It's doing no good just sitting here and watching."

"No," she whispered. "I guess not."

Someone must have told Regent they were on their way home, because he was waiting in the kitchen with mugs of hot cocoa on the kitchen counter when they arrived back.

"You made cocoa?" Maxim asked in disbelief. "Do you even know how to make cocoa?"

"Obviously, since I just made it. Bring them over to the table, will you? I couldn't carry it."

"I didn't even know that you were aware of how to operate the cooktop. Or where the cocoa was," Maxim stated as he carried the mugs over.

Regent glared at his youngest brother before turning to her with sympathy in his face. "I'm sorry about the bakery, Gracen."

"Thanks," she said, sitting. She rested her elbows on the table with a sigh. She was so tired. Sad. Drained. "I don't know why it's hitting me so hard. I wasn't planning on going back there to work. That chapter had already closed."

"But maybe you hadn't said goodbye yet," Maxim offered.

She managed to give him a small, sad smile. Of all the Malone men, he was, surprisingly, the most sensitive. Sometimes she wondered if he played up the playboy image to hide what was really going on with him, but she'd let him keep his secrets.

"I guess that could be it. There were still things in the bakery I wanted to take with me. I mean, I know they were only things . . . but they had sentimental value. There was this old egg mixer that Grandpa always swore made the best meringue even though we had a newer industrial mixer that did five times the volume. It's silly, but I wanted to keep that."

"It's not silly," Victor growled, leaning over to lift her into his lap. "There's nothing wrong with being sad or sentimental."

Both Regent and Maxim stared at him in surprise.

"Oh, how the mighty have fallen," Maxim said quietly.

"What does that mean?" Victor asked.

"Nothing." Maxim held his hands up. "I've just never known you to be sentimental over anything. You're usually quite, uh, pragmatic."

"This is different," Victor said.

Maxim met her gaze with a wink. "It certainly is."

Victor grabbed a cup of cocoa, handing it to her.

"Thank you." She wrapped her hands around it. She took a sip and nearly spit it back out.

Holy. Crap.

"How is the cocoa?" Regent asked, almost looking anxious. But that couldn't be right. He was always super confident. Was this really the first time he'd made cocoa?

Actually, she could totally believe it was the first time since it seemed he'd forgotten a key ingredient.

Like sweetener.

"Oh, it's really nice. Well done."

Maxim eyed her skeptically then grabbed a cup. She widened her eyes, trying to shake her head without Regent seeing. But Maxim either didn't see her, or he'd decided to ignore her because he took a long sip. Then his eyes widened. He swallowed it hastily.

"Shit! Regent, how much cocoa did you put in this?"

"Uh, I don't know. About a cup. Why, isn't it enough?"

"No, no, it's plenty, and how much sugar?" Maxim asked.

"You're supposed to add sugar?" Regent frowned. "That doesn't sound very healthy."

"Cocoa isn't supposed to be healthy, that's the point," Maxim told him with a shake of his head. "Your education is sadly lacking."

"I'm sorry, Gracen." Regent grimaced.

Reaching over, she grabbed his hand and squeezed it. His eyes widened in surprise. She got the feeling people rarely touched him.

"I appreciate the thought."

Regent sighed while Maxim rose to make a new batch of cocoa. "I fear this might be my fault."

She gave him a surprised look, aware of Victor stiffening beneath her.

"How could this be your fault?" Victor asked in a low growl.

Reaching down, she rubbed the side of his thigh soothingly.

Regent ran his hand down his face, looking exhausted. He carried so much on his shoulders. More than she thought he ever let anyone know.

"You know that we've been making things difficult for the Ventura gang."

She nodded.

"We've been hitting them where it really hurts—their cash flow. And we haven't been subtle about it. Victor has been working to cut off their supplier. We're slowly destroying them. What if they found out that you are part of our family now?"

That's why he thought it was his fault?

"By that reasoning, it could as easily be my fault," Victor rumbled. "I haven't been subtle either. And I took out two of their guys. Whoever they answered to in the gang likely knew they were going there that night. He could have figured out something happened to them there and burned down the bakery as retaliation."

"Or this might have nothing to do with retaliation at all," Maxim said as he stirred hot cocoa on the stovetop. "Could have been an accidental fire for all we know. Maybe we should wait and see what it's ruled as before we become conspiracy theorists."

Regent tapped his fingers against the tabletop as Maxim came back with several mugs of creamy cocoa topped with tiny marshmallows. She took a sip. Perfect.

"I don't believe in coincidences," Regent said.

Maxim sighed. "Well, did anyone check the cameras yet?"

Victor grumbled. "Why didn't I think of that?" He shifted her onto one knee then pulled his phone out.

"Can you put it on my computer?" Regent asked. "It would be easier for us to see it on a big screen."

"Yeah, I'll send the feed through." Victor set her on her feet, then picked up her drink for her as they walked into Regent's office. They crowded around his desk as he opened it.

"I'll go back three hours," Victor said.

They shifted through footage until finally, someone moved through the bakery's entrance. They had a beanie on their head and gloves on and they were carrying . . .

"Is that a gas container?" she asked.

"Yes," Victor replied grimly. He pulled her in close to him. "Bastard."

"Wait, there's someone else," Maxim said, pointing at a smaller figure. Definitely shorter than the first person. And this one had hair falling out the bottom of their hat.

"Is that a woman?" she asked. Surprise filled her. Not that women couldn't commit crimes.

"It appears that way," Regent said grimly. "Can we focus in further on what's on the back of his jacket?"

"I can try," Maxim replied. He did something on the computer and the image was blurry, but there was no mistaking it.

She let out a short gasp.

"What is it?" Victor asked.

"I've seen that image before. On the back of a jacket."

"Whose jacket was it?" Victor asked.

"Ice's," she whispered.

"Uh, guys," Maxim said. "Look at this."

They turned back to the computer screen. They'd moved on from Ice dousing the bakery in gasoline.

To where the second person was staring right up toward the camera, and her stomach sunk. She'd been hoping she was mistaken. Or that Ice was working with someone else.

But there was no mistaking her niece's face.

∾

VICTOR PACED UP and down the downstairs hallway the following evening. Pausing, he glanced toward the kitchen.

What was she doing? Was she all right? Should he go to her?

He hated being this indecisive. Not knowing what his girl needed.

"You're giving me a headache," Regent called out from his office. "Either go to her or get in here and sit down."

"She said she needed some time to herself." They'd spent most of today dealing with the fire investigator and the cops. Then he'd taken her down to look at the remnants of what was left of the bakery. They'd gotten home at dinner time and after heating them up some meals, she'd asked for some time alone.

He didn't like that she'd skipped dinner. Even though she'd heated up some of the meals Gerald had left for the three of them.

The fire investigator had told them that it appeared to be arson, but that a proper investigation would likely take weeks. He'd seemed somewhat intimidated by Victor's presence. But that was his problem.

Regent had suggested that they didn't tell the investigator or police about the camera feed. He didn't want the cops using it as an opportunity to look into anything else, like Ice and his ties to Santiago and the Ventura gang. Or what they were doing to the gang.

He needed to make that bastard Ice pay. Anita, too, but that was trickier. Victor could tell Gracen was conflicted about the whole thing.

The problem was, she wasn't talking to him. And he hated that. He didn't like there being anything between them. She'd asked him for some time alone, though. And he had to give her that.

No matter how much he didn't want to.

So now she was in the kitchen, baking up a storm and he was out here, annoying Regent.

He walked into his brother's office and sat on the chair across the desk from Regent.

"Do you know where Maxim is?" Regent asked.

"I think he went out to check on the clubs. He took guards," Victor added.

What was she doing? Had she eaten anything? What if she was sitting there, crying?

He was nearly at the point of sitting her down and forcing some food into her.

Regent looked up at him. "How is Gracen?"

"Not great. She asked for some time alone." He clenched his hands into fists, feeling helpless. "I should be out there searching for Ice. Teaching the bastard a lesson." He was torn between being here with her and destroying the asshole who'd hurt her.

Regent leaned back in his chair. "I've got my guys searching for him. Once we find him, you can take care of him."

Good. Nothing would make him happier.

"I received some interesting images from my informant just now," Regent said. "I'm just printing them off."

Victor grunted. Regent had managed to turn one of Santiago's men. But at the moment, he could care less about what was going on with Santiago. All he cared about was his girl and what was going on in her head.

"Victor? Are you listening?"

A knock on the door had them both turning to look. There was only one person it could be. Victor jumped up to find Gracen picking a big, silver tray off the floor where she'd obviously set it while she knocked. It had a pot of coffee on it, a couple of cups, sugar, creamer, and two large pieces of what looked to be lemon cake.

"Baby, you shouldn't be carrying that," he scolded. "It's too heavy."

"I know it might not seem like it lately, but I'm not weak."

He took the tray with a scowl. "Nobody said anything about you being weak. But that still doesn't mean you carry around heavy things when I'm here to do it for you."

"But you won't always be here."

He was planning on being with her as much as possible.

Victor set the tray on Regent's desk then turned to study her. She looked tired. He knew she'd hardly slept last night because neither had he. He'd kept expecting her to say something about her niece, but she'd been surprisingly quiet on the subject.

He didn't like it.

Running his finger along the underside of her eye and down her cheek, he pressed it under her chin, tilting her face back. "You're exhausted."

She just shrugged, her lower lip trembling before she took in a deep breath. "I'm all right."

Leaning in, he whispered in her ear. "You know better than to lie, little bit."

A small shiver ran threw her.

"Have you eaten?"

"Uh, no. But I'm not hungry."

"You need to eat." She looked drawn and pale. "Why don't I go make you some grilled cheese?"

That was something he could make.

"Or I could find a meal to heat up that Gerald left."

"I'm really fine, Victor. Would you both like coffee?" She reached for the carafe, but her hand was shaking.

"Allow me," Regent said smoothly. "What's this?"

"It's lemon cake. I baked it earlier. I didn't put icing on it since I know you don't like things too sweet. Would you like to try it?"

Victor sent Regent a look over her head. He better fucking say yes.

"I would be privileged to try it," Regent told her.

"Sit down, baby. Did you have any cake? Do you want coffee?"

"Uh, no. I don't think I need more caffeine. I feel a bit jittery already."

She needed sleep. As soon as he could, he was carrying her upstairs and putting her to bed. Even if he had to tie her to it.

A plan in place, he settled on the chair next to her.

"I've been . . . I've been thinking about my niece." She straightened her shoulders, staring from Regent to him. "I think I might call her."

Victor sucked in a breath. "Are you sure, baby?"

"I need her to know that I know what she did. To tell her how upset I am with her. I just need to get these feelings out."

She had her hands clenched tightly into fists and her body was vibrating with emotion.

His poor girl. He wished he could take away all of her anxiety and worries. Her niece had a lot to answer for. Gracen had taken the girl in when her father died, given her a home and a job, and this is how she repaid her?

He didn't care that she was just nineteen. This wasn't the way you treated family.

Lifting her to his lap, he carefully pulled her fists apart, rubbing gently at the red marks her nails had made in the skin. "Don't hurt yourself, baby."

"I didn't mean to. I didn't feel it."

Which worried him. But if she wasn't able to take care of herself, then he was here and willing.

"If you feel you need to, then I don't see the issue in calling your niece," Regent told her. "You realize that you may not get any apology or real closure, though."

"I know. I just want to know why."

"She might not tell you that either," Victor said.

"No, maybe not."

"But we might also be able to figure out whether it was your niece's idea or her boyfriend's. Because there are some interesting connections going on here." Regent tapped a photo in front of him. "Recognize this man, Victor?"

He turned an image around to show them.

"Where were these taken?" Victor asked.

"At one of Santiago's clubs. My informant was able to take these images of a meeting in the backroom. See that man there?" He pointed out a scrawny, middle-aged guy who was wearing an ill-fitted suit. "That's Snake."

"Snake?" Gracen asked. "His parents give him that name?"

Victor realized then that Regent was showing how much he trusted Gracen by allowing her to see these images and hear about his plans. He didn't usually believe in including women in meetings like this. Well, the only woman that had been around them for any length of time was their sister. And Regent was hugely protective of her.

But he guessed that Gracen had a stake in this.

"Snake?" he asked. "The leader of the Ventura gang? He's meeting with Santiago?"

"Yes," Regent replied grimly. "And doesn't he look stressed? Probably because he's bleeding cash at the moment thanks to us. Interesting how things keep leading back to Santiago, isn't it?"

"So, you think they're working together?" Gracen asked. "Santiago and the Ventura gang? That might explain how Ice got a job with Santiago. He's not officially a part of the gang, but I got the feeling that eventually he'd join."

"So, Santiago could be working both with Patrick and the Ventura gang? What is he trying to do? Find partners who will help him build an empire?" Victor asked.

"That's my guess, yes," Regent said. "The Ventura gang aren't that powerful, but they have plenty of foot soldiers Santiago could use. What Patrick brings, I'm not sure. Connections? Ideas?"

"Or maybe he's the ringleader," Gracen suggested as she

glanced over the photo. "And he's bringing all of these people together."

Regent stared at her for a long moment. "Maybe."

"Was Patrick at this meeting?" Victor asked.

"No. Our informant believes he's laying low. Could be he's getting Santiago to recruit for him. There wasn't anyone else interesting in the room." He turned the other images around. In one, Snake was shaking Santiago's hand. In another, Santiago was looming over a slight, red-haired woman. He seemed to be upset with her if his tense stance was anything to go by.

Gracen took in a sharp breath, growing tense. "Little bit? You all right? What is it?"

"Who . . . who is that?" With a trembling finger, she pointed to the red-haired woman.

"I don't know," Regent said. "I just thought she was some fling of Santiago's. I've heard rumors of a long-term girlfriend. This could be her."

"I think this is the woman who approached me in the bathroom at Matteo's," she said, turning to Victor. "The one who thought that you'd hit me. She offered to help me. Only, her hair is different. But why would she be there?"

"And why does it look like she's having an argument with Santiago?" Regent mused.

"She could be the girlfriend," Victor said.

"She doesn't look happy. Perhaps she was reaching out to me because she needs help. It sounded like she'd helped other women, why would she be with him?"

"Maybe she helps them in secret," Victor mused. "In which case, she could be in a lot of danger if Santiago discovers what she's doing. Especially if any of the women work in one of his clubs."

"We need to help her."

"Or she could be working for Santiago," Regent suggested.

"Maybe she saw you with Victor at Matteo's and knew that Santiago was working against us with Patrick and wanted to gain your trust."

GRACEN BIT HER LIP, trying to think.

She rubbed her temples. She had a raging headache.

"You need sleep." Victor rubbed at the knots in her neck. "And something to eat."

She wished she could. But she felt nauseous every time she thought about eating. After they'd gotten to bed in the early hours of the morning, her mind had been too busy to sleep. She'd lain there, secured in Victor's arms, the only thing keeping her grounded.

"Talk to me, baby," he practically begged.

Guilt filled her. Poor Victor. She knew he was having fits, not knowing what to do to make her feel better.

"I'm all right. I just . . . I didn't get the feeling she was lying to me. I know that's not a lot to go on. I mean, I'm obviously not a great judge of character. I didn't even know what my own niece is capable of . . ." she trailed off.

The sense of betrayal was enormous. She felt like she'd been through a whole rollercoaster of emotions. Disbelief. Denial. Anger. Sadness. Now, she was kind of numb with exhaustion. But she also wanted some resolution.

"That doesn't mean you're wrong about this woman," Regent said gently. "Let me find out what I can about her. If she is what she seems to be, someone who's helping other women, then she might be someone we can use."

"Use?" Gracen asked. "We shouldn't use her, we should help her."

"I apologize," Regent said. "I used the wrong word. Maybe we can help her, and she can help us."

"But even if she can't help us, we should help her," Gracen insisted.

Regent nodded slowly. "That would be the right thing to do."

"Do you want to call Anita now?" Victor asked. "Why don't you try to get some rest first?"

"I don't think I can rest. Not until I talk to her." It was like a beast under her skin, pushing and prodding. Wanting freedom.

"You are welcome to use my office," Regent said. "I'll go clean the kitchen or something."

"You will?" Victor asked. "Do you know how?"

"Very funny. I am not completely hopeless."

"That remains to be seen. Now, if you manage to load the dish-washer, I'll die of shock."

Regent shot him a cold look as he picked up his crutches and swung his way out of the room.

"That wasn't nice."

Victor scoffed. "Remind me to check the dishwasher before we go to bed. He'll probably stick dishwashing liquid in it or something."

She just shook her head, then let out a loud sigh. Climbing off his lap, she dug her phone out of her pocket.

"You don't have to do this, little bit. Not right now or at all."

"No, I have to do it. I can do it. I'm just nervous about what she's going to say."

She tapped her niece's name, then set it on speaker before pacing up and down while she waited for her to answer.

"Aunty G," Anita answered coolly. "I haven't got much time to talk. I got a new job, and I'm about to head out."

"Well, that's good you have a job."

Even if you are a criminal.

"I thought you'd be happier for me than that. I got it all by myself."

"Anita, the bakery burned down last night."

She held her breath. There was still a part of her that hoped her niece would have some explanation. That she would come clean and tell her that Ice had somehow tricked her or threatened her. Not that she was hoping her niece was threatened . . . or that she genuinely thought that was a possibility.

"What? Really?" Anita replied with fake shock.

She closed her eyes, taking a deep breath.

In. Out.

Strong arms wrapped around her from behind. Sheltering her. Keeping her in the here and now.

Victor was her rock and she needed him now more than ever before.

"Aunty G? I really gotta go, so if that's all you've got to say . . ."

What? She couldn't even be bothered to try and pretend to care? Tears welled in Gracen's eyes, but she wouldn't let them fall. Not yet.

"No, that's not all," she said in a hard voice. "I know it was you."

A fake laugh came through the speaker, tinged with worry. "What? Aunty G, you on something?"

"No, I'm not on something." Feeling exhausted now, she leaned against Victor, who easily took her weight.

And she was back on that emotional rollercoaster.

"I know it was you, Anita. I saw you and Ice on the cameras I had in the bakery."

"Oh. My God!" Anita screeched. "You had cameras and you never told me? Do you realize what a breach of privacy that is? I could sue you."

"No. You can't," Gracen said. "Because you burned my bakery down."

There was a beat of silence. "So, what you going to do about it?"

Her breath came in sharp pants. "What am I going to do?"

"Yeah. Come on, Aunty G, you should really be thanking me. I mean, that bakery was never going to make any money. The place was run-down and shit. At least now you'll get the insurance money."

"Insurance money? You think there will be insurance money?"

"Well, yeah. Of course."

"Anita, I don't have insurance. The landlord might have it on the buildings, but that will go to him. If he's even insured for arson. I don't even know how that works. And besides, I don't care about the money. There were items in that bakery that were sentimental. Things that reminded me of my grandparents. You took those items from me. Not to mention the damage that was done to the surrounding buildings. What if the landlord doesn't have insurance? What if this is completely out of pocket for him?"

"That's his problem, I guess. So, what are you saying? That you're mad at me? Because Ice reckons that you must've stolen the money that daddy had left when he died and that it should've come to me."

"What?" Gracen was flabbergasted at the accusation. "You think I stole from you?"

"Well, yeah," Anita said, sounding slightly unsure.

"Anita, after I sold anything we could there was about five hundred dollars which I gave to you. You blew most of it on clothes. I paid for his funeral out of my own pocket. I can't believe you'd accuse me of that. And yes, I'm mad and I'm upset. I am shocked that you'd do something so stupid and criminal! You broke the law!"

"You're going to turn me into the cops? Some aunt you are! My dad would be horrified by how you're treating me."

"No," Gracen replied coldly. "Your father would be ashamed of you." She ended the call with a shaking finger.

And then she collapsed.

23

Victor caught her, of course.

She lost it on the floor of Regent's office, crying with huge, gulping sobs. She shook so badly she worried there was something wrong with her.

Victor didn't try to quiet her. Didn't say anything. He just sat on the floor with her in his lap, his arms tight around her as he rocked her back and forth.

When the tears started to dry up, probably because she had no liquid left inside her, he stood with her in his arms. Setting her down on Regent's desk, he grabbed some tissues from the box on the shelves behind the desk.

Did a lot of people cry in this office?

The thought came out of left field but she'd rather focus on that than what just happened.

Victor cleaned her up gently, wiping away her tears. He held the tissue to her nose. "Blow."

"Ew. No. That's not going to keep the romance alive."

"We'll find other ways to keep the romance alive. Blow." The last word was said in a stern voice.

She blew.

Gross.

But he didn't seem fazed at all as he wiped her nose.

"You'll make a good dad," she murmured.

He froze, then threw the tissue into the garbage can.

"I'm sorry," she said hastily. "That was kind of a weird thing to say. I didn't mean . . . perhaps you don't want kids . . . I . . ." she trailed off. Why had she opened her big mouth?

"I never thought I would have children."

"Right, yeah, cool."

Cool? Was she serious right now? How was that cool? She really shouldn't be having this conversation when she was beyond exhausted.

"Because I never thought I would find someone I would want to spend my life with."

"Oh, so you do want children?"

He sighed, tracing his finger over her lower lip. She opened her mouth and nipped the tip. He stared down at her sternly, but she saw the twinkle in his eyes.

And the relief.

Yeah, he'd been worried about her. And she definitely wasn't feeling a hundred percent better. Talking to her niece had been both cathartic and utterly soul-destroying at the same time.

But she could piece herself back together. And maybe, while she was trying to do that, Victor could be her glue.

"I don't know if I'll make a very good father."

"What? Are you kidding? Yes, you will. You're patient. You're a good listener. You're protective. And you don't mind wiping snotty noses. All you need is the ability to deal with scrapes and injuries as well as vomit and poop and you'll be there. Oh, and you already don't need a lot of sleep. So, you're the one designated to get up with the screaming baby in the night."

He stared down at her in amazement.

Getting ahead of yourself, Gracen.

"That's assuming you'd want to have babies with me," she added in a quiet voice.

"Gracen, I plan to spend the rest of my life with you. Who else would I have babies with?"

She stared up at him shyly. "Okay, then. That's nice."

He shook his head but then warmth filled his eyes. "Yeah, baby. I guess it is. But I wouldn't mind having you to myself for a while first."

"I wouldn't mind that either." She heaved out a sigh. "I shouldn't have said that to her. I should really call her back and tell her I didn't mean it."

"That you didn't mean what?"

"That bit about her father being ashamed of her." She lowered her eyes, ashamed herself. She shouldn't have sunk that low.

"Baby, look at me."

When she raised her gaze to his, she found his eyes firm and serious.

"Would he have been ashamed?"

"Yes," she whispered honestly. "But he might have been ashamed of me too."

"I don't think so. But maybe those are the words she needs to hear to get her out of her own head. Or maybe she won't pay any attention and keep going on this path. The fact is, none of it is your fault. Understand me?"

"I guess so." That headache was back, worse than ever.

"I know so. It's up to her now. Although, we can still give that footage to the cops. Or I can go have a chat with her." There was a dark gleam in his eyes.

"No, I don't want that. She's all I've got left. My only family."

"No, baby. You're one of us now. A Malone. We can make it official as soon as you like."

Her eyes widened. "Victor Guillaume Malone."

"You have really got to tell me who told you my middle name. So I can murder them. Slowly and viciously. It was Maxim, wasn't it?" he growled.

"You cannot seriously be proposing to me right now."

"Why not?"

"B-because I just cried my eyes out on your lap, and you had to wipe my snotty nose."

"Still love you."

"I've barely slept. I look like a complete fright."

"Still love you."

"I just confronted my niece who set my bakery on fire, and she didn't even care."

"Still love you."

"You don't have a ring," she whispered.

"I do have a ring."

What? Was he serious? He picked her up in his arms, carrying her bridal style. She'd given up telling him that he couldn't carry her like this. When they got to the door to his room, he set her down and walked inside. She followed him in slowly while he searched through his drawers.

He picked out a jewelry box. It looked a bit worn. How long had he owned this? Longer than he'd known her.

"We've only been on two dates," she whispered as he got onto one knee.

"Still love you."

"I have no job, no money, and no idea what I'm going to do with my life."

"Still love you."

Tears dripped down her face. Seemed she did still have some moisture inside her.

"We've only known each other a short while."

"And I know that I will love you every day from now until I die. And after. There has never been someone in my life like you. I live in the darkness. I've done terrible things. I don't deserve you. Probably never will. But no one will ever love you like I do. Gracen Rose Stall, will you marry me?" He opened the jewelry box and she gasped as she saw the most beautiful ring she'd ever laid eyes on.

It had a pale pink sapphire in the middle and clusters of diamonds on each side.

She dropped to her knees on the plush carpet and held out her shaking hand.

"Yes." It was all she was capable of saying. Tears streamed down her face, and she sobbed with happiness this time as he slid the ring onto her finger. It was slightly tight, but it went on.

"We'll get it resized," he told her. "It was my grandmother's ring. She left it to me to give to someone special."

"It's stunning. Thank you. Thank you!" She threw herself at him.

He held her tightly, kissing the top of her head. "Stop crying now, baby."

"They're happy tears." It was insane how she'd gone from feeling the lowest of lows to the highest of highs.

Which might be why she was feeling woozy and out of it.

"I know. But I'm worried you're going to dehydrate."

Setting her aside, he stood then lifted her. When he stood her on her feet, she wobbled.

Okay. She probably should eat something.

"Whoa. Are you all right? What's wrong?" he asked in a sharp voice.

"I'm fine. I just feel a bit light-headed."

A grim look came over his face. "You need a doctor."

"What? No! Really, I'm not sick. I just . . . it's been a lot and I haven't had much sleep. Or food. I'm fine, Victor."

"That's it. You're going to bed." He picked her up, then laid her down on the bed. "I'm going to get you into your pajamas. Then

I'll get you something to eat and drink. You're going to spend all of tomorrow in bed resting."

"I'm not spending all of tomorrow in bed resting."

"Yes, you are. You're wearing my ring now. That means you obey me."

She made a scoffing noise. "You're dreaming, buddy."

He stared down at her with soft eyes. "If I am, I hope I never wake up."

She melted. He was the sweetest guy.

24

The man was a tyrant.

Actually, he made tyrants look good.

"Victor, I'm not sick. I slept all night. I feel fine."

"You don't look fine," he countered as he fussed with her covers.

This kind of felt surreal. This huge man with the scarred knuckles, who'd actually stalked her at one time, was fussing over her bed covers like they were the most important thing to him right now. He was determined not to let her out of bed today, which was crazy.

"Why? How bad do I look?" She tried to scoot out his side of the bed, but he placed a hand on the mattress, keeping her in place.

"You look beautiful."

She glared up at him. He couldn't have it both ways. "You said I don't look fine."

"You look pale and tired. But still beautiful. Now, what would you like to eat?"

"I just had breakfast."

"And now it's time for a morning snack."

"I'm not hungry."

He frowned. "I don't like your lack of appetite. I think I should have Regent call for the doctor."

"I don't need a doctor." But he might if he kept this up. "I just haven't done anything to work up an appetite. And not all of us are sized extra-extra-large."

"You calling me fat?" He gave her a mock-scowl.

"No one could ever call you fat. But it takes a lot of calories to keep you going. Me, not so much."

He still didn't look like he agreed. "Fine, no snack. You're still staying in bed."

"Victor!"

"But I'll let you watch some television."

She folded her arms over her chest. "Wow. That's so generous of you. Is this what I have to look forward to? Being bossed around the rest of my life?" She still couldn't believe he'd proposed last night.

They were engaged.

"Yes. I'll have it written into the vows. By the way, the word obey is going in there."

"It is not!" She knew she wasn't pale now. Nope, she likely resembled a tomato.

"Absolutely it is." He flicked through the channels on the remote until he found the home improvement show she liked. She sighed. Looked like she was staying in bed a bit longer.

At least until he left the room, then all bets were off.

He settled in next to her, his arm wrapped around her shoulders.

"Uh, don't you have somewhere else to be?" she asked.

"No."

"Are you sure? You don't have to work?"

"Trying to get rid of me, little bit?" he asked, giving her a suspicious look.

"Yes. Is it working?"

To her shock, he grinned at her. "No."

"Drat." She gazed down at her ring. Damn, it was beautiful. "Did you tell anyone yet?"

"No, I thought we could tell them together."

"If you'd let me out of bed, we could tell them now."

"Good try."

Obviously not good enough since she was still stuck in this bed.

His phone buzzed and he groaned. "Crap."

"Oh, you've got to go?"

"Try not to sound so happy about it, brat." He bopped her nose with his finger. "I just need to talk to Regent for a moment. I'll be back soon. Don't get out of this bed."

"Aye, aye, bossy tyrant."

"I mean it. Stay there."

Almost as soon as he left, she was out of the bed. She stretched with relief and raced into the bathroom to pee and brush her teeth and hair.

Hmm. How long would he be? Long enough for her to sneak out of here and get some coffee?

Victor had refused to give her more than one cup this morning, claiming that it would stop her from resting.

But she was dying for another cup. Her head was still throbbing slightly after all the crying she'd done yesterday. She wanted to avoid taking painkillers and she was hoping a dose of caffeine would help. Not to mention that asking Victor for painkillers would probably send him off on a tailspin. Or have him calling for a doctor.

Quickly throwing some clothes on, she grabbed her phone and tiptoed her way downstairs and into the kitchen.

"Ooh, someone's going to get her butt spanked," a voice sang at her from the pantry.

She jumped with a cry, turning to find Maxim standing in the pantry, eating a piece of red velvet cake.

So far, Regent hadn't liked any of her efforts that much. There had to be something he liked, though.

"Jesus. What are you trying to do? Scare me to death? Do you know how long I'll have to stay in bed if I have a heart attack?"

"Who had a heart attack?" Regent asked, coming into the room.

She groaned as a scowling Victor followed him. He glared at her, coming over to stand in front of her, his arms folded over his chest.

"I gave Gracen a fright," Maxim said. "Although, I think it was her guilty conscience that made her jump."

"I don't have a guilty conscience."

"Are you supposed to be out of bed?" Regent asked, giving Victor a look of reproach. He sat at the table, setting his crutches down next to him. "I thought you were going to make sure she rested?"

"I was. Until you called me down."

"I don't need to rest, I'm fine."

It was Maxim's turn to frown. "I don't know how you can be with everything that's happened, doll."

She stared at all three men, looking back at her with different levels of concern.

"I really do have a family, don't I?" she whispered.

Victor's gaze warmed and softened. "I told you that you did, baby."

She nodded. "I'm just realizing it, I guess." She turned to Regent. "Victor was making sure I rested. However, he only let me have one cup of coffee this morning, and I'm dying here." Looking over at Maxim, she gave him a small smile. "And I meant that I'm fine physically. Emotionally, it will take me a lot longer to get over what happened. Thank you both for worrying about me." She walked over and hugged Maxim. He held onto her until Victor gave a warning growl.

Leaning back from her, he winked. He loved to pick at his brothers.

Moving to Regent, she saw him eye her warily. Was he worried she would hug him? Or that she wouldn't?

Didn't matter, he was getting a hug.

Leaning down, she wrapped her arms around him, gratified that he hugged her back. He didn't strike her as overly demonstrative.

She slid away from him. He caught her hand, looking from her ring finger to Victor. "Is there something you both wanted to tell us?"

"Yes," Victor replied, taking hold of her other hand and tugging her over until she was pressed to his side, his arm around her shoulders. "We're engaged. She's mine. So, you all need to stop touching her."

That announcement just meant another round of hugs. That included Victor this time. He grumbled through them, but she could tell he was happy by the glint in his eyes.

"This calls for a toast." Maxim clapped his hands

"It's not even noon," she pointed out.

"Special occasion." He reached into a wine fridge and drew out a bottle of what was likely insanely expensive champagne, pouring out glasses and handing them around.

Regent held his up. "To Victor and Gracen, may they live happily ever after."

Somehow, she knew that would come true.

25

"I think I've cracked it. Try a piece of this."

She walked into Regent's office with a plate of blueberry and lemon muffins. Not too sweet. Not too sour. Hopefully just right.

Victor walked in behind her.

"These are actually really good," Maxim said as he entered, eating a muffin.

"How are you so slim?" she complained. "Honestly, it's not fair to the rest of us."

She set the muffins down on Regent's desk then turned back to look at Maxim in disgust.

Victor moved in behind her, wrapping his arm around her waist. "That better not be a putdown."

"What? No! No negative comments here." She'd been about to say something else but had stopped herself. Just as well. Her bottom still felt a bit tender after he'd spanked her last night for getting out of bed without permission.

The man had been on a total power trip ever since she'd said yes to his proposal. Although, to be fair, he'd been on a power trip before then.

"Better not be." He patted her ass gently, then held out a chair for her. He sat next to her while Maxim sat on a corner of Regent's desk.

"Maxim," Regent said in a low voice.

"Yes?"

"Get your buttocks off my desk."

"But they're so comfy on your desk. They're on their own power trip. They're sucking up your mojo."

"They're about to feel something else of mine if you don't get off my desk."

"Okay, okay, no need to get nasty." Maxim sat and put his feet up on the desk instead.

Regent shook his head. "Right, I've been investigating who this mystery woman is and I've got a name and some details."

"Wow, you work quickly," she told him.

"I have to. Jardin and his family came home last night. The boys need to get back to school. I've got guards on them, but it can't go on indefinitely."

"Bet Ace and Keir are loving that," Maxim said dryly.

"They are. The school, not so much," Regent said dryly.

"With what you donate to that school, I doubt they're complaining," Victor added.

She knew that Ace and Keir were Thea's brothers and that they lived with her.

"Who is she then?" Victor asked.

"Her name is Lilia Montague. So, she told you the truth about her first name. And she's not Santiago's girlfriend, she's his stepsister. Her mother married Santiago's father when Lilia was just thirteen and Santiago was nineteen. There's not a lot of information about her. It looks like she moved back here about three months ago. But I can't find any concrete information about where she's been or what she's been doing."

"If she's his stepsister, she might not be interested in going against him," Maxim said.

"This is where it gets interesting. My informant seems to think that Santiago is obsessed with her. And that she didn't want to return to him. Although it seems she has some freedom to move around the city. But she could be in an ideal place to help us. If she wishes to."

"I have her number," Gracen said. "Do you want me to contact her?"

"I think it would be a good idea," Regent said slowly.

"I don't like it." Victor shook his head. "What if she's loyal to Santiago?"

"I could just sound her out first," she offered. "Ask her if she needs help. See if she offers any information."

Regent looked to Victor.

"She might know that Gracen is with me," Victor said.

"If it's in a public place, though, it would be safe, right? Or I could text her a place at the last moment."

"That could work," Maxim agreed with her.

Victor made a low noise.

"She tried to help me, Victor. And I believe she was sincere. I want to see if she needs help. Please."

"Fine," he said after consideration. "But if there's any sign of danger, I'm getting you right out."

"I know you'll take care of me," she reassured him.

"Now, onto Ice," Regent said. "So far, we haven't located him. It seems he's gone into hiding."

She frowned. "Anita will know where he is. I suppose I could ask her."

Gracen's phone rang. She frowned. "Speak of the devil, it's Anita."

"Are you going to answer it?" Victor asked. "You could ignore it."

She could, but she wouldn't. With a sigh, she answered the call as she walked into the hallway.

"Hello?"

There was silence. That was odd.

"Anita?"

"A-aunty G."

Gracen frowned. There was clear fear in her niece's voice.

"Anita? What is it? What's wrong?" She moved back into the office and Victor stood, looking at her with obvious concern.

"Aunty G, I'm s-so sorry. But, p-please, you have to h-help me."

"What's going on?" Gracen stared at Victor, worry beating at her.

"Hello? Is this Gracen Stall?" a smooth, male voice asked.

Her heart skipped.

"Put the phone on speaker," Victor demanded quietly.

She fumbled with the phone, getting it on speaker. "Who is this?"

"Am I on speaker?" the voice asked, not sounding perturbed at all.

Regent frowned and Victor came over to get her, leading her back to a chair. She set the phone on Regent's desk.

"Yes, you are," Victor replied. "Who is this?"

"I'm so upset you don't recognize my voice. This is Carlos Santiago."

Her breath came in stuttered gasps. "Why do you have my niece's phone? Is she all right? I want to talk to her again."

"Oh, I'm afraid I can't allow that right now. But she's fine. I'll send you some photos of her. I'm afraid I can't say the same about her boyfriend. He suffered an unfortunate accident."

Unfortunate accident?

Was that why Regent had been unable to locate Ice? Because Santiago killed him?

"Ice is dead?" she whispered. "Why? He was working for you! What are you doing with my niece?"

"Did you know that your niece got a job with me?" Santiago asked instead. "Good little stripper she is too. Nice, perky tits."

She was going to vomit. That was Anita's new job?

Oh, Anita. What have you gotten yourself into?

"Too bad she doesn't know how to keep her mouth shut," Santiago said.

She heard someone weeping in the background. Was that Anita?

"She's not very loyal to you, is she? In fact, she was rather angry at you when she came to me and told me that her aunt was dating Victor Malone. She even explained how she burned down your bakery. How must it feel to be stabbed in the back by family?"

Oh, Anita. You idiot.

She'd obviously thought that Santiago would value that information. And he did. What he didn't value was the person who brought that information to him.

"What do you want?" Regent asked coldly.

"I want a meet. You've been creating a lot of problems for me and my associates," Santiago replied. "I'll send a location and time when I'm ready. Oh, and daily pictures of your little bitch niece. Don't worry, I'll treat her really well."

The call ended and Gracen placed her hand over her mouth, sobbing. Victor pulled her against him.

"What do we do?" she asked. "I can't . . . I can't let him hurt her." Or worse. "She's still my niece."

"We need to get in touch with Lilia," Regent said. "I'll also check in with my informant. He might be able to get your niece out. Or at least give us a heads-up about the location and time for the meet ahead of Santiago telling us. He won't give us any time to prepare."

"Don't worry, baby," Victor whispered to her soothingly. "We'll get her back."

She just hoped it didn't cost her everything.

GRACEN TOOK a seat in the busy café at the back of the bookshop. She'd chosen the place and the others had agreed. Nerves filled her stomach. She hadn't slept a wink last night or eaten since Santiago's call. She'd been too worried about Anita.

Victor was in complete overprotective mode, fretting over her. But she knew that she wasn't going to feel better until they saved Anita.

Her foot bounced up and down. Where was she? Would she come?

She'd texted Lilia last night after Santiago's call asking her to meet her today but hadn't given her a time or location. Then about an hour ago, she'd sent her details for their meeting. Luckily, the other woman hadn't seemed fazed. Finally, she spotted her dark hair coming through the crowd. Was it a wig?

Lilia slid into the table across from Gracen.

"Hi, Lilia," Gracen said. She had to stop herself from immediately asking her if she'd seen her niece. Or knew what her evil stepbrother was up to. "Would you like something to drink? Eat?"

"No, I don't have much time, sorry." Lilia looked around worriedly.

Okay, this was a good chance to bring things up. She had a recording device on so the others could listen, but she couldn't hear them.

"Are you all right?"

"What? Yeah, fine. We're here to talk about you. Do you want help leaving that asshole?" Lilia asked.

"Actually, Victor isn't an asshole. We're getting married." She held out her ring to show her, aware that her hand was shaking.

"Oh, girl. If he's hitting you—"

"He's not. I promise. Really."

Lilia leaned forward. "Then why am I here?"

"Because you were willing to help me when you didn't know me. And I kind of got the feeling you were the one who needed help."

Lilia looked surprised then resigned. "Who are you?"

"What?"

"FBI? Local police? DEA? Something else?"

"Uh, no. None of those."

"I'm not here because you're worried about me. I'm here because you want something from me and if you're not going to tell me then I'm gone." Lilia stood.

"Wait, please!" She knew Victor would kill her. But she had this feeling that she was right about the other woman.

Lilia paused.

"You're right. I do want something. But I'm hoping we can help you too."

"We?" Lilia glanced around then sat.

"My family. We . . . Lilia, are you safe? With your stepbrother? Is this where you want to be?"

"You do want something from me. Because of him."

"Yes, but not like you're thinking. I'm not law enforcement." She lowered her voice. "I'm engaged to Victor Malone."

Lilia went pale then sat. "Shit, girl. Do you really know who my stepbrother is?"

"Yes. That's why I'm here. He . . . he called me last night." She sucked in a breath. "He has my niece."

"Oh, fuck." Lilia bit at her thumbnail, then seemed to realize what she was doing and set her hands down on her lap. "He has my mother."

"Oh, no."

"He's holding her captive to keep me in line. He's always . . . he's always wanted me." She shuddered. "My mom is ill. She has cancer. Anytime I do something he doesn't like, he threatens to take away her care, the drugs she needs to keep her comfortable."

"Lilia, I'm so sorry." She wished she knew the other woman better, she really wanted to hug her.

"I escaped him a while ago with help. But he kidnapped my mom and forced me to return. He's a terrible person."

"A monster," she agreed. Who threatened to withhold a person's medical care? "But we can help you get away from him. You and your mom."

Lilia chewed her lip. "God, I'd be stupid to trust you. I don't know you. At the same time, there's something about you that tells me you're genuine."

"I feel the same about you. Victor won't be pleased I just spilled everything to you like I did."

Lilia's gaze narrowed. "Sure you're safe with him?"

"I'm sure."

"Well, if anyone can help me, I guess it's the Malones. Carlos is power hungry, but it wasn't until he started working with Patrick McMahon that he figured out a way to build his empire. Patrick is the brains. Carlos isn't smart enough to go against Regent Malone. Then they brought in the Ventura gang, mainly for the manpower."

Gracen was kind of surprised she knew all of this.

"Carlos likes to have me with him at most of his meetings. I think he likes to show off or something. He doesn't realize I have a brain in my head. He thinks I'm not paying attention. But knowledge is power."

Gracen nodded. She got that.

"I haven't seen your niece, though. I can try and find where he's hiding her."

"That would be amazing. But only if you can do it safely. The thing is . . . he's told us he wants a meeting, and he'll give her to us."

"He won't do that."

"We know. It's obviously a setup. You're right, he's not that smart."

Lilia made a scoffing noise. "I wonder if Patrick knows what he's doing. He's out of town at the moment."

Shit. Regent would be upset.

"If I find out any information about the meeting, I'll tell you."

"Thank you."

"I've got to go. I had to slip away from my minder."

"Is that why . . . are you wearing a wig?" she whispered.

"Oh yeah, my natural hair color is too easy to spot. Don't worry, I slip away all the time, so no one will be that worried. But eventually, I have to let him find me or he'll tell Carlos. Be safe."

"You too."

SHE DIDN'T HEAR from Lilia for another two days. She was nearly a complete wreck by that time. And Victor was close to breaking. He'd actually threatened to tie her to the bed and force a sedative on her.

Thankfully, a message had come through from Lilia giving them a time and location.

Regent had quickly set things into motion to protect them. He'd stuck Jardin and his family on a private jet out of the city. Victor had wanted her to go with them, but they'd already had this argument.

She had to stay in case Santiago insisted on her being at the meeting. Of course, he'd argued about that too. But both Regent and Maxim agreed with her.

When Santiago's message came through, it was with the same details. But with an order for all of them to come. Unarmed.

Including her.

And now, Victor was really losing his shit. He picked up the closest object in Regent's office, which was probably worth more than most people's mortgages and threw it.

Thankfully, Maxim managed to catch it before it could smash into a wall.

"Victor, calm down," Regent said sternly. "We don't have time for you to freak out."

"She's not going. No. Fucking. Way."

"If I don't go, he might kill Anita," she said frantically. "I can't live with that, Victor."

"Come on, brother. We talked this through," Maxim added.

"Yes, but it's not your woman walking into a dangerous situation," Victor roared. "Not your heart."

Maxim winced.

Gracen knew that only she could get through to him. Walking over, she reached up on her tiptoes to place her hands on either side of his face.

"I have to do this, Victor."

"No."

"Yes. We've gone over and over this. And I'm not worried. Know why?"

"Why?"

"Because you'll be with me and you'd never let anything happen to me."

He closed his eyes, then opened them. "Nothing better happen to you, not even a fucking scratch."

"I know," she whispered. "I love you too."

26

Despite the fact that she'd argued to be here, Gracen was nervous as hell.

She reminded herself that they were prepared. Regent's men were all in place, ready to strike. They had people on the inside.

Nothing was going to go wrong.

Well, she hoped it wouldn't.

Regent climbed out of their vehicle, leaving his crutches inside. She knew that he didn't want to walk into this abandoned-looking warehouse showing any sign of weakness.

But she just hoped he didn't do more damage to his leg.

If things went to hell, Maxim was to grab her and keep her safe. She hated that Victor would still be in the line of fire, but she knew he needed to do this. He'd pulled Maxim aside and lectured him for an hour on taking care of her.

Poor Victor, he really wasn't happy that she was here.

Nerves filled her stomach. As they stepped into the dimly lit warehouse, three men strutted toward them, full of attitude. The warehouse was cavernous with glass windows set up high in the walls. Most of them were broken. There were empty crates seemingly positioned at random around the place.

They stopped in front of them. One of them reached out for her, and she spotted a familiar tattoo on his forearm.

A viper twirling around a huge V.

Victor grabbed his hand before he could touch her, spinning him and pressing his arm up his back until something snapped. The man howled in pain.

"Do not touch her."

Suddenly, two guns were aimed their way. Maxim and Victor stepped in front of her. Was this it? Were they going to be shot before they even saw Santiago?

"Hey, what the fuck are you guys doing?"

She glanced toward the voice, recognizing the man who'd spoken as Snake.

"This asshole broke Rat's arm!" one of them complained.

Rat? Really? That was the name of the guy who was now sobbing pitifully?

"Just search the guys and leave the bitch."

It was a dumb move. Seemed Snake wasn't any smarter than Santiago since she was carrying a knife in a scabbard in the small of her back. It was there in case things didn't go as planned.

Please let them go as planned.

After patting Victor, Maxim, and Regent down roughly, they followed them further into the warehouse and around some crates that had hidden the rest of the warehouse from view.

In the middle of the room stood Santiago, smiling at them maniacally. Snake moved up to stand behind him. Beside Santiago, her hair a matted mess, her clothes torn, looking drawn and pale, was Anita.

Gracen sucked in a sharp breath and had to remind herself to stick to the plan. She couldn't go to her. Couldn't talk to her. She had to stay close to Maxim.

"Aunty G!" Anita called out with a cry. She tried to run to her, but Santiago cruelly grabbed hold of her hair and dragged her back. The younger girl fell to the ground with a cry of pain.

Gracen had to work hard not to show her anger or fear. She'd been warned that Santiago would be looking for a reaction from her.

"Please come in," Santiago called out cheerfully. "Welcome. You're on time. I do love punctuality."

Was he insane? He was acting like they were coming for dinner or something. They moved forward, stopping about fifteen feet away from him. And that's when Gracen noticed that Lilia was here. She stood off to the side, with a guard on either side of her. Gracen didn't make eye contact. Didn't stare at her.

The last thing she wanted was for Santiago to find out that Lilia was on their side.

Santiago scowled as he took them in. "Where's the other brother?"

"He's out of town," Regent said smoothly. "You know he has nothing to do with the family business. What do you want, Santiago?"

"What? Straight into negotiations? No pleasantries?"

He'd kidnapped her niece and held her for days, and he wanted to exchange pleasantries?

"What do you want?" Regent repeated.

Gracen knew that Regent's men had eyes on the inside of the warehouse. They would wait for Regent to give them a signal and then they would attack.

"That's no way to talk to me when I've got a proposition for you," Santiago told Regent.

"What kind of proposition?" Regent crossed his arms over his chest.

"I heard you've got a real hard-on for Patrick McMahon," Santiago said slyly.

"I think that's common knowledge by now. I heard you've been working with him."

"Not for much longer if you agree to my offer."

This wasn't what they'd been expecting.

"Snake and I are tired of working with Patrick. He seems to think that we should take all the risks and he gets all the rewards. So, our proposition is this, we will work with you against McMahon."

Gracen was aware of how Victor had tensed, although she doubted that anyone else would notice. Would Regent take the offer? She didn't know. She knew he wanted this Patrick guy. But surely he knew he couldn't trust Santiago and Snake.

"As tempting as the offer is," Regent said slowly. "I'm going to have to decline."

Santiago's face tightened in anger. He drew out a gun, aiming it at Anita's head. "Then I'm sorry, but the girl is going to have to die."

Anita let out a frightened squeak. Gracen thought she was going to vomit. She forgot about everything Regent and Victor had told her and tried to run toward her. Maxim wrapped his arm around her tightly.

"No, wait. Stop!" Regent held up his hand.

That was the signal. Maxim picked her up, throwing her behind some empty crates as bullets smashed through windows.

There were screams. Cries of pain and fear. Maxim drew out his gun then crouched over her, one hand on her back.

Please keep everyone safe. Please.

Was Victor okay? Was Lilia all right? What about Regent?

And what about Anita?

The shooting seemed to go on forever. Then she heard more men yelling. Some more shots. She whimpered, terrified that at any moment that Victor would get hurt.

"Fuck! She's shot!" someone yelled.

"Get a vehicle close!" Regent ordered.

Who was hit? She moaned. Who? Oh, God. Who? She tried to wriggle her way out from under Maxim, but he held her down.

"Stay down, Gracen. We need to wait."

Tears rolled down her cheeks as she sobbed.

"Maxim, let her up."

Relief filled her at Victor's voice. Maxim stood and she scrambled up onto her feet. Victor stood in front of her, his gun in one hand, his eyes filled with cold fury. He looked intimidating and mean.

She didn't care. She went to throw herself at him but he held up a hand. "I'm covered in blood."

"Is it yours?" she asked hoarsely.

"No."

"Then I don't care." She flung herself toward him, and he caught her with a grunt, holding her tight.

"Maxim! Get over here and help us!" Regent yelled.

"Victor? Are you sure you're all right? Are you hurt?" She pulled back so she could pat his body, searching for injury.

"I'm fine, baby." He drew her against him again, holding her tight.

"What about everyone else? Regent? Lilia? Anita?"

"Regent is good." Victor pulled away from her and nodded to something behind her. "So is Lilia."

Lilia stood there, talking to one of the guards who'd been with her earlier. Was that the guy that Regent had turned to their side? She looked pale but unharmed.

"Lilia? You're all right?" She tried to walk to the other woman, but Victor wouldn't let her move.

Lilia came to her. "I'm fine. Just a few scrapes and bruises."

Yeah, Gracen likely had the same. But she couldn't feel anything. She was numb.

"Lilia?" Regent called out. "Some of my men will go with you to get your mother and clear Santiago's house."

Lilia nodded. Then she turned back to Gracen. "I might not see you again."

Gracen wrapped her arms around the other woman. "Call me if you need anything. At all."

With a shaky nod, Lilia walked away with several men accompanying her. Regent said something to her, then pressed a card into her hand. With his phone number? Maybe.

"What about Anita? Santiago?" she asked, looking around frantically. A number of people were gathered in the center of the room.

"What's going on? Anita?"

Victor gave her a look filled with sympathy. "I'm so sorry, Gracen. Anita's been shot."

GRACEN SAT in the waiting room chair.

She leaned her elbows on her thighs and tried to breathe. Her entire body was trembling. The shock was almost too much. She could feel herself shutting down.

Just stay with it a bit longer.

It didn't help that she hadn't been sleeping or eating properly. And that she'd just been through something horrific.

Just as well that the Malones owned this hospital or else they'd be dealing with the cops right now.

At least Snake and Santiago were dead. Regent and Maxim were on clean-up. But Regent had called to let her know that Lilia had gotten her mother and they were leaving the city.

So Lilia was safe.

But Anita had been shot. She was in surgery, fighting for her life.

What would she do if she died?

She'd failed her.

"Baby." Victor sat beside her, placing his hand on the small of her back. "You need to come rest."

"I can't leave."

"You don't have to. I've got a bed ready for you. Come on. You're resting. And if you argue, I have a doctor ready with a sedative."

Tears dripped down her face as she crawled into Victor's lap. "You're always threatening to drug me."

"I've only threatened that a couple of times. And you're really starting to worry me. If we don't get you some rest you're going to end up in here as a patient."

He lifted her into his arms. Right as a doctor walked into the room.

"Ms. Stall?" the doctor asked.

"Yes?" She didn't care that Victor was carrying her. "Is my niece all right?"

"She's strong. She came through the surgery. It's still going to be a long recovery, but her vitals are good at this point."

"Oh, God. When can I see her?"

"She's in ICU and she'll be out for a while. Why don't you get some rest and come back later? We'll take good care of her."

When the doctor left, she turned to Victor. "I think I should stay—"

"We're not staying," he told her in a gentle voice. He brushed her hair behind her ears. "You've had a huge shock. This isn't something you're used to. Your body needs proper rest. You need something to eat. Anita is fine for the moment. She has plenty of people to look after her. My job is to take care of you. And that's what I'm going to do. So we're going home and you will rest. And once I have determined you've had enough sleep, you can return. Understand?"

She thought about arguing. But she was so exhausted. And she could admit that she was near the end of her tolerance. She could feel fine trembles rocking through her body and she felt nauseous every time she moved.

"All right," she whispered.

Twenty minutes later, they arrived home to the Malone mansion. Brax was driving with Ajax in the passenger seat. She wondered if things would ease up now with Santiago and Snake dead.

Victor led her inside and into their bedroom.

"I want a shower," she whispered.

"How about a bath? Then I can get you some food and something to drink while you soak."

"I'm not hungry."

"I want you to try and eat something. Please."

The please did it for her and she nodded tiredly. After drawing her a bath, he helped her undress and climb in.

He stared down at her in worry.

"I'm okay, Victor," she murmured.

"No, you're not. But you will be. I won't have it any other way. I'll be as quick as I can. You won't fall asleep, will you? Maybe I should have Aero come up here."

"You wouldn't!" Her eyes widened as she gaped up at him.

"Not inside the bathroom. I'd cut out his eyes and feed them to the birds," he growled.

"Ew, if I wasn't feeling nauseous before, I am now."

"You're nauseous? You didn't tell the doctor that at the hospital."

He'd insisted that she get checked over, even though she hadn't really been anywhere near the action.

So overprotective.

"Because I'm tired. That's all. I promise."

He studied her, then nodded. "If you're still feeling ill tomorrow, then you're staying in bed and I'm calling the doctor."

"Okay," she agreed, knowing it was pointless to argue.

Ten minutes later, he was back with some cheese, crackers, and grapes, which he fed to her by hand.

If she'd been feeling better, she would have appreciated that more. She made a mental note to revisit this some time.

He quickly showered off, then lifted her out of the bath and got her ready for bed. He did everything. Brushed her hair, got her in her pajamas, he even brushed her teeth. She felt like a doll.

But despite her exhaustion, when he tucked them both up into bed, her mind was still running. Victor pulled her to lie on top of him, rubbing her back gently.

"Go to sleep, baby. Just let it go."

"I don't think I can."

Trembles started to rock her.

"Baby," he crooned softly. "You're okay. You're all right."

"You could have died," she said brokenly. "What would I ever do without you?"

"I hope you never have to find out. I'm determined that you won't. But if it ever happens, you know you'll be taken care of. You're part of our family now."

That didn't really make her feel better. She wasn't certain that anything would.

"It's all over. We're all safe. Everything is going to be all right. You and me, we're going to get married, have a pile of kids, and live happily ever after."

"Do you promise?" she whispered.

"I promise. What can I do to help? Is there anything that will make it better?"

"Can I have your fingers?"

Immediately, his hand was in front of her face, and she sucked lightly on his fingers. She loved his hands, no matter what he thought of them.

She sucked on his fingers, then kissed along the back of his hand.

"Baby, you don't want to kiss my hands."

"I do. These are the hands that love me. That take care of me. These hands are beautiful."

He let out a deep breath. Pushing up, she stared down at him. Then she kissed him lightly on the lips. "You're so beautiful."

"Stop it," he said huskily. He'd dimmed the bedside light, but she saw a light blush on his cheeks.

She nuzzled into his chest with her cheek, then took his fingers into her mouth again. But it wasn't enough. She needed more.

"Baby?" he asked huskily.

"I need more."

"Take what you need."

She slid down his body, kissing his bare chest and sucking lightly on each nipple before getting to his semi-hard cock.

"You're getting hard," she murmured as she pushed down his boxers and pajama pants.

"Don't worry about my needs. We need to take care of you."

She wrapped her lips around the tip of him, sucking gently.

Oh Lord. This was what she needed.

She had no idea why this helped. Why the thoughts in her head started to quiet and she could now relax.

But it did help. And she decided not to question it. This wasn't about sex. She always found him sexy as hell. But right now, she didn't want anything but comfort.

And he gave it to her. When she was slumped against him, her mind finally quiet, she slid back up so she lay on top of him.

"Need anything else, baby?"

"Just you."

"You have me, baby."

"I love you, Victor. So much."

"I love you too. But if you ever insist on putting yourself in a dangerous situation again, I'm going to redden your butt."

The threat made her smile. Because there was her bossy, protective man.

And she wouldn't have him any other way.

EPILOGUE

"I think I've found it," she said cheerfully as she walked into the office where all of the Malone men sat.

The cheer might have been a bit false, but they didn't need to know that. Although, the way that Maxim, Regent, and Victor looked at her told her that she wasn't as good an actor as she'd hoped.

Jardin didn't know her well enough to tell when she was faking.

"You baked something, baby?" Victor asked in a soft, relieved voice, getting up to grab the tray from her.

"The boys wanted to make chocolate chip cookies," she explained.

She got why he was relieved. She hadn't baked since the warehouse.

Since Anita was shot.

She swallowed heavily.

"Did they help you bake them?" Jardin asked with a grimace.

"Um, yep," she replied with a small smile. "Thea and Carrick are helping them clean up the mess. I didn't think it was possible to get cookie dough on the ceiling, but those boys managed it."

"Well, better than them breaking something, I suppose. I'll go help." Jardin gave her a small smile before he left the office.

"What did you make me?" Regent asked, picking up a piece of the slice.

"It's something I created just for you. I'm calling it Regent's Rum Delight."

He raised his eyebrows.

"It's got a rolled oats base, sweetened with a bit of honey. A creamy rum filling and a dark chocolate topping."

He took a bite and she waited anxiously. Surprise filled his face. "This is actually good."

She rolled her eyes, but her insides danced. Victor pulled her down onto his lap and she settled into him. Since the shooting, he'd been fussing over her like crazy. But she'd kind of needed it. She hadn't coped well. She'd been waking every night screaming with nightmares. Eating regularly was a distant memory. And worst of all, she couldn't bake.

But when Keir and Ace begged her so nicely to help them make some cookies . . . well, she couldn't say no to those two cuties.

And she actually felt a lot better, more like herself.

"Really? Or you're just saying that?"

"I never say things I don't mean," Regent replied.

"I can attest to that," Maxim said dryly. He'd been different since the warehouse too. More serious. Quieter.

"Did you hear from the facility?" she asked in a small voice.

Anita had spent two weeks in the hospital. She'd had two surgeries to repair her shoulder, which had been shattered by the bullet. Gracen had spent almost every day at the hospital with her. But things weren't exactly right between them. Gracen couldn't forgive her niece yet for what she'd done. Even though she'd actually apologized for everything, including setting fire to the bakery. She claimed that Ice talked her into it. She'd also confessed that she'd been regularly taking money from the cash register. Something Gracen felt stupid for not realizing.

And Anita was a different girl. Quiet and withdrawn.

Instead of opting to move in here with Gracen after being discharged, she'd gone to a rehab facility.

Gracen had been secretly relieved, which made her feel guilty. But she didn't think she had it in her to have Anita here. In her safe place.

"I did. She's settled in well."

"Good." Victor was paying for the facility, but he probably thought it money well spent if he didn't have to have Anita in his house. "I hope she gets the care she needs."

"She will," Regent told her.

There had been a bit of a power vacuum with Santiago and Snake dying. Regent was managing everything, but he had no interest in Santiago's businesses. Victor said he'd likely find someone to take them over.

She didn't really care. She might not know what she was going to do next, but for the moment everyone she loved was safe.

And that was the most important thing.

"WHAT DO YOU THINK?"

"I think it will look beautiful." Gracen sighed happily as she glanced down at the house plans, then over at the piece of land where they intended to build their four-bedroom, two-bath house with a wraparound porch.

It wouldn't be a full-time house. They still intended to spend most of their time in New Orleans. But this would be their getaway house where it could be just the two of them together.

Which would be nice. But she also loved living in the Malone mansion. Maxim had started to spend three or four nights there each week. She liked having him under their roof.

When Victor had asked her if she wanted her own place in New Orleans rather than living with Regent, she'd told him no. The mansion was her home. The Malones were her family. Next weekend they were all going up to New York to an art exhibition which featured Lottie's paintings.

She couldn't wait.

Six weeks had passed since the warehouse incident. She hadn't heard from Anita since she'd gone into the rehab facility. And she wouldn't lie, it hurt.

Maybe one day their old hurts would be mended. But not today or tomorrow. Regent said that when Anita was ready to leave, he'd reach out to her to offer help. She was grateful for that.

"Good. I think it will too." Victor turned her to him. She was still having the occasional nightmare, but they were lessening. And she knew eventually they'd go away completely.

But there was one thing bothering her. Victor had been treating her with kid gloves. For a while, she'd needed that careful care. Him watching over her closely, even feeding and bathing her sometimes. Holding her tightly when she cried or shook with nightmares.

However, that had to stop.

"You know, I'm really looking forward to our trip north next weekend," she said as Victor put the plans into the back of the car. "I especially can't wait to see Nico."

Shot loaded.

"He's so hot."

Shot fired.

"You did not just say that." Victor stalked toward her.

She stepped back with a laugh. "It was a joke."

"Not a funny one."

"Oh, yeah? What are you going to do about it? Spank me? We know you won't do that. Fuck me? You won't do that either."

"Little bit, you better run."

With a scream, she turned and took off toward the trees.

"I'm coming for you!"

He definitely gave her a head start, though. She wasn't a fast runner, and her legs were far shorter than his. He caught her before she got to the tree line. Then he threw her over his shoulder.

"Victor! It was a joke. I don't find Nico sexy."

Slap! Slap!

His hand landed on her ass. Hard.

She squealed.

"You never said sexy."

"Because he's not!"

Smack! Smack!

Shit. That hurt.

He turned her over and then sat on a stump and pulled her over his lap.

"No, Victor! I was just trying to rile you up."

"Mission accomplished," he told her as he pulled her shorts down.

Shit!

Maybe she'd done too good of a job.

Her panties went down next. And then his hand laid into her.

Smack! Smack!

She kicked her feet, and tried to reach back to stop him, but he gathered her hands up in the small of her back.

"I just wanted you to stop treating me like I'm fragile."

"Guess you got your wish."

She wouldn't quite put it that way. By the time he was finished spanking her, her ass was searing hot.

"Promise you won't ever look at another man."

"Victor, I wouldn't. I promise. I'm sorry. It was a joke."

He turned her over, then stood her in front of him, between his legs. He quickly started to strip her. "I didn't find it funny."

"I'm sorry. Really. I just . . . I needed you to see that I'm all right, Victor. Better than all right. Because I have you."

He pulled her onto his lap, so she was straddling him. Then he kissed the hell out of her. One hand cupped her breast, toying with her nipple while he teased her clit with his other hand.

He drove her insane for the next ten minutes, driving her up to the peak then drawing back. By the time he stood and set her on her feet, she was a mess.

"Please. Please."

"Shh, baby," he told her while he undid his jeans, then drew them and his boxers down. "I'm going to take care of you. I promise. Lean over, put your hands on the stump. Good girl. Spread your legs. That's it. Fucking beautiful."

Breathing heavily, she glanced over her shoulder to find him running his hand up and down his thick shaft.

Then he grabbed her hips, pulling her up onto her tiptoes before he slowly pushed his cock inside her.

"Just relax, baby. That's it. Fuck, you feel so good." He gave her an inch at a time, stopping every so often so she could adjust. He was always so careful of her.

But she just really needed him to move.

"Please, Victor! Please, fuck me!"

"Easy, baby. Easy. I'm nearly there. Damn, you look so fucking gorgeous taking me."

She really needed to come.

"Please, oh, God. I can't bear it."

"There we are. You are such a good girl, taking all of me. That's it. Fuck, yes." He started sliding out of her. Then he pushed back inside her.

Hell. Oh, shit.

"More. More," she begged.

He started to move faster. He kept this thrusts short and fast. Then he drove in deeper, with long, slow glides.

Yep, he was driving her nuts. Her body trembled. She needed more. She was stretched around him, just on the cusp of coming.

"Baby, I can't last much longer. I want you to come with me. Flick your clit. That's it. Come with me! Come, now!" he commanded.

She screamed as she came, her pussy clenching down around him. His own roar of release followed as he pushed inside her, his hands around her hips, holding her to him.

Carefully, he pulled out of her. Then turning her, he lifted her into his arms, holding her against him with his arm under her ass.

"I love you, baby. You're my world. My heart. My everything."

"I love you too, my gorgeous, protective, bossy hairy fairy godfather."

I HOPE you all loved reading about Victor (aka the hairy fairy/Vicky) and the woman he adores.

The next book in this series is going to be Maxim's. Unfortunately, that won't be until 2023, but we will be back to visiting those wild Texan Malones in the Haven, Texas series soon!